WOLF SLAYER

—

LINDA THOMAS-SUNDSTROM

ISBN-13: 978-
WOLF SLAYER

Copyright © 2013 by Linda Thomas-Sundstrom

All rights reserved. Except for use in any review, the reproduction or utilization of this work in whole or in part in any form by any electronic, mechanical or other means, now known or hereafter invented, including xerography, photocopying and recording, or in any information storage or retrieval system, is forbidden without the written permission of the publisher, Harlequin Enterprises Limited, 225 Duncan Mill Road, Don Mills, Ontario, Canada.

This is a work of fiction. Names, characters, places and incidents are either the product of the author's imagination or are used fictitiously, and any resemblance to actual persons, living or dead, business establishments, events or locales is entirely coincidental.

This edition published by arrangement with Harlequin Books S.A.

For questions and comments about the quality of this book, please contact us at Customer_eCare@Harlequin.ca.

® and ™ are trademarks of the publisher. Trademarks indicated with ® are registered in the United States Patent and Trademark Office, the Canadian Trade Marks Office and in other countries.

Recycling programs
for this product may
not exist in your area.

978-1-335-62947-0

Wolf Slayer

Printed in U.S.A.

Dear Reader,

South Dakota. Hills. Forests of trees. Secluded cabins in the woods. Acres of uninhabited space. Can you picture it?

This is where I've set the latest book in my Wolf Moons series, and I've been excited to explore the extremely fragile and always volatile relationship between werewolves and the hunters who go after them. Because not everything is ever as it seems with these two sides of the supernatural spectrum...and well, sexy is sexy, no matter where we find it. Right?

Two opposites, attracting. Forces beyond their control pitting a man and a woman against each other, and against what each stands for, as a truly dark entity comes prowling.

This is *Wolf Slayer*.

Imagining stories like this one is the reason why I enjoy writing about the werewolf world. I always look forward to finding out what these tall, edgy, gloriously sexy weres can do to make my blood boil. And then I hunt, as they do, for just the right adversary in the form of a strong, independent woman who might turn up. In this case... plenty of sparks fly!

I hope you'll love *Wolf Slayer* as much as I loved writing it.

Please do check out my website to keep track of what's coming up next. Connect with me on my Facebook author page. Stop by and say hello. I'd love to hear from you.

Cheers—and happy reading!

Linda

LindaThomas-Sundstrom.com

Facebook.com/LindaThomasSundstrom

To my family, those here and those gone, who always believed I had a story to tell.

Chapter 1

Tess Owens didn't like dark things. Or the full moons that brought dark things out of hiding.

Standing in the front yard of her secluded South Dakota home, she could see a vague imprint of the moon rise over the treetops. Familiar sensations tied to the big silver orb flooded her system in waves. Flush of heat. Spikes in her pulse. A sudden upswing of anxiety.

Full moons messed with her nervous system in a way Tess supposed similarly affected the creature she'd go after tonight when the stars came out. Although it was only late afternoon, her body was doing its thing, readying, gearing up for the time when adrenaline would push her beyond normal human limitations and she'd become the thing she had been created to be. *Hunter.*

Tonight, she'd need every ounce of strength she possessed if she met up with the dark thing that had taken up residence in the area. Because tonight was going to be special.

Rumors about the newcomer had been spreading throughout the towns nestled in the hills of South Dakota for a few days, and those rumors didn't begin to address the level of danger this new threat posed. She had been aware of the trespasser since it arrived.

The thing in these woods wasn't human. Its otherness was rich and dangerous. Acknowledging it gave her a thrill, because hunting anomalies is what her family had done best when they were alive. As bad luck would have it, she just happened to be the only Owens left in this part of the Dakotas, so the job was hers.

Hunting big bad creatures after nightfall wasn't for everyone and definitely not for the faint of heart—especially the kind of hunting her family was known for among certain circles. As far back as anyone could remember, the Owenses had been big-game specialists, not after lions or tigers, but wolves of a certain variety—the kind that walked upright on two legs and often looked like everyone else until a full moon rolled around.

"Plenty of light tonight," Tess muttered.

There were no clouds and not one hint of a storm system rolling in…unless she counted that damn newcomer as a special kind of storm. The werewolf that had dared to come here.

"Wolf," Tess said, standing near her front gate and searching the area west of the tall pine trees. "I know about you. I can taste your presence."

The fact that ninety-nine percent of the world's population didn't know Weres existed was a testament to how talented that species was at keeping secrets. But Tess and her family had been wolf hunters for nearly as long as werewolves had been around.

She was going to have to be careful, though. The nervous twitch in her shoulders suggested that this sucker had an ominous vibe. Tonight wasn't going to be easy. Even now, Tess breathed in the uniqueness of this creature's essence.

Either a particularly powerful new werewolf had moved to the neighborhood, or she wasn't worth the *O* carved on the hilt of her hunting knife.

O—the symbol for a pledge some ancient-based Owens had made to cull werewolf numbers.

O—a sign that was symbolic for zero, as in the number of werewolves that had gotten past her family since they had moved to the Dakotas thirty years ago.

O—for the look on miscreant werewolf faces when a well-placed silver knife or arrow terminated their freakish existence.

"And now you," Tess said, pacing the yard. Although some were rumored to be good, she hadn't seen the good stuff in any of the man-wolves she had hunted. Those creatures left a lot of damage behind. And she had never set eyes on a full-blooded Were, male or female, because Lycans, as those purebloods were called, tended to run in secretive, close-knit packs.

"So why are you trespassing where you don't belong?" Tess whispered. "It's my duty to catch you, you know. My job. My calling. I take my vows seriously."

After her first hunting expedition with her father

at the age of eight, she had accepted her role and had never looked back. At the ripe old age of twenty-four, she had the family name to live up to and didn't take that honor lightly.

She was fast, strong. Her life depended on those things. One mistake, one too many hesitations and death would be the result. Even talented hunters didn't usually last very long.

"I know you're out there somewhere, wolf. Will you offer me a game of hide-and-seek or just magically appear?"

South Dakota wasn't a hotbed for supernatural activity, unlike big cities in the West and East. There were slim pickings here for monsters, so a werewolf hadn't crossed her path in months.

"Until you."

She paused to scan more of the forest. Being alone for so long had made talking to herself out loud an acceptable habit.

"A beast like you took down both of my parents, leaving me without backup. But don't assume that means I'm weak."

On the contrary, the loss of her mother and father last year had energized her need to take care of problems that arose. So here she was, fighting back, fighting hard and willing to go to extremes in order to deal some payback to the creatures that had taken so much from her.

"I will find you. That's a promise."

If luck was on her side, the new Were wouldn't get wind of her before she found it. Out of necessity, she had become good at stealth, but werewolves also had keen, fine-tuned senses that were apt to be better than hers. She bore the scars to prove it and wore those scars like notches in her belt to mark the fights she had not only survived but won.

Would this guy know about her?

"Twelve," she said. "Twelve half-crazed werewolves have ventured too close to this part of South Dakota for their own good."

She ran a hand down the left side of her face, tracing a line of lightly raised scar tissue. "Number seven did this to me, and regretted it."

She raised an arm, showing off ridges on her left wrist. "Number nine."

If the people in town knew about what she did—about how far she had to go and how much she had sacrificed to protect them from the monsters—her loner status would make sense. But they could never know.

"Can you hear me, wolf?"

Maybe it could hear her. And maybe not. Though the keenness of werewolf hearing was legendary, it wasn't miraculous. They weren't gods. Weres were just one of nature's peculiarities.

Then again, possibly this one's hearing was better than most.

Straightening up with a sudden jolt of insight that demanded her full attention, Tess focused harder on the trees.

Someone was out there.

Chills arrived before the next rush of heat obliterated them. That familiar flash of warmth, originating in her chest, quickly radiated outward to kick her adrenaline levels through the roof.

The creature was here.

Watching her.

The air around her vibrated with a telling whisper that said, *Male werewolf. Big. Strong. Intense.*

Tess gritted her teeth in anger. By coming here, that Were had crossed a line.

"I don't care much for trespassers and haven't asked for company," she announced at a reasonable decibel. "Especially yours."

No reply came.

He was sizing her up.

Tess shifted from foot to foot as a sudden external wave of heat blew in to raise her own rapidly escalating body temp even further. The damn heat wave was like being caught in a lava flow and so hot, her stomach turned over.

Tess widened her stance to meet that heat wave head-on. But it was gone as suddenly as it had come. Just like that, and as if the trespasser had merely called it back...

Leaving Tess breathless.

Jonas Dale stopped five feet short of the chasm dividing his land from his neighbor's. Exceptional sight allowed him to peer through the trees.

The air was cool. An acrid odor of woodsmoke left a tang on his tongue. Aside from the normal forest fragrances of pine and scrub, he could detect a human.

He had heard about Tess Owens, of course. Word traveled fast and went something like this: *hunter in residence. Wolves beware.*

Coming here had been a risk. But he needed to be in the remote hills of South Dakota and about as far from his home in Florida as was geographically possible.

The choice of this location hadn't been made without careful consideration. Tess's family's reputation preceded them. If the thing chasing him knew about the Owens family, surely it wouldn't imagine he'd come here, so close to one of them.

In this case, he was using Tess Owens as camouflage.

Since word had come of the Owens deaths last year, Jonas figured he might get away with this. Still, extra caution would be needed when dealing with any member of that clan. Cunning and the power of persuasion might be the ticket to keeping Tess off his back if she would listen to reason.

Would she be open to hearing anything he had to say when her family was notoriously unforgiving to his kind?

He had come here today, near her home, for a quick look and to judge for himself about Tess. Finding her had been easy. She was standing in her yard, near enough for an agile werewolf with a grudge to take her on without the benefit of any moon-induced physical changes. He wasn't that wolf, however. Not today. Not ever, hopefully, since his energy was needed elsewhere and he had little time to spare.

Underscoring the mixture of woodsmoke and wildflowers near the Owens cabin were hints of other scents that only a Were's imagination would acknowledge. Energy. Anticipation. Blood.

Danger had its own unique fragrance, and this Owens offspring had Were blood on her hands. Her head was lifted, her posture tense. If she was good at what she did, there was no way Tess wouldn't already have a bead on him.

It was a standoff, from a distance, before they had even gotten to hello.

Looks were fairly deceiving though, Jonas had to admit. Tess Owens didn't look so formidable in person. She was tall but delicate, small-boned, long-limbed and young. Her shape was sleek and accentuated by tight jeans and a skimpy shirt that showed off too much skin and failed to reflect the current coolness of the afternoon temperature.

She had long, fair hair, most of it twisted into a braid that hung halfway down her back. A few unruly strands blew in the same breeze that had carried her scent to him, and those wayward strands were the only bit of wildness in her that he perceived.

The fair hair was a surprise, though. For some reason, he hadn't expected this werewolf slayer to be a blonde. Not that the color of her hair made a difference in the long run. It's just that he had a soft spot for golden-haired beauties. Still, Jonas wished he could see her face to witness firsthand the malice that had to be reflected in her eyes.

There were other curious particular details about her as well. Tess's skin was paler than any outdoorswoman's skin should have been. That little discrepancy seemed odd since she had to maintain her shape somehow and the great outdoors was her backyard.

Her shoulders were gracefully curved. Slender arms showed good muscle definition, as if she worked hard at something other than chasing Weres. Tess was visibly lean and fit. Too bad she wasn't a Were, Jonas mused, because he appreciated her looks and could have made the most of them in other circumstances.

Lean, wiry, fierce females were his preference. Females who could hold their own and give back what they got. Females who didn't usually bend unless they wanted to. He would have liked to run a palm over all that bare skin. Equally as pleasurable for him would have been to touch those silky golden tendrils currently hiding her face.

Wild was, after all, every werewolf's middle name. In his twenty-eight years of dealing with his species, he had come to recognize the extremes of Were needs and wants…and tamp them down when he had to.

No such luck here, though.

Shaking his head scattered the impossible images taking shape in his mind. The only way he was going to touch Tess Owens would be in self-defense when she came at him with an intent to kill.

That was a shame because he knew instinctively that Tess Owens was something special and so much more than the reputation that preceded her.

He just couldn't put a finger on how he knew this.

As his body shuddered with a mixture of appreciation and wariness for this new opponent, Jonas spoke softly so that Tess wouldn't be able to hear what he had to say.

"Possibly that's your greatest asset in dealing with my kind? We tend to underestimate you after a first glance? Pretty girl all alone in the woods?"

Inwardly, he also added, *I vow not to become one of the suckers overly intrigued by those things. All I have to do is stay out of your way and hope you can determine friend from foe.*

He prayed that Tess Owens might turn out to be an ask-questions-first kind of predator, just like he was. But this wasn't the time for introductions and more wayward thoughts having to do with Tess's tight jeans. Any hunter with a rep like hers wouldn't let a full moon go to waste. Tess Owens would make the most of tonight and come knocking at his door fully armed and ready to rumble.

He had to keep her from doing so.

"I'm not what you think I am, Tess. I'm here, not to mess with you, but to protect a secret of my own. I'm needed. Someone else's life depends on what happens here and what I do, and you just need to stay out of my way for a while."

Did she get those confidences sent across the distance separating them? Jonas watched her turn her head as if she might have. He also felt a pull from somewhere behind him, an indication that he had to get back to his temporary home.

Having an Owens next door was one strike against him. The other creature that was looking for him was far worse.

Death was coming and would find him eventually. The black-cloaked, soul-catching bastard was the greater opponent, the mightier threat, and the monster he needed to keep at bay. Besides himself, there was only one member of the Dale family left, and his sister's life depended on his ability to protect her. That had become his goal in life.

The bad news was the wave of aggression coming from Tess Owens and the silent words he swore he heard slip from her lips.

"It's a date, wolf. Tonight. Don't be late."

At this point, so early in their association, probably nothing he could have said in return would have changed her mind.

Chapter 2

Tess paced the room as night began to descend. Wearing leather pants, a black shirt and black boots, she took a quick look in the mirror to make sure she hadn't forgotten anything that might make the difference between life and death when dealing with a werewolf.

She looked good enough, Tess thought, though people in town stared at her for other reasons when they met her. More than one of them had probably wondered where she might have gotten so many of the scars that crisscrossed the side of her face.

"Will he keep our date? What do you think, Tess?" she asked herself as she strode down the hallway of the cozy, eight-room, wood-paneled cabin.

Determined to find out the answer to that question, Tess entered the weapons room and chose a knife with a gleaming silver blade. She slung the bow and quiver of arrows over her shoulder, adjusting easily to the added weight, then rolled her neck to ease the tension building there.

Gloves on, weaponed up, she walked out of the front door. After giving the cabin a last glance, she set her sights on the trees and slipped into the dark.

"It's okay."

Jonas spoke softly to his sister, though he wasn't sure how much of what he said ever sank in. There hadn't been a verbal response from her since she had been attacked in a Miami park not too far from where they had lived.

Gwendolyn Dale had grown frail and lethargic on the outside—the parts others saw if they looked. He hoped the darkness he now sensed inside his sister would eventually fade away and be replaced by the happy-go-lucky sister he had always loved.

Sometimes, though, he wasn't so sure about the darkness's staying power.

Jonas tended to believe the attack in Miami had left Gwen with a black spot on her soul, and that she had been marked by Death in some way. This had to be the reason there seemed to be a specter on her trail. He thought it likely that his sister wasn't supposed to have survived that attack, and that she had been slated, fated, or whatever the hell happened in the big cosmic scheme of things, to have died that night in Miami.

In the end though, what did he really know about such things? His entire repertoire of ideas was based on nothing more than conjecture and supposition.

"I have to go out, Gwen. Just for a while."

Jonas laid a hand on his sister's shoulder and winced at its thinness.

"I'll be back soon, so take care while I'm gone and don't do anything I wouldn't do."

Gwen would have laughed at the last part of that statement if she had been with him mentally as well as physically. Out of everyone else around them, his younger sister had been the most like him. She had been developing a similar kind of power and strength, even though neither of those things had helped the night she slipped out of the house with her friends without telling anyone and had encountered true darkness.

Gwen had been the only victim left alive out of the four young girls…if the term *being alive* could describe the state they had found her in. It had taken weeks of seclusion for her to recover enough to move her to this remote location. She hadn't said a word to anyone since that terrible night.

Gwen was haunted. He knew that. She grew paler day by day and seldom ventured outside. Jonas wanted to believe she understood every word he said now, even as he could see her slipping further and further away.

"Your new companion will be here tomorrow," he said lightly. "You probably need a female around. I think you'll like her. She'll stay for most of the day and go home before sundown. You know why she can't stay here after dark settles in. That's my shift. If you like her, we can see about having her spend more time here."

Gwen's pale blue eyes stared up at him as if she had

heard him this time. She offered nothing in the way of facial expression.

"Right, then," Jonas said. "I'm off to meet our neighbor. She sent me an invitation."

In the old days, Gwen would have pleaded to go along. But even before her accident, she hadn't yet been in full possession of the kind of skills that could have helped against things like experienced wolf hunters. It wouldn't have been long, though, before his sister would have outshone every other Were in the area.

Gwen was an anomaly within an anomaly. A special being within the Were species. He wasn't sure if she knew this.

"Wish me luck." Jonas leaned over to place a kiss on his sister's forehead and then headed out, knowing his meeting with Tess Owens couldn't be postponed.

Keeping beneath the shadows of tree cover didn't isolate him completely from the moon's effects. Dappled light on his shoulders instigated sparks from nerves that buzzed, snapped and roused the wolf nestled inside him. His claws had appeared. Both shoulders ached. This was all part of the deal when the moon issued a come-hither.

After covering another acre of rocky, forested hillside, he got his first good impression of what was coming his way. Tess's scent was in the air—that same mixture of smoke and flowers that had led him to her earlier.

The scent grew stronger as he walked. So did the moonlight. Jonas resisted the urge to shape-shift. Tess was here, just ahead, waiting for him. She had met him midway between the two cabins, which probably meant she knew where he was staying.

Tess Owens stood near a large rock pile at the crest of the hill overlooking property lines, surrounded by trees. She was partially camouflaged by shadows. The fact that she wore black would have helped to hide her from human eyes, but not from a werewolf's. Jonas located her with a complex system of sight, scent and the image presented to him by way of her body heat.

It was showtime.

"Don't bother to hide," she called out in a tone that was both combative and dangerously sexy in equal measures. It was a deep voice for someone her size.

Jonas hadn't counted on her ability to tune in to him so quickly, though. This was yet another detail that added respect and wariness to his initial assessment of her.

She seemed to be looking straight at him when she couldn't possibly see that far. Night-vision goggles might have helped her to pinpoint him, but she wasn't wearing them. Maybe she had heard his approach? The snap of a twig? A rustle of branches? He used to be better than this.

She spoke again. "These days I'm fairly good at what I do, and I get better with age and practice."

Careful not to make a sound, Jonas inched forward with his wolfishness twisting his insides. A human growl stuck in his throat. The claws that had appeared made his human hands ache. His wolf side was willing to take on this threat, but it wasn't time to let that happen. He doubted if Tess would take aim at a human form with the silver-tipped arrows he could now smell. Hunters rarely did.

"Are you coming out, or should I welcome you with a silver-coated handshake?" she challenged.

All hunters knew about the Were aversion to silver and a few other metals. Tess Owens seemed pretty confident about that aversion.

Blaming his comeback on his reaction to her voice, Jonas decided to oblige her request, at least in part.

He said, "Handshake? I wasn't aware that you had social skills, Owens. People in town told me you rarely show your face there. To some of them, you're more of a ghost than a neighbor."

He wondered what that remark might do to her self-confidence and if it would shake her up in a way that might lead him to find a crack in her admirable armor.

"People in town don't actually know me," she returned, showing no sign of being affronted either by his remark or the fact that he had not shape-shifted like he was supposed to.

Jonas took another step forward, keeping to the darker spaces. His wolf urges were rising by steady degrees, drawn to the moon, drawn to Tess Owens, ready to take its turn in this face-off.

"Don't stall the inevitable on my behalf," she continued. "There's no need to fight your true nature. You know you want a piece of me."

"What nature would that be?" Jonas asked.

"The kind that howls."

"I think I'd prefer to meet you on a more human basis, at least on this occasion," he said.

"Should I be honored?"

"That's up to you."

"Show yourself and get this over with."

"Put down the bow and I'll think about your request."

"How about if you reel in your claws?"

Her comeback was testy and insightful since she couldn't actually see his claws. Wild guess?

Jonas asked, "What if I'm not what you're thinking I am? Don't you ever make a mistake when pointing a weapon at someone?"

"Only one mistake, and I won't make it again."

She might have been alluding to the death of her parents a year ago. But now that he was closer, Jonas finally got a good look at her face.

He suppressed a growl of appreciation. Tess was incredibly beautiful. All the right stuff was there, in all the right places. She had an oval face with perfectly symmetrical features and large, light eyes. Her brow was wide beneath a fringe of fair hair. Angular cheekbones gave her a regal look, though the deep hollows beneath them accentuated her thinness.

All in all, she didn't look anything like any wolf hunter Jonas had ever seen.

However, she wasn't perfect. Overlaying all that beauty was a trail of scars. Lavender lines, like crawling vines, crossed one side of her face, running from her forehead to her chin.

Jonas recognized those scars and knew what had made them. Tess had been mauled by a wolf, and that wolf had done some damage. Because she was here now, it was easy for him to see who the winner of that previous skirmish had been.

"Are scars the reason you stay away from town, or are hunters loners by necessity?" he asked, earnestly wondering about that.

A shudder of disgust ran through her, but Tess didn't drop the aim of the arrow pointed in his direction. Still, Jonas thought he might have found that crack he'd been searching for, however small it might have been. Those scars bothered her.

"Old wounds come with the territory," she said calmly enough.

Jonas nodded as he took another step toward her. She still wouldn't be able to see him clearly, and he wasn't going to allow verbal taunts or silver-tipped arrows to mess up this crucial meeting. Two more steps to his right and into the moonlight, and he would become the target she was looking for. He had to stave off that shape-shift. He had to hold on, sensing how badly she wanted to let that arrow fly.

Tess wasn't just a hunter out to score. Her level of palpable aggression told him that she had a personal vendetta against the creatures she hunted. Six years on the force with the Miami PD had taught him a lot about dealing with emotion and the concept of revenge. Tess's hatred for his kind left a sour taste in his mouth.

"Claws also come with the territory," he said.

"Then use them. Do your worst. Or try to," she taunted.

"Having animal in my DNA makeup doesn't make me stupid, Tess."

His use of her name surprised her. Her right cheek quivered.

"If true, that kind of insight would be a first," she noted.

"You have no reason to fear or hate me. I'd like to offer a truce," Jonas said.

"Like that will happen."

"What can I do to force the issue? I have an agenda

here that doesn't include you. My reason for being in the area is important to people other than myself."

"People?" She picked up on that word, emphasizing its misuse when pertaining to him.

Jonas wasn't used to this kind of treatment. In Miami he was a respected detective on the job, fighting crime both in and out of the shadows. To Tess Owens, he was nothing more than an animal.

Turns out that she was formidable enough, he supposed. But she was also quite a sight standing there— a delicious, leather-clad, angry sight.

He wondered what she'd think if he mentioned how exotic he found her voice or how good she looked in that black suit. He could have bet she'd have been insulted then.

"I applaud your goals," he told her. "But I'm not one of the bad guys."

"Wouldn't bad guys use that line?"

"Not around me," he said.

Would Tess believe that Weres didn't like bad guys of any species, including their own? Would she change her mind about werewolves if she knew how many decent wolves there were in the world, and how they fought behind the scenes to further the concept of peace and justice for all?

What if he showed her his badge?

"Most of the time, human is what I appear to be," he said. "That's what the world believes I am."

"Except for those of us who know better."

"Yes. But I'm not part of the reason you do what you do, and I've already stated that my intention for being here isn't to cause you or anyone else around here harm."

"Why here?" she asked, unshakable on her aim with that arrow.

"It's as far away from others as I could find on the spur of the moment," Jonas replied truthfully.

"What others?"

"People."

"That's rich," she said. "And it would also be a point in your favor, if anyone was counting."

All right, Jonas thought. *That's it.* He had said more than he had intended, and Tess Owens had no right to question him further. Meeting her here had been a courtesy. He had hoped she'd see reason and leave him and Gwen alone, but it didn't look like that was going to happen.

It was likely that Tess was driven to exterminate every werewolf she came across and had made up her mind about him being included in that goal.

"I suppose there's no reasoning with you then," he said.

"Reason? I'm pretty sure werewolves don't know the meaning of the word."

He nodded. "Well then, it's been a pleasure, Tess."

The calmness of his closing remark also seemed to surprise her. Another shudder ran through Tess that was sizeable enough to make her leather suit creak.

"Show yourself," she demanded, though her voice was softer, lower, and almost a purr.

Her tone stirred Jonas's insides in a strange way, as if he could feel its vibration from where he stood. That purr melted into his skin, sparked his nerve endings in a way that created its own electricity.

"I don't think that would be a good idea, do you?" he asked.

"What it would do is make things a whole lot easier."

"For whom? You?"

"Yes. For me," she said.

"You believe that killing every Were you meet will bring your parents back? And that every Were is bent on carnage and destruction?"

She didn't hesitate. "Yes."

"Then you don't know much, wolf hunter, and your education has been sorely lacking."

She spoke quickly. "You're suggesting that you are not like the others? That you're different?"

"I can't speak to the actions of those others. I can only repeat that I mean no harm to you or anyone else around here and leave it at that."

"Can you prove what you say?"

"I can prove it by turning my back and leaving you alone and in one piece."

"Or by showing yourself," she suggested with more tension on the string of her bow.

Okay. If you say so...

Jonas stepped into the moonlight, allowing the rain of silver light to wash over him. The wolf inside him barreled upward so fast, his shape-shift was completed in the few seconds it took him to reach Tess Owens. So fast, she didn't have time to use her lightning-fast reflexes and let loose of that arrow.

She might have been primed and fighting fit, but she was no match for a full-blooded Lycan who had been shifting since his teens. She was no real match for a werewolf who was twice as fast as any werewolf in his pack and shifted without recognizing the pain of each physical transformation.

And she was no competition for a Were whose sole

purpose in life currently was to guard the sister who stood on the brink of death.

He had the bow in his hands before Tess could blink or utter a groan of protest.

He had her knife in his fingers, her hand in his, and the tip of the razor-sharp blade she carried tight up against his chest. Her blue eyes, wide with shock, met his.

Growling was the only way Jonas now had of speaking to her. That growl rumbled menacingly as he held her gaze and pressed the tip of the blade into his own flesh.

Do it if you don't believe me, wolf hunter. Go ahead.

Whether it was the shock of his shift, his appearance, or his speed that stayed her hand…

Or maybe it was the look in his eyes as they met hers…

Tess Owens didn't make that thrust. She stood there, staring at him as if momentarily confused.

And since the advantage belonged to Jonas, he took it.

Chapter 3

The werewolf in front of her was huge, muscled, and faster than anything Tess had ever seen. The adrenaline punch that hit her when she looked into his eyes was a stunning blow to her confidence.

His eyes were blue and way too human.

Those eyes were intelligent and intense.

And the face…the werewolf's face…was disturbingly human, as well.

He had angular features and no sign of anything that even hinted at a wolfish outline. No five o'clock shadow, let alone the typical werewolf's layering of fine hairs and elongated bone structure. This guy actually was different. He was resetting the stats on everything she had known about werewolves. Meeting him, seeing him like this, sent the damn rulebook spinning.

Why had he turned the knife on himself? One

thrust of the blade and he'd be toast. One plunge into that broad, naked chest with the sharp end of her silver dagger, and she would come out the victor.

That's what she had to do. That's what she had been trained to do. Raised to do. Taught to do. Remember… Too many hesitations and death will be the result.

Then why didn't she edge that knife deeper into the wolf's flesh? And why wasn't he tearing her apart? He made no move to hurt her. The damn werewolf was waiting for something. She thought she saw a flash of curiosity in his eyes.

"Who are you? What are you?" she asked after a long overdue breath.

Because of their closeness, the next growl that rumbled from the Were's throat also rumbled through her. Tess kept a tight hold on the hilt of the knife. Her bow, along with the arrow, lay on the ground where he had tossed them, and far from reach, but they wouldn't have helped in this awkward situation anyway.

Push the damn blade.

He's not human.

None of them are human. They ate my parents and made me a freak.

The wolf's response to her question was to inch closer. A trickle of blood began to seep through the small hole where the blade pierced his flesh, and yet he didn't blink.

What was he doing, though? Did he want to die, or was this merely a tactic to confuse her?

Well, damn it, she was confused, and had to either get her mojo back or suffer the consequences in the next few seconds.

One of you killed my family…

Nevertheless, whatever he was trying to do with this odd turnaround stayed her hand. After several more seconds of alarming eye contact and a lot of pulse acceleration, Tess stepped back with her heart beating way too fast and the bloody knife clutched in her hand. A brand-new kind of fear was setting in. She had never come up against anything remotely like this Were.

"If you think this changes anything, you're wrong," she said. "We're on opposite sides of the game, and in any game, there can only be one winner."

She watched the alarmingly large Were shake his head as if he understood what she had said, as well as the promise in it. True to his word though, he didn't make any move to harm her. This close to him, she couldn't see his claws or imagine what he might gain by holding back on his end.

So she waited for his next move, already planning hers. She'd duck to the side, come up to his right and use the knife. She wouldn't be facing him then, wouldn't have to look into those sympathetic blue eyes.

Yes, that's what she had seen in them after the flash of curiosity. Sympathy.

"Who the hell do you think you are?" she demanded in a voice that didn't sound as strong or as confident as she meant it to be. "One of us has to do the honors. If that's you, so be it. If it's me, all the better. That's how this works."

When he failed to respond, Tess's gaze went to the blood dappling his broad chest. Red blood. Half men, half beasts had red blood like the humans they emulated.

She continued to eye the tiny hole in the Were's chest until he began to back away. Given some distance, Tess's nerves fired up, white-hot. Her arms began to quake with the need to do something—show him who she was and what she could do. She'd just had an intimate tryst with death and was still standing.

The Were was a good three feet away now and facing her. Tess's first real look at the whole package he presented, head to foot, was another nerve-jangling revelation.

In this incarnation, the Were actually did seem more man than beast. Well over six feet of undulating muscle and sinew made it appear that he was moving when he wasn't.

He had chiseled cheekbones, sun-streaked brown hair and blue eyes. If there had been an image of the perfect specimen of a man-wolf in that wolf hunter rulebook, this guy could have been the model. The real deal. The epitome of an evolved enemy.

She was looking at a Lycan. Tess knew this now. This guy was a pure-blooded example of the species. Her first.

No longer able to manage the internal quakes shaking her, Tess widened her stance. Her pulse was skyrocketing. Her fingers were bloodless from her grip on the knife. Confusion caused this delayed reaction, she told herself. She needed to lunge.

Do it now.

End this.

"If you go now, I will find you," she vowed. Encouraged by the strength in her tone, Tess added, "Why prolong the inevitable? Tonight has to be the night. We both know this. Wolf and wolf hunter is the way this goes down. Werewolf and hunter."

The wolf blinked his big eyes and then he shook his head. Within seconds, his body was against hers and she was wedged between his considerable bulk and the shadow-covered rock face behind her.

It was over. She had lost with supernaturally unlucky werewolf number thirteen. It was inevitable that this minute would come someday.

Tess closed her eyes.

Without sight, all of her other senses became acute, serving to enlarge every small detail of these last few seconds she had left. Her opponent's breath was heated and slightly sweet. With the Were's chest tight up against hers, she felt the steady rhythm of his heartbeat and the way his muscles twitched. Was he eager to win? Holding back for what? The hope that she might plead for her life?

Never...

With the weight of his body squeezing hers into submission, Tess discovered how close to humans Weres could feel physically. All of the masculine stuff was there, in spades. With her eyes closed, she might never have known what this bastard was and the extent of the danger she found herself in. Even his musky masculine scent was pleasantly unique.

"Sorry, Dad, Mom," she whispered, ready to draw that last breath.

The Were's muscle rippled as the shocking sound of muscle pulling on bone made Tess look up to meet the blue eyes that would be the last thing she'd ever see... and found them looking back at her from an exceptionally handsome human face that was a lie, at best.

* * *

"I told you I mean no harm," Jonas repeated in a hoarse voice that hadn't fully recovered from the shift. "What more do I need to do to prove that to you? What part of my explanation didn't you get?"

Tess was barely breathing, and staring at him.

Jonas tried again. "We're not all bad guys. Most of us aren't, in fact."

She said, "You could have fooled me."

He could see she was scared, though not as frightened as anyone else in her current position would have been. Tess Owens had faced more than one werewolf with grit and dedication, though it was clear that she had never met anyone like him.

She expected trouble. Clearly, she was awaiting her death by his hand. Her face had paled to transparency. In that milky whiteness, her scars took on a pale blue cast.

Jonas touched one of those scars with a finger no longer blessed by a claw. The scar he chose was the one nearest to her temple. In response, she drew back as if she'd been struck. Her head hit the rock with a thud. She swore out loud, which seemed to make her feel better if the light that appeared in her eyes meant anything.

"Do it," she challenged. "What are you waiting for? There's only one way to end this, because I'll never stop hunting you."

She was so damned determined to fix this situation, so stubborn and brainwashed on the werewolf issue that Jonas had to smile. The smile kicked up the flames of her anger.

"Promise me something," he said. "If I let you go, you'll need to honor that promise."

"I don't owe you anything," she snapped.

He pushed more of his weight against her. "No?"

"I'd rather die right here than to owe you anything at all," she said.

He shook his head. "We both know that's not really true. You have a calling and I can't stop that. I wouldn't stop that. Bad guys are bad guys."

"Wolves," she corrected.

"But I'm not one of those bad guys. This, I solemnly swear."

"What would the world be like if I believed that line from every werewolf that trespassed here?"

"Did you give any of those Weres the chance to prove it?" Jonas asked.

"I caught them in the act. Devilish stuff. Killing sheep. Killing horses. Stealing. Brutally attacking people in the dark. Were those things supposed to continue without intervention? Knowing what those creatures are, was I supposed to allow it to go on?"

He said, "If that was the case, it's likely those creatures deserved what they got. I might have done the same things you did in order to keep the peace."

Her eyes narrowed. "You mean in order to keep your species a secret, don't you? You'd condone culling a few bad seeds in order to keep most of you safe from the world discovering your existence?"

She had more to say. Jonas waited.

"So why here? Why have you come here?" she asked again.

"I'm here to keep something very bad from happening."

She struggled against him. Jonas held her firm as he continued.

"I have a life, Tess. But I needed to come here to take care of an issue that arose. When that's done, I'll go back to my life, get on with my life, hopefully having helped to save someone very dear to me."

Chances were slim that she might believe him. Nevertheless, Tess stopped struggling.

"Promise me you'll let me do what I need to do here without interference and that you'll give me time to take care of the thing I came here to do," Jonas said. "That's all I ask."

"You're kidding, right? Turn my back? Let you have free rein?"

Her tone hadn't softened and yet her body had lost some of its stiffness. Hints of a darker ivory color were slowly returning to her cheeks. Jonas hoped this meant he was making progress.

Although the situation remained tense, his mind wanted to focus on Tess the woman, rather than as his rival. He was a male after all was said and done, and Tess Owens was young, strong and interesting.

Her tight leather vest cinched in her breasts in a way that made her appear almost boyish with a first glance, and yet pressing against her gave Jonas a good impression of what lay beneath all that leather. Her hips were narrow, but feminine. Prominent hip bones accentuated her leanness. Her legs were shapely and firm.

In her current position, Tess didn't offer up one good quake. This hunter was all about secrets and the art of camouflage. Wasn't his life similar in those respects?

Jonas swept a slow glance over Tess's face, noting that her expression was blank. Though her eyes were intent on him, she didn't meet his gaze directly. Tess might never have been up close and personal with a werewolf in human form.

In any case, she didn't cringe, cower or plead for mercy. If she had a plan for getting her edge back, she had seconds to consider how to accomplish it. Barring that, he could see that she'd accept the ramifications of a meeting gone bad with dignity.

Tess Owens hadn't done her homework regarding Lycans and the abilities that set them apart from other Weres, and he had just offered her a fast track to enlightenment. What she did with that was up to her. After a few more moments of body-hugging closeness, he'd let her go if she promised to behave.

"Get off me," she said curtly.

"You haven't spoken the magic words."

He was angering her further and wasn't enjoying that, but shattering her old habits would take time he didn't have. And when she looked up, when her eyes finally met his, what he saw in them shook him up slightly. He saw sadness.

His body reacted with a twitch of understanding that was visceral. Tess had tucked that sadness so deep inside of her, he was witnessing only its tip.

"Go to hell," she said.

She tried to shove him back, but was trapped.

"Promise me what I've asked for, and I'll let you go," Jonas said.

"I can't do that. Won't."

"Because you're too proud to admit what happened here, or because you have a stubborn streak?"

Flashes of defiance raced through her blue eyes, but she unwaveringly held his gaze. He couldn't look away, couldn't untangle himself from the sensations rushing over him. Lust, greed and hunger were all there, piling up. But there was also something else nagging at his consciousness that was at the moment misty and ill-defined.

Jonas had to force himself to speak. "Time is what I need. Then I'll be gone and out of your life."

Her lips parted as though she was going to challenge that statement, but no words came out. Reluctant to lose the eye contact that made him so interested in what lay behind those eyes, Jonas finally dropped his gaze to her mouth.

What would Tess Owens, werewolf hunter, taste like? He wondered if anyone had tried to find out.

If she rarely showed up in town, what were the odds she'd have a lover? Given what she did for a living and the secrets she kept, what kind of normal man could handle her or her choices? This could be the cause of her sadness. Tess was lonely.

Actually, he decided, a wolf would have been the better choice for someone like her, if the world turned on a different axis. If Gwen hadn't been waiting for him, and if he hadn't set himself up as his sister's protector, he might have desired a lot more time with Tess Owens. As the only person in South Dakota who also knew about him, they might have been friends in some parallel universe. They might even have been lovers.

His body liked that idea. Both man and wolf sincerely appreciated the thought.

Tess's lips moved again, keeping his attention there. He wasn't allowing her much room to breathe, so either she was trying to take in air or a new protest had gotten lodged in her throat.

"What issues brought you here?" she eventually asked. "What are you escaping from?"

"That's personal."

"Maybe you just made it up to play on my sympathy," she suggested.

Jonas liked the way her mouth moved. He liked the way Tess smelled. Again though—and a tough reminder here—they were, for all intents and purposes and according to Tess, enemies.

"Still waiting," he said without easing up on the pressure that pinned her to the rock.

"If it's a promise for me to turn my back, then you'll wait a very long time," she returned.

Jonas swore under his breath. Niceness wasn't getting him anywhere.

"What you need," he started to say, almost giving in to the impulse to tell her about Lycans and Miami and about his gig as a cop. But there was an interruption in the form of a sound that didn't belong to the reasonably intimate moment he and Tess were sharing.

And Jonas knew without a doubt what that sound was, and who had made it.

Tess was screwed and hated to admit it.

She waited for death, knowing there was no one to mourn her and that not one soul would realize she'd been gone for some time.

This was not okay. It sucked. And yet here she was, pressed tightly to the body of a werewolf who had shown her both sides of himself in a matter of minutes and who had drawn the better hand in this game.

Not necessarily the winning hand, though.

She was a fighter, and not fully onboard with giving up. When the bare-chested werewolf, who was way too human at the moment, lifted his head and tore his attention away from her to tune in to a sound she barely heard, Tess stiffened in reaction. Without his eyes on her, she felt colder and even more alone.

Those reactions made no sense.

She saw that he was irritated by whatever he had heard in the distance. After tossing another glance over his shoulder at the moonlit field behind him, his attention returned to her.

His expression registered his disappointment over the timing of this potential interruption in their strange getting-to-know-each-other session. She, on the other hand, wanted to cheer and would have shouted to whoever was out there if the man pressed against her wasn't a monster masquerading as a man.

When she felt the urge to speak, the wolf in human skin held up a warning finger. Then he did a strange thing. Leaning closer, he brushed his lips over her cheek—a surprising move that sent her insides skittering. One quick, light touch. The cunning bastard smelled like pine.

He didn't bite her or break her neck. Nor did he shift to his scarier form. After that touch, he backed up and pulled her forward until she stood on her own. Then he nodded to her. His eyes never left hers. It seemed to Tess as though he was attempting to send her a message and willing her to keep her mouth shut.

What had he seen or heard out there?

Who was coming?

Why am I shaking?

Tess had to gather herself if she had any chance here. She closed her eyes and sent more of her senses outward, hoping to discover what had disturbed the Were because she couldn't afford to be caught like this any more than he could. Hell, she was in possession of a bloody knife and a quiver of silver-tipped arrows. What kind of picture did that paint?

The Were turned. He took a few steps, daring to keep his back to her, leaving her the opening she had waited for. The knife was in her hand before her next big breath. She readied for the attack.

Before she could make that move, he said, "Trust me, Tess. Leave now. Go home. What's out there isn't something you'll want to face tonight."

And then he took off running.

Chapter 4

Tess stared after the Were's retreating form for a few ticks of her internal clock before following him. In the pit of her stomach, she knew he had been upset by whoever this intruder was and that whatever was out there presented another kind of threat.

Since she had detected nothing in the periphery, she had no idea what that might be. Nor could she imagine what could be more dangerous to her, more lethal, than a Lycan with a jump on the human hunting him.

He ran like the wind, covering ground as if he actually was a wolf with four legs, instead of two. Tess knew she couldn't catch up. Nevertheless, she wasn't ready to give up. Not after the strange encounter with this Were that had set the hunter's rulebook on its ass.

The werewolf had let her go. Not only that, he had tried to reason with her. He had issued a warning, presumably in an attempt to save her some future grief over whatever that other thing out there turned out to be.

His thought had been to help. What kind of werewolf wanted to protect the hunters who came after them? This one had told her he wasn't one of the bad guys, but again, weren't they all bad? Every last one of them? Weren't they, by definition, monsters, or was there something she didn't know, proving that her education was indeed sorely lacking, as this wolf had warned?

No time to ponder that...

She was geared up and anxious to find out what had made that wolf turn his back to her and what had made him turn the tip of the damn knife in his direction. She could have used that knife. If she had, this would have been over. Instead, she was charging after the Were as if she was part of his tag team, bringing up the rear.

Confusion didn't begin to describe what she felt. Tess couldn't shake off the memory of the moment she had looked into his eyes, and the feelings that came with that connection. Absurd feelings. Impossible feelings about wayward longings that had made her pulse thunder.

To say she was interested in this guy would have been an understatement when what she actually felt was something else entirely.

"You have to know that I'll keep coming," she said as she ran, needing to get those words out and into the open, hoping they might somehow reinforce her need to believe them when she now had doubts.

When a new thought touched her mind—one that

wasn't of her making—Tess nearly tripped over her own feet.

"Please go home, Tess. Do as I ask. Trust me just this once."

It was him. His thought. She recognized the tone, if not the voice. The damn Were was speaking to her telepathically.

"Ridiculous," she muttered. "Can't do that."

Weres could only link minds telepathically with other Weres, so the stories went. Still, other than the werewolves themselves, no one could possibly know that for sure.

The wind seemed to come alive with this guy's next utterance.

"Now isn't the time. We will meet again, I promise."

Speaking with a tight jaw, Tess shouted, "No way, Lycan. This is my turf!"

But suddenly, unbelievably and as if another creature had simply dropped from the sky, Tess saw two forms running near the base of the hillside. One of them she recognized, having been close to the big Were. The other animal was a real wolf, on all fours, with fur that glowed silver-white in the moonlight as it streaked through the woods at the Lycan's side.

There had been no warning for her of another wolf in the area, Were or otherwise. She didn't smell that other wolf now.

What the hell was going on?

Mesmerized by the sight of the pair running in the field, Tess pulled up…and stared.

The sadness Jonas had seen in Tess's blue eyes had moved him. Being a werewolf meant keeping company with his own kind mostly, so what about her life? Tess's life?

Was culling werewolves her only form of excitement? He supposed that doing her job might make up for whatever else she lacked in terms of family and friends sometimes.

Looking into her eyes had left him with a flood of strange sensations. Staring into her eyes had created ribbons of light in the dark recesses of his soul. He had connected to Tess on a level new to him and somehow had been able to tap into her emotions. The depth of that connection, as well as the speed with which it had occurred, was disturbing.

Were to Were was how those rapidly formed internal bonds usually happened. *Imprinting* was the term used for the union of two souls, a state that only happened between Were couples destined to be mated for life. This sudden bond with Tess felt like a similar version of that, though he hadn't experienced it for himself before. And she wasn't a Were, so this had to be something else.

He couldn't dwell on that now. His attention was needed elsewhere. He was needed elsewhere.

Gwen hadn't listened to his instructions. In a rare out-in-the-open appearance, she was beside him—this unusual creature in his life who was so special.

Tess would have been even more surprised if she knew that his sister was a Lycan throwback to the earliest form of the werewolf species.

Gwendolyn Dale was a carrier of the original form of Lycan DNA—the only Were he knew of these days who was able to transform into a full wolf, and with no hint of wolf scent. A pure white wolf. Gwen's presence on this earth made the necessity for secret-keeping all the more imperative.

And she had followed him.

He ran through the shadows of the trees in human shape for several more minutes with Gwen on all fours, dancing at his heels, before the moonlight performed its neat trick of setting his inner wolf free. Yet Jonas's stomach stayed tight. He had been unprepared for Gwen's latest streak of rebelliousness.

His sister had possibly just blown their cover, placing them in as much danger here as they had been in Florida. She had left the cabin and shown herself to anyone who might have been looking. If Tess had seen her, there would be a hefty price to pay. If Death's minion had been here, the final fight for Gwen's soul would soon be upon them.

They ran in silence, covering ground on legs burning with energy. Gwen's white coat took on a silvery sheen in the moonlight. Few Weres had white hair or fur. Colorlessness would come from having survived heinous wounds, the way his sister had survived hers. Ghost wolves, these wounded warriors were called. Only one wolf remotely connected to the Miami pack had become a ghost, and that was another cop named Colton Killion.

Within their pack, his sister was to be revered. The unique blood in Gwen's veins that allowed her to possess these special traits and the ability to avoid detection was going to be cherished. If passed along, the special ancestral particles in her bloodstream could reinvigorate the entire Lycan species.

No pressure there.

So he had to take extra care now to keep her safe

and away from Tess Owens, who brandished silver-tipped weapons instead of claws. Blue-eyed Tess, who shouldered so much sadness.

One thing was for sure. Their circumstances had just gotten a hell of a lot more complicated. And if that wasn't enough, there was the rather startling fact that he couldn't wait to meet Tess again. The sooner, the better.

Tess swore out loud.

Unbelievably, she had let those wolves go. Now, she promised herself this was only a temporary setback. The werewolf wasn't going anywhere anytime soon. He had told her that, though his explanation for why he was here had been missing a few details. Like all of them.

This guy had even seemed reasonable.

Could that be right? Possible?

The fact that she had chosen to believe him might have made her an idiot and a shameful member of her clan.

Another hiccup in a night full of them was that this Were actually ran with real wolves. Rare ones with white pelts. Maybe there was a connection between pure-blooded Lycans and the wolves their species had sprang from. Lycans, who were the equivalent of werewolf royalty, had lineages that went way back.

This guy was a stunner. Up close, he had reeked of enough raw male power to make her feel tingly all over. Still, she wasn't ready to concede and let this wolf chalk tonight up as a victory. Anger was flooding her with heat. She felt antsy, anxious and ready for a rematch. This time she would be prepared, she told herself.

"I know every inch of these woods and hillsides," she called out, hoping her voice would carry. "So it won't take me long to find you."

Setting off again in the direction the unusual Were had taken, Tess imagined he sent a reply.

"Wait for me, Tess, but give me some time."

Hell, that couldn't be right. She could not have heard him. She couldn't even see him. What she could do, however, was follow the trail of the scent that this big sucker left behind that was now deeply ingrained in her lungs. The scent underscoring the inexplicable tickle at the base of her neck and causing an internal shakeup. Her new target was both unbelievably handsome and monstrously unique. He was a worthy adversary and as powerful as Weres came.

She had met a Lycan, and he had not killed her when he had the chance.

All of those things factored into her renewed desire to find the bastard and put an end to whatever this was, and before she was declared certifiably insane.

"Give you time?" she muttered. "I don't think so."

She added a thought, *"Got that, wolf?"*

She didn't expect a reply and absorbed another ripple of shock when one came.

"We are more alike than you know, Tess. If you hunt me, I will haunt you in return."

"BS!" Tess shouted to the otherwise quiet hillside as she stood on another rocky ledge dividing her property from the property that she now knew had to be his. But she didn't go any farther, bothered by the word *haunt* and inexplicably willing to give that damn Were one more night to get his act together.

Haunt her in the future?

Hell, he already was.

Chapter 5

Sleep was elusive. Jonas hadn't stopped pacing since he and Gwen had returned to the safety of the cabin. Chastising her would have been useless and might have driven her further from him, so Jonas kept his fears to himself.

Tonight was the third time he had seen his sister shape-shift. The sight was both a blessing and a curse. He couldn't foresee what kind of future Gwen might have if they made it back to Miami. The thought of taking her back there made him sick.

He doubted that anyone else in his family had known about how special she was. She would have been too precious to everyone in the Lycan community to be allowed to roam freely among the packs.

When they got back to Miami—and if they did—there would be a highly detailed plan for her to breed and pass along her genes. By bringing Gwen here, he had granted her the gift of more time away from all that, besides the other pressing issue of keeping her alive long enough to see that future.

In any case, his sister hadn't yet fully healed from her injuries and needed more time to do that.

Jonas stood for a while at the window, searching for any hint of the things that would eventually come their way.

The night was quiet. Tess hadn't followed them here, and he silently thanked her for that. As for the darker thing on their trail, Jonas hoped they would have a few more days of relative tranquility before that battle took place. He also hoped he'd have time to meet Tess in more reasonable circumstances, though that wish seemed like a stretch.

Already, and from his first sight of Tess, she had become an unshakable fixture in his mind. When Jonas closed his eyes, she was there. Each breath he took seemed to bring her closer. Leather, smoke and flowers were her calling card, and his cabin seemed to be full of those fragrances.

He glanced at Gwen's door and sighed. Leaning a shoulder against the wall, Jonas sent his mind outward to test his theory about his uncanny connection to this hunter.

"Do you sleep, Tess? Are your dreams peaceful, or are they filled with dark things?"

It was stupid of him to believe she might hear him from this far away, and yet he could swear he felt his thought travel over the distance separating them. He almost felt himself beside her, as if his threat to haunt her had come true.

She would have a small bed in a small room, Jonas envisioned. Her fair hair would be loose and spread like sunshine across a lavender-scented pillow, because Tess Owens was actually a creature of sunlight, like other humans were.

What would you be wearing tonight, hunter?

He pictured her in something comfortable and light, rather than silks or satins. Tess wasn't a girly girl.

Maybe you'll rest in leather in case a werewolf comes calling?

After letting her go, she would be doubly on guard. She would have her knife handy. It was obvious that she knew how to wield a blade, as well as what she could have done with one if she had wanted to.

"Expect me, Tess," he sent to her. *"Rest tonight. Sleep in peace. Meet me tomorrow in the sunlight when the dark things are hiding."*

Did he see her open her eyes and turn from her pillow to listen? Was there actually a possibility she had heard him?

What would it mean if you are listening? Am I wrong about a bond forming between us?

He imagined Tess covering her ears in an attempt to ignore his mental invasion. But he also felt her tuning in, as if she were merely in the next room and straining to listen to him speak.

As the images floated away, he realized that Tess probably wouldn't fall sleep in that bed tonight, and that wishful thinking on his part didn't ease things for either of them.

"Tomorrow," he said aloud. "Meet me tomorrow."

He felt an unusual drag on his thoughts that made

his heart pound and sensed that this new bit of aware-ness carried no hint of Tess Owens in it.

Jonas turned to find his sister in the doorway with a questioning expression on her face.

Had his thoughts been too loud?

Tess sat up in bed after tossing and turning her way through two hours of thoughts. After checking the corners of her room for werewolves a tenth time, she threw off the covers and walked to the window.

She couldn't see out. The shutters were closed and locked tight in case *he* showed up unannounced. With-out fresh air, the closeness in the room made her feel claustrophobic.

Tess doubted if she'd be ever able to sleep again until this werewolf issue was settled. She had an in-tuitive feeling that tonight wouldn't be the time for a second meeting but had to remain on guard. There was no telling what this unusual Were might do.

"Get out of my head," she muttered, shaking the shutter to assure herself that it was in place. Wood planks would be easy enough for a strong werewolf to destroy, but there'd be enough noise to alert her if one tried.

Tomorrow...

Since she'd first heard his invitation, the word had floated in and out of her consciousness with the tone of a whispered command.

"Get out," she whispered again, forgoing the bed in favor of a trip to the front door.

Palming her knife, Tess left the cabin in her shorts and tank top to look up at the moon. Sensing no wolf presence, she sighed with relief and spoke out of frustration. "I accept, in case you're the one sending this invitation."

Brush rustled. Night birds sang. Bugs chirped as tree branches swayed in the wind. All this was normal. Usual. Except for one thing: the feeling of dread that invaded her as Tess studied the moon.

She dropped her gaze to search the area. Her skin bristled. Nerves again began to buzz. Something else was out there, and she didn't know what. She didn't recognize the sensations hitting her system. This was no wolf. So, what?

The air changed. Night seemed to darken as the overhead stars were erased. The moon disappeared as if a black curtain had descended over them and everything else. Tess looked at her knife. The silver blade had been swallowed by the roaming blackness. Its surface was dull. The shadows in her peripheral vision appeared to be moving.

Feelings of dread brought on a chill. Her knees felt oddly weak. But as quickly as it had arrived, the strange sensations drifted away as though this had been a bad dream.

The stars and moon reappeared. Tess took a breath and let it out slowly, listening for anything that might explain what had happened. She looked to the west, the direction the Were had taken after leaving her earlier that night, wondering if he had been responsible for what she had just experienced. The rolling blackness had moved off in that direction…toward her neighbor's place and the wolf who had taken up temporary residence there.

"It's coming," she said, feeling silly for thinking the

Were she had been hip to hip with a couple of hours ago would be able hear a warning he might not need.

And why would she warn him, anyway?

Tess cleared her throat and repeated the warning, concerned about why she would care what happened to a creature she was going to take down anyway when the next full moon came if he hadn't caused that blackout.

I'm here to keep something very bad from happening, the Lycan had told her. *Promise me you'll let me do what I need to do here without interference, and that you'll give me time to take care of the thing I came here to do. That's all I ask.*

A small shiver of incomprehension ran through Tess as she remembered those words. For the life of her, she could not imagine a greater threat than having a werewolf next door. But somehow she sensed that was about to change.

Chapter 6

Jonas smiled at his sister. "Sorry, Gwen. Did I wake you?"

She eyed him thoughtfully.

"It's okay," he said. "You can rest."

Gwen didn't move from the doorway. Her gaze moved past him, heading for the window.

Jonas looked out. "Has something else disturbed you?"

He felt the quake that ran through his sister from where he stood and turned to look at her.

"What is it? What do you see?"

If ever there was a time for Gwen to speak, Jonas would have liked that time to be now. But she didn't oblige and continued to stare at the window as if expecting someone to show up.

He didn't like this. Didn't like the lack of expression on Gwen's young face as she waited for whatever she thought was out there to come knocking.

Gwen might be tapping into other special powers that he had no knowledge of, but would that include an awareness of the presence of things no one else could see?

Chills dripped down Jonas's back, taking their time, hitting every vertebra one by one. He had a really bad feeling.

"I can't read your mind," he said. "You'll need to tell me what I need to know."

When Gwen's head tilted to the side as if she were listening to sounds other than his latest request, a cascade of pale hair slipped to cover half of her face. Her hair had been brown once, like his, before the attack that had rendered her speechless. Brown, straight and shiny. Massive injuries had instigated the change in this pretty teen and nothing could alter that.

Gwen was disturbed as she looked outside, and her inner distress was contagious. Jonas liked to believe he was still close enough to his sister to understand a few things, but until she decided to speak, he needed another way to find out what was going on.

"Gwen," he said, hoping to get her attention. "I'm trying to protect you. Please help me do that."

Her gaze traveled to him before again bypassing him in favor of the window. Feeling helpless, Jonas placed himself in front of the glass.

"What do you see?" he asked, his concern growing. Gwen's skin had begun to ripple the way his skin did when a shape-shift was imminent.

Jonas held up a hand. "No. Stop, Gwen. Now isn't the time. It isn't safe. We aren't alone out here. Our neighbor knows what we are."

That last statement was only partially true, Jonas

amended inwardly. Tess might know about him, but as for Gwen...

Gwen was something Tess Owens had no idea existed and would label a nightmare if she did.

His sister now had claws—ten short white claws nearly as colorless as her hair. She had become hyperaware of an issue she considered a problem and couldn't fill him in.

"Shit," Jonas muttered without daring to go to her, fearing that too much protesting might set her off in ways he wouldn't be able to corral.

Gwen sidestepped him with a graceful move and joined him at the window. She pressed her face to the glass and ran her claws down the wooden frame hard enough to leave visible tracks in the finish.

Jonas took hold of one of her wrists and turned Gwen around to face him. He adopted a stern tone when repeating his last warning, hoping a repeat of the same stuff would get through to her.

"No, Gwen. Now isn't the time."

She raised her chin and looked directly into his eyes. What Jonas saw in those eyes frightened him more than the idea of what might eventually be out there somewhere.

And then he heard what Gwen must have heard: the echo of a distant voice.

"Whatever the hell this thing was is heading your way."

The effort of absorbing that warning required Jonas to turn for the door.

Though she hadn't meant to move, Tess found herself running.

Curiosity had gotten the better of her as to what

that engulfing blackness had been, and yet she wasn't a fool. Her property line would be the stalling point in going after it. She just wanted to see that thing again to make sure she hadn't made it up. After all, not much about tonight had been usual. The wolf next door had seen to that.

And okay, maybe she was a fool for falling for his line about being needed elsewhere and about being a good guy. She found it difficult to explain the leniency of her actions and his. The damn Lycan's face had been painted in her mind ever since.

It was in her mind now as she sprinted over the rocky ground in her bare feet, ignoring the discomfort, feeling lighter without her boots. The flimsy tank and shorts she slept in wouldn't help her fend off claws if she bumped into that Lycan and his friends, but she didn't think she would meet them. There was no sense of that Were's closeness in spite of all that imagined telepathic mumbo jumbo. She just needed a better view of the fields.

Nevertheless, her heart hammered inside her chest, pushing adrenaline to the right places to fuel her muscles. The chill she had felt several minutes ago melted away as rising body heat took over.

It didn't take her long to reached the crest of the hill where she had encountered the Were. Stopping, Tess waited in silence with her eyes trained on the valley beneath the rocky ledge. No new anomaly stood out as far as she could see, and yet she couldn't shake the return of an inexplicable undercurrent of dread.

And then she saw something down there. It wasn't a moving black curtain or the Were she had encountered earlier. This thing moved like the wind, like a white missile, close to the ground and heading straight for Tess's home turf.

It was the white wolf. The Lycan's pet.

Without hesitating to watch that ghostly apparition in action, Tess turned and retraced her steps, heading for home, clutching the knife in her hand and hoping to beat that animal there.

When she got to her fence, she found the place quiet. Nothing moved or jumped out at her, but she still felt a wolf's presence. Inching toward the gate by walking backward, Tess scanned the yard.

"I know you're here."

Those words had become her mantra lately and seemed terribly inadequate for tonight's level of activity.

"Cat got your tongue?" she asked with her heart banging against her ribs.

Cool air swirled around her as she waited. No big, hunky Lycan stepped out of the shadows. No rolling mass of darkness descended. Her only visitor could be the four-legged animal she had seen running in the valley—the real wolf she had seen loping along in the Lycan's wake.

"No use hiding," she said, hoping to lure that wolf out of the shadows, though it was, she supposed, silly to think that an animal could understand human speech.

The wolf emerged from beneath the trees as if it had understood her request, moving just far enough out of the shadows for Tess to see the brilliance of its silver-white coat in the moonlight.

"I have no problems with wolves. Real ones," Tess said, speaking more for herself than for that animal.

As soon as she had spoken those words, however, Tess began to comprehend that this was no mere wolf after all. The vibes coming from it were altogether new and different. And honestly, she was getting sick of things being so far out of the norm.

The white wolf's muzzle lifted as it sniffed the air. Tess couldn't see its eyes or determine the animal's actual size. After seeing the animal's head, she guessed this visitor was a lot larger than any other wolf she'd seen in the wild. Twice as big, maybe more.

"This place is protected from the likes of you," Tess said, moving toward the gate that would seal her off from immediate harm.

Her knife dangled from her hand.

"Try it, wolf. Take me on and see what kind of skills I have developed to ward off claws."

Her dare was punctuated by a rustling sound in the brush. Tess couldn't look there. Dividing her attention could amount to suicide.

Her heart could not have pounded harder. The fingers holding her knife were turning white due to the tightness of her grip on the hilt.

Damn it... There was another visitor. His approach hit her hard. Coming up against this particular presence was like running into a familiar wall.

"Tess," the Were said, as if they were friends.

She refused to look for the speaker, already knowing who it was. No one else said her name like that, in the tone of a caress.

"Is that wolf with you?" she demanded with her gaze fixed on the white wolf.

"This wasn't planned," the Lycan said. "I'm sorry you were disturbed."

Tess rallied. "This is the second time you've come here and gotten too close to where you aren't welcome."

The white wolf growled in response to Tess's clipped tone. Tess raised the hand holding the knife.

"It's all right," the strange Were said in a placating whisper that reached Tess from a short distance. "I'll take her home."

Her?

Hell, Tess didn't want to know what a werewolf might do with a female animal like this one. She was sorry she had believed this guy to be truthful and handsome. His looks might have been exceptional, but werewolves were still monsters in disguise. Being handsome and convincing didn't mean he was exempt from her reaching current goals.

"We'll go," he said with the adamancy of a promise. "Turn your back, Tess, and we will be gone."

"What sort of an idiot do you take me for?" Tess returned.

"She won't hurt you. I won't let her."

"Do you have a leash? The beast keeps a beast for a pet?"

The white wolf growled again, forcing more of Tess's attention there.

"She doesn't like trouble," the Lycan said.

"Then why is she here?"

"She sensed trouble and came to investigate."

"Then she knows about me?" Tess asked.

"Yes, in theory."

Tess turned toward the direction his voice had hailed from. "Because you told her, and she understands English?"

The problematic Lycan didn't take on that question.

Catching a hint of movement in the brush, Tess backed again toward the gate with the knife raised and ready. Her sworn enemy didn't make an appearance, and it looked like he wasn't going to.

She heard him speak in soft tones to someone else. He had to be addressing the white wolf. But that wolf didn't budge.

"Perhaps you've lost some of your power of persuasion," Tess suggested nervously.

There was a lull before he spoke again.

"She believes trouble is near," he said.

"I'll second that," Tess muttered.

"Maybe you can tell her it's okay," he suggested.

Unbelievable...

"Am I to invite her in and offer tea and cookies, too?" Tess fired back.

"I'm pretty sure that won't be necessary. However, if you want her to go, you'll need to let her see that there's no cause for concern."

"Because there isn't?"

"Not from us. Not from me. Not from her. Not tonight."

Tess thought back to their earlier encounter. "Is this wolf part of the reason you let me go without a fight? She is one of the things you're protecting?"

It seemed that no replies to those questions were forthcoming, so she tried again. "Do you hold yourself up as some kind of wolf warden?"

"No," he replied. "Nothing like that."

The white muzzle shifted slightly before one silvery leg appeared. Slowly, that wolf left the shadows, and the sight of this animal robbed Tess of more breath.

The largest real wolf Tess had ever seen moved toward her with a growl rolling in its throat.

Chapter 7

Jonas lunged forward just as Gwen glided through full moonlight to reach Tess. He barked a command that Gwen ignored. His sister was interested in Tess. Whether that reason was a bad one that involved seriously twisted intentions, Jonas couldn't tell.

He reached Tess seconds before Gwen did. Gwen butted her head against his thighs as if she would go right through him, but Jonas held steady and barked a stream of protests in return.

The moon was overhead, and he was standing beneath it. His claws popped before he had time to stop them. Neck muscles began to spasm. "No, Gwen," he said with the last vestiges of a voice everyone here would understand. "Not today."

He could see that Tess was both fearful and annoyed by his interference. Jonas sensed the silver blade she held without having to see it, remembering the way it had burned into his flesh. That knife would hurt Gwen when she had already suffered enough. He had to keep Tess from using it.

Tess's hands were like fire on his back when she tried to push him away. Gwen growled again, letting him know that she also wanted him to move. Maybe this is the fight Tess had anticipated tonight...not with a rogue werewolf, but something more. Something priceless to the Were world. His sister.

He could not let that fight happen.

When Gwen hurled herself at him, he caught her by the fur on the back of her neck. Tugging hard, he maneuvered his sister to the side as his Were genes, triggered by the light, fully kicked in.

He heard Tess's surprised intake of breath as he tightened his grip on Gwen's fur and spun the white wolf around. Tess sprang forward with her knife in her hand. Gwen panted and growled, showing treacherously sharp teeth as she struggled to get free. But he was far stronger than either of these characters. He proved it now by lifting Gwen's front paws off the ground until his sister and Tess Owens stood eye-to-eye with a distance of only six inches between them.

Tess froze. Gwen stopped growling. It was a scene straight out of a horror movie and yet as the hunter and the very special white wolf eyed each other, Gwen began to whimper. Hearing that, Tess, who seemed to be equally as stunned, lowered her blade.

Jonas hoped that Tess had seen something human in Gwen's eyes that wasn't obvious in the form his sister was able to take. He hoped his sister would accept the temporary truce of Tess's lowered blade and take the opportunity to disappear.

He could have cut through the tension in the air with that damn blade in Tess's lowered hand.

With the lull in aggression, however temporary it might have been, Jonas raised his face. He let loose a howl directed at the instigator of this current round of trouble. The moon. Then he hauled his sister back, gave Tess a quick bark of warning to stay back and led Gwen away from the big bad wolf hunter, who for some reason hadn't been at her best tonight.

Lesson learned, Tess. Some of us truly are different.

He kept hold of Gwen by digging his fingers into the scruff of her neck fur, careful not to let his claws do any real damage. After her initial reluctance, Gwen allowed him to lead her away from the Owenses' front yard.

Jonas had no idea what his sister might have been thinking by coming here. Lycans of her caliber had thought-blocking techniques probably unknown to every other Were, and that was damnably inconvenient.

On some level, he realized that Gwen had been as surprised as he had been by coming face-to-face with Tess. One close look at the hunter and Gwen had made sounds he'd only recently heard her make—sounds shockingly similar to the groans she'd uttered during the difficulty of her recovery from the injuries she had accrued on the night of her attack.

When standing eye-to-eye, she and Tess both had been privy to a sudden wave of insight that had quelled their urge to fight, at least for the time being. Jonas had no idea what that might have been but was thankful for the respite.

Show-and-tell time was over. Introductions between these two had been made. Tess didn't know that the white wolf was a Were in wolf form, or that she was his sister. Full-wolf shape-shifts, so rare these days, would be new to Tess, since they were virtually unheard of outside of a sanctioned few elders and the families that lived with these rare beings.

If Tess setting eyes on Gwen wasn't bad enough, the Owens woman had seen him shape-shift twice in a single night and might be wondering about that as well.

He wanted to know why Gwen had come here and if it could have been nothing more than a desire to meet the neighbor.

Perhaps Gwen had scented the hunter in the same way he had, and her instincts for survival had taken over. Maybe the strange DNA in Gwen's makeup retained memories of hunters from times in the past.

Those thoughts were legitimate ones. Nevertheless, Jonas had a hunch the reason for Gwen's visit could be blamed on neither of those things. Warning flags in his mind were waving. Gwen wasn't struggling half as hard against his hold as he thought she might. He hadn't even broken a sweat.

"Your big brother is keeping watch, Gwen," he silently messaged his sister, pulling her along without pausing to address her second act of rebellion as a real issue. Just because he couldn't hear his sister's thoughts didn't mean she couldn't access his.

"Possibly you need to learn to use more control, hun."

Jonas let her go in a spot near the rocky overlook and placed his considerable Were bulk between Gwen and the path behind them, daring her to try to get past him.

Gwen waited without moving for a minute or two before turning to focus on that path in a way that made Jonas's neck chill.

Tess hadn't been content to let the two Weres go. He should have known the white wolf would pique her interest and get her hunter blood pumping. Could he blame her? In Tess's place, he probably would have done the same thing by following them. She was coming now.

Unfortunately, there was more at stake here than Tess Owens hoping to do her job. And he was caught between two females on opposite ends of the DNA spectrum that had gotten a good whiff of each other. Two females with the power to mess things up before the real mess began.

Christ, he could feel that other thing he had feared getting closer. The thing he dreaded most. The air was thicker, wetter. He didn't want to lose Gwen. Besides his own feelings, the future of his species might hang on her survival.

In Jonas's mind, the woodsy fragrance of the wolf hunter's cottage was suddenly blotted out by the odor of impending doom. He now had Tess and Death to worry about, and it seemed that his worst nightmare was about to come true.

"Run," he sent to Gwen, giving her a gentle shove. For once, his sister did as she was told. She took off, heading west like a bullet shot from a rifle, leaving him standing on the rocks with his claws raised.

* * *

To Tess, this felt wrong—not only for the fact that she had let her family down, but because of the entire night and the way things had gone.

She had never seen a wolf like the one the Lycan had tamed into submission, and that brought the tally to two firsts in one night. It had been two wolves against one hunter in her front yard, and yet the handsome Were hadn't allowed the white wolf to take her on when that would have served him better.

Uttering a string of curses and oaths, Tess again sprinted through the trees and brush. There was still time to put things to rights, she told herself...at least there would have been time for that if she hadn't become so interested in this Lycan and what he was up to by showing her a sensitive side.

Not only had he not gone after her tonight, he had kept the white wolf from doing the same. *Why?*

What was his connection to that white wolf? Had his hesitancy to fight been due to his desire to see that real wolf unharmed?

She wasn't dressed for this. Her feet hurt like hell and there was a good possibility she wasn't thinking straight. The only weapon she had was the blade. One damn blade against that Lycan's cunning and mounds of muscle. She was going after a werewolf in an outfit that amounted to little more than sleepy-time underwear.

What a pretty picture that presented.

But it was okay, Tess supposed, since it wasn't in the Lycan's favor to let her catch up with him. Additionally, he had no reason to want to see what she'd do next since he had gotten the better of her twice already without lifting a claw.

The differences between this Were and other werewolves she had dealt with were major and lent an air of fantasy to the craziness of this night.

If she could only get him out of her mind...

If only her wits would return and warn her that a strange attraction to this guy was surely going to be her downfall...

But she was fighting those what-ifs and in need of other answers. Tess wanted to stop the madness that had been caused by meeting this guy, no matter how interested she was in his behavior. She didn't have to admit to anyone, including herself, that she was curious about him for more reasons than his actions alone.

That face.

The sculpted physique.

His deep voice.

It was strictly forbidden and an unforgiveable sin for wolf hunters to cozy up to their prey. They were two different species. Leniency showed weakness. If word about her inability to do her job were to spread, other monsters would arrive.

Still, deep down in Tess's mind lay another reason for her interest in this guy that scared her more than anything else.

Having been tight up against him had caused her well-tuned willpower to backfire. In man form, he was mesmerizing. In the other shape, he was forbidding, but with an intelligent gleam in his eyes.

She wasn't caving on the job. She just wasn't sure what had happened tonight.

"There is something about you..." she said aloud.

"And I will probably regret finding out about whatever that actually is."

Against all inner warnings, though, Tess didn't turn back. Sensing a change in the atmosphere, as if the moonlight had somehow suddenly grown brighter, denser, she slowed, then stopped to look up at the rocky ledge above her with her blade ready and her heart in her throat.

He was there. Contrary to everything she had just thought about the situation, he stood in the open—this tall, muscled, wickedly formidable and one hundred percent Lycan werewolf. He seemed larger than life and looked to have been carved from the surrounding stones.

Even in this setting where animals prowled, this guy with his bronze skin and light brown hair stood out as another kind of being entirely. Her new nemesis was a crazy anomaly within his species. Something new and exciting.

Maybe that's why her heart was beating so rapidly she could barely draw a breath. Maybe it was also the realization that running wasn't what had winded her. She was breathless because she found this Lycan so fascinating.

He had seen her. The growl he issued was soft, low, and did things to her that Tess refused to acknowledge. She didn't speak, didn't reply. Couldn't do either of those things.

Though he was motionless, the werewolf wasn't at ease. Tess sensed the tension flowing through him, and like an airborne contagion, that tension quickly transferred to her.

He was looking at her, not as if she might be his

plaything, but as though he wanted to say something to her that his shape-shift had prevented him from saying several minutes ago.

Having witnessed his ability to manipulate his shifts so quickly, Tess observed him carefully, fully on guard. When she could draw a full breath, she said, "I don't think I like whatever kind of game it is that we're playing."

He sank to a crouch. In other werewolves, this would have meant he was ready to spring. This guy didn't translate that kind of intention to her. It was as if he didn't want to appear too large or menacing.

He was still bare from the waist up and wearing faded jeans. The guy was a magnificent example of this species, and only by looking at him through narrowed eyes did Tess see the more wolfish parts. The harder she tried to zero in on those things—the extra layer of muscle and the claws—the less she saw. The wolf aura surrounding him hinted at the term *werewolf*, rather than anything pertaining to the purely physical aspects of his countenance.

Tess had seen him run. She didn't take her eyes from him now. Man and wolf were such an unlikely combination, who else but the few people in the know would have believed anything like this possible?

She showed him the blade. "This is all I have at the moment. Will you challenge?"

When their gazes connected, heat streaked through Tess that was akin to having gotten too close to the sun. Her pulse thundered in her neck, pounding out beat after merciless beat that lifted the skin beneath her ears.

Her interest in him would be her death.

"So tell me," she said, pitching her voice low to hide any telltale signs of quavering. "Is the neat trick of attracting the hunters who are hunting you some special kind of power you possess?"

The beast perched on the rocks above her couldn't answer that question unless he used more of his magic Lycan voodoo to transform himself into a more vocal version of the one he presented to her at the moment. It was entirely possible that he wouldn't change back, so that he could avoid answering her altogether.

His tension had become like a separate living thing. Swallowing back a lick of fear and determined to ride this out, Tess asked, "Do you also have the ability to call real wolves? I'm wondering if they realize what you are and that you might at one time have been related."

The Lycan's shoulders twitched briefly before quickly settling back to stillness.

"Why don't you jump? I'm standing here like an idiot, breaking every rule I've ever had pounded into me about dealing with the likes of you," Tess said.

The Lycan's next growl was more like a touch than a sound and caused Tess to lean toward him. "Stop it," she commanded. "I came here to ask you about another thing as well. That veil of darkness that blew in and passed over before you and your four-legged friend appeared on my doorstep."

Breaking eye contact, he turned his attention to the distance.

"It rolled west, toward you," Tess continued. "I liked it about as much as I like you. Still…"

Her voice trailed off.

The werewolf on the ledge above her took that jump

and landed beside her. The blade in Tess's hand was useless. Her lungs were useless, and so were her legs. She found herself in the Lycan's arms, being swept off her bare feet.

Then they were moving in the direction of her cabin, and any protest Tess might have wanted to make would have sounded like the next growl that came from the Lycan's throat.

Chapter 8

Jonas was frightened by Tess's mention of a rolling darkness. He and Gwen had barely settled in, so it didn't seem feasible for Death's minion to have found them already.

It was possible, reason told him, that the darkness Tess had spoken of had nothing to do with that. There had been no hint of it at the cabin. His sensation of having felt that darkness earlier hadn't panned out, and Gwen had seemed more concerned with Tess than anything deadlier.

Maybe there was time, and they were safe at the moment. Possibly Tess was wrong.

Jonas looked down at the woman in his arms. He could sense she was allowing him this leeway only out of curiosity and to see what he was up to. Her left arm dangled as they moved. The knife was ready in her hand.

No surprise he could have offered her would have thrown Tess too far off her mark, he supposed. She was watching him closely and was far from relaxed. One slice with that blade across an artery in his neck or thigh, and he'd be hurting.

Jonas had wanted to touch her again and had taken the liberty, figuring he didn't have long before she'd put up a fight.

He liked holding her. She was a good fit in his arms.

Tess's unique scent was backed by the fire of determination and grit. She might be tough, but underneath that trained exterior lay a woman who was alone in the middle of nowhere out of necessity and loyalty to a cause.

She was light in his arms and weighed next to nothing. Her leanness was necessary for speed and for sidestepping any trouble that came her way, though it was also misleading. Tess Owens was nobody's fool.

Jonas waved off the desire to shift back and speak to her, thinking about what he could have said to explain things better. What words would best describe a Lycan who was willing to break with tradition and treat himself to time with a fair-haired morsel like the one in his arms, when other situations were dire?

Her gaze was similar to the fire in her scent, though Tess's skin was cool. She wore shorts, exposing long, slender legs that were as ivory as her face. Her thighs were shapely. Her calves were soft. Jonas tried not to concentrate on her knees. Against the skin of his forearms, those bare legs felt like silk.

She didn't touch him back; didn't sling an arm around her neck for balance. Beneath her blond lashes, blue eyes the color of an afternoon sky invaded his privacy by seeming to look right through him.

Her gaze was intimate to a degree he could never have anticipated, and continued to jolt his insides. He should have been able to understand the reason for their unexpected connection. Weres and humans weren't a good mix, and yet his desire to be close to Tess felt as necessary to him as the moon was.

Things were more treacherous here than he had anticipated. After two short meetings, he was developing unusual feelings for Tess that were reserved for she-wolves. Those feelings of lust, need and an intense longing to possess her, were all part of the emotions he couldn't shake off.

Getting this close to an enemy was a game, as Tess had suggested, but that game had already gone too far. As soon as either of them stopped playing, the situation would change. She would change.

How far will you let me take this, wolf hunter? Are you also searching for something in this forbidden closeness?

He might not have intended to soak in more of her delicious details, but that's also the way this back-and-forth sizing up worked. With Tess pressed against him and her heartbeat matching his in the way talented hunters had of tuning into their prey, their bodies were absorbing things that couldn't be found any other way. Naked skin to naked skin. A brief meeting of their eyes.

Oh yes, you're good at this, Tess Owens.

She was no amateur when it came to reading her opponents either. Part of her plan might have been to give him a false sense of accomplishment, and then, when ready, she'd challenge that.

They had only gone a few yards from the outlook before that moment came. With a slick move he almost hadn't seen coming, Tess had the silver blade against his throat.

"Really, wolf," she said. "Do you think I'm completely insane?"

Tess knew it would have been easy for the magnificent Lycan to have tossed her aside. Being in his arms had given her new insight into the power his body commanded. Her knife seemed insignificant in light of that, and yet he had stopped and was waiting for whatever she might do next, when she didn't know what her next move might be.

"What do you say if we cut this out and get on with things?" she suggested, hearing lingering echoes of that same request from their first meet-up.

The problem facing her was that this Lycan just didn't look like a werewolf. She couldn't slide the blade into his bronze-skinned throat and not feel as though she'd be hurting a human. There was no wild and wooly fur. No gleam of moon madness in this wolf's blue eyes. Those eyes were on her and focused. Inside them, golden lights danced.

He was alive, warm, masculine. Like her, this guy more or less lived on the fringe of society where secrets ruled the shadows. He might also be a loner and at times in need of company other than the kind with fur.

And maybe not.

Tess thought about closing her eyes to distance herself from those ideas, but that would have been her next ridiculous move in a night already full of them. She was blowing things, big-time.

"For your information, no one is less interested in being a damsel in distress than I am," she said, turning the blade slightly to emphasize the importance of that remark.

"I met the first of your relatives when I was a kid. Wolves have been my sole addiction since then. So you can put me down and face me. Show me how much of an animal you are and that everything I've learned hasn't been wasted."

Instead of acknowledging her words, the Lycan again began to walk, dismissing the silver blade biting into his throat as if it were merely a minor inconvenience. As Tess saw it, this left her only two options. She could shut her eyes, bury the knife in this guy and never look back…or postpone that part and find out what else he had in mind.

He was continuing to look at her as if reading her mind was part of his Lycan skill set. When he shook his head, soft strands of shiny brown hair tickled her face, bringing back that deep inner rumble she had worked so hard to hide from him and from herself— the one that had kept her from dispatching this guy to werewolf heaven so far.

Letting him get on with this charade had been a very bad idea, though. In truth, she actually was a fool, a complete idiot and no longer to be considered trustworthy.

Taking the silver blade from his throat, she let her hand fall. His reaction was to nod his head and smile.

"Time's up," she said, irritated by that smile. "Make a stand."

He obliged enough to put her down but didn't back off. A third option for dealing with this, and him, suddenly presented itself.

She could just walk away and be done with it.

Given this Were's refusal to fight and the nearly naked state they were both in at the moment, that third option seemed like a good one. The only one.

Then he did another strange and unexpected thing. Still unable to speak, he pointed a lethally clawed hand toward her bruised, scratched and slightly bloody bare feet. Tess didn't like what he might have been insinuating by that either. Had he offered to cart her back to her cabin so that she wouldn't hurt herself any more than she already had, and out of the kindness of his little Lycan heart?

Damn it...

Acknowledging the pain in her bare feet wasn't part of the deal. *You are the deal, wolf.*

As if he had heard that thought, as well as the half dozen others Tess had kept to herself, he backed up slowly, facing her without offering a growl and taking his incredible heat with him.

Realizing he was done for tonight and that he was going to be the one exercising option three, Tess waited.

After backing into the shadows, the Were turned from her and walked off. Tess watched him go. She couldn't call him a coward when this wolf was the most formidable opponent she ever had met. But she could pin the coward label on her own sorry backside for letting him go, again. She muttered something to that effect as she watched the magnificent Lycan melt into the darkness.

There would be another full moon next month, and by then she'd be better prepared to deal with her first Lycan. She made a vow to honor that idea as she waited by the rocks, anticipating the time when his scent would disappear, while knowing it wouldn't. The Were's musky maleness was in her lungs and on her clothes. It was like a new layer of her skin and clung to several strands of her hair.

This guy had tainted her with a magnificent presence and had turned her world upside down.

The worst thing of all was daring to admit to herself how much she had liked it.

Jonas didn't want to go. Didn't want to leave Tess. He was torn but not quite as confused as she was by the suddenness of their implausible attraction to each other. Out of everyone around, wolf hunters knew the Were species best, and this kind of intimate knowledge might have been what forced a connection.

He dealt with humans on a daily basis in his job with the Miami PD. He crossed paths with humans, rubbed shoulders with them and helped them out of situations that sometimes pointed to the bad guys of his own species. He and other Weres had made covering up those inconsistencies an art form.

Tess Owens wasn't like any of those humans he had met. And as impossible as it seemed, other than a threat or two with the sharp edge of her blade, she hadn't pounced.

Why had she backed off?

Another question nagging at him had to do with

Gwen's behavior tonight. The noises his sister had made when she got close to Tess suggested Gwen had also connected with the wolf hunter in some strange way.

Impossible?

Pure imagination?

No. Because he got it.

Tess was tuned in to his kind, and Gwen had also sensed this.

"You need to trust me," he sent to Tess as he walked. *"But I have other obligations that override any feelings I might have developed for you."*

Feelings? Jonas repeated that word to himself and shook his head. A brief look behind him let him know that Tess hadn't moved from the spot where he had left her. He had never been more thankful for his gift of enhanced sight than right now. Tess was an elegant eyeful. She was a fragrant, golden-haired enigma.

He wanted to run a claw over her, tear those shorts from her body and discover what kind of delights lay beneath. He wanted to force her to explain what this thing between them was and how the night had gone wrong.

Picturing those long legs of hers stretched on soft white sheets, bare and inviting, left him hungering in ways he had never acknowledged. But there was nothing he could do about it.

Sunrise wasn't that far off. At the very least, he could be thankful for what a new day without moons, realigning bones, silver blades and dark shadows might bring. In a calmer state, he'd gain a new perspective on what was going on with this hunter and reason things out. Far away from Tess Owens, he might again be able to fully concentrate on why he had brought Gwen here and how important that objective was.

Far from Tess.

Far from you, wolf hunter.

With those words filling his mind, Jonas took off at a run, heading home, sensing no danger in his surroundings other than the one he had just left behind.

Really, the only true darkness he felt at the moment was the vortex of emotion rolling through him that didn't belong there and made him want to turn back.

Tess was thinking about him. He felt it. Some part of her was reaching out to him in ways she or any other human being had no right to utilize. Her energy charged across his nerve endings. Her voice lingered in the recesses of his mind. And that was never a good thing when he was supposed to be concentrating elsewhere.

Do you know how badly I want to return, and what I want to do to and with you, wolf hunter...all of which involve a mattress and some sweat?

Was there the slightest chance that would actually happen if the two of them remained in close proximity?

Not only could he visualize it happening, he could taste it.

This, Jonas growled to himself as he picked up speed, *can't possibly end well.*

Then again, whoever said that things had to be easy?

Chapter 9

Tess gave up her position by the rocks when it became clear that the wolf and his four-legged sidekick weren't going to make a return appearance.

"Now what?" she asked herself over and over as she returned to her cabin. For once she had no clue what the next hours and days might bring.

She didn't want to meet this guy in the daylight or face him any other way but in his wolfed-up shape. Seeing him tonight as a human, however brief that appearance had been, caused a major hole in her agenda. She had never encountered a Were in its alternate form. In order for her to believe in the job she was destined to do, she had to meet the beast.

The fact that he could shape-shift more or less at will showed that this guy's talents and abilities fell well beyond the norm. Especially since it hadn't seemed to pose any problem for him at all.

It was a huge problem for her, though.

Did he know she wouldn't be able to hurt a Were who looked and talked like a man? One who appraised her the way a man might and seemed to enjoy making her uncomfortable?

Tess's anger flared as she faced those unanswered questions.

As she stood in the small space that served as a dining room, her home suddenly seemed truly isolated. She felt a separation between herself and the living, breathing world around her...something that hadn't bothered her until now, and until she had confronted a Were who had made her feel so completely alive.

Leftover sparks were keeping her energy output in high gear with no sign of a letup.

If that way-too-alluring Were had been playing with her, hoping for a notch in his own belt and to humiliate her, his methods had worked. Meeting him had been like a dream. She had behaved as though she were in a trance. No one else was to blame for her fumbling. She had to own this one.

"At least I'm alive. Ego-bruised and confused, but alive."

After face-palming on the dining table, Tess sank into a chair by the shuttered window, wondering how she was going to live this down and what kind of information about the Owens hunters the damn werewolf was going to pass along to his friends...if he had any friends that actually spoke in words and sentences.

The white wolf was another enigma that required careful consideration. Pure wolf? Real wolf? Those haunting blue eyes had seemed to suggest there was more to that animal than met the eye.

Tess stared at the window. Her sense of the Lycan was acute. Instead of leaving the area, he might have remained relatively close by.

She got up to rest her hand on the shutter, imagining he might spread his fingers on the other side of the same panel. If that were the case, Tess wondered who might go through that window first.

Reality came stumbling back with the awareness of another anomaly pressing in.

She listened hard.

The house was utterly quiet and yet it felt full, as if she shared the space with someone else. Maybe an uninvited visitor had gotten inside when her attention had been turned elsewhere.

Whirling to reach for the knife she had left on the table, Tess took a stand near the window and waited for whatever was going to happen, thinking to herself that this was the longest and most complicated night ever.

"Gwen?"

Jonas called out to his sister as he closed the door behind him. The cabin was quiet, the front room chilly. But he wasn't alone. His sister was here somewhere in wolf form.

He couldn't help thinking that she might have liked to remain on all fours forever, shunning the shift to her other side to avoid the pressure of someday having to deal with the reasons for her withdrawal. This kind of shunning was one thing among so many others that spelled out their differences.

He liked both man and wolf states equally. Then again, he didn't have the gene that would allow him to look like a real wolf, like his sister did, so he couldn't actually begin to think he understood her.

The uniqueness that had been sealed into Gwen's genes made sharing parents a radical idea, but who was he to question that or the age difference between himself and his sister?

He just couldn't be sure if Gwen's recent desire to keep her human side at bay and remain in her relatively mindless state was intrinsic or the result of the attack and loss of her friends that Gwen had suffered. He had lost a few friends along the way, both as a cop and a Were.

"Gwen? You can come out now."

Jonas turned toward the sound of claws scraping on the hallway floor. "Why don't you change back and rest? It's very late. Or early, depending on how we want to look at it."

The white wolf rounded the corner in a slinking posture that showed off the same thinness Gwen's human-like shape had. For all her genetic glory, Gwen had for a while seemed to be wasting away.

She expected chastisement for ignoring the directions he had given her, and Jonas couldn't bring himself to harp when no one on the planet knew what she had gone through in that Miami park. No one except for him, that is, since big city detectives dealt with assaults and other heinous crimes on a weekly basis.

Gwen padded closer to him with her head down. Although Jonas didn't want to encourage her present shape, he reached down to give her a loving pat.

"Please change back," he said. "I want to see my sister and believe that she will speak to me sometime soon."

Huge blue eyes found his, but she didn't honor his request. Gwen went to the window to press her muzzle against the glass, wanting out again. The moon wasn't yet down but was invisible from the cabin.

"Not again," Jonas said with a stern shake of his head. "We've had plenty of excitement for one night, don't you think?"

Gwen wasn't listening. From deep in her chest came a low whine that nearly shattered his heart to pieces. His sister wanted something that lay beyond the confines of the cabin.

What?

He looked at Gwen with a sudden flash of insight. Gwen wanted to see Tess again after having gotten a close-up of the young wolf hunter.

Take a number, hun...

Jonas rested a hand on Gwen's fur and closed his eyes. When Gwen whined a second time, Jonas checked the front door to make sure it was bolted. If Gwen wanted out of here, she'd have to change back and grow some fingers to work the lock.

"Later," he said. "We're not going anywhere, though this might strain the reputation of our new neighbor."

With a tight hold on Gwen's fur, he turned her toward him. "You do now understand what Tess is, and that she despises the likes of us? She is what most wolves fear. She hunts wolves, Gwen. She hunts us."

Gwen's eyes were far too bright, Jonas decided, and he was unable to read what was going on behind them.

"We've postponed the showdown with this hunter. God knows why things have turned out this way, but it's not to our benefit to get close to her again. She will be waiting and watching for a mistake that she can use against us."

Gwen's quake of understanding mimicked the quakes he had felt run through Tess. What caused these quakes, though, in both wolf and wolf hunter alike, lay beyond his pay grade.

What, exactly, did both females understand about what went on tonight? Had Tess seen the differences that separated him from other Weres she might have encountered? Had she, for a few brief moments, believed what he'd told her?

There was no way he could allow Gwen a second look at Tess, even when he desired the same thing with every fiber of his being.

"Tess will be wary. She might expect another visit and not be so lenient this time on the whole 'destroy all werewolves' thing," Jonas said.

She would also be angry. Who the hell knew what she'd be going through? There were so many unanswered questions, Jonas's head hurt.

"No," he said to his sister. "Not tonight. No going out there. I'll build a fire and you can curl up beside it if you'd like to. Are you cold?"

Gwen's answer was to pull away from him. She turned from the window and jumped up on a chair that was too small for her wolf body, though she made it work and seemed to settle in.

At least Gwen wanted him to believe she had settled. But then, Jonas recalled with sorrow, he had seen this false sense of security before on the night she had sneaked out to meet her friends in a park that was notorious for after-hours crimes.

And look where we've landed, Gwen, he didn't say

out loud. He could never blame Gwen for any of this when he also had been a rebel in his teens.

At the window, Jonas gazed out at the night. He wasn't going to be able to sleep. There was a good probability that Gwen would keep her eyes on him until the sun came up.

With far too much understanding, Gwen seemed to realize how badly he wanted to go back to the woman who would just as soon hang his pelt on a tree as admit that she was thinking about him that minute.

Jonas felt Tess's attention as strongly as if she had been in this room with him. There was no mistake about that.

Can't go... was the message Jonas wanted to send to Tess to quell his need to return to the brave and beautiful wolf hunter. *Can't.*

Tess Owens had gotten under his skin. With her lush scent in his lungs and the memory of her taut body pressed tightly to his, he had been thrown offstride.

"There is just something about you," he whispered without meaning to say those things out loud.

When he turned to Gwen, it was to find that the white wolf had gone, replaced by a frail teenaged girl who no longer appeared to belong to either world, wolf or human, but somewhere in between.

"It's just you and me," he said to his sister.

That wasn't the truth, though. Not anymore. Tess was in the room with them, if only in his mind.

Chapter 10

"What new menace have you brought here, wolf?"

Jonas stood up straighter, startled by the voice in his mind and sensing the hidden fears behind those words. *Her* words.

Tess had spoken to him and he had heard her, which was impossible. There was no way their connection could have developed that much or that far unless Tess had a special gift that he hadn't been aware of.

This confirmation left him feeling uneasy.

Menace was the word she had used. Had she been referring to him? To Gwen? To the fact that she hadn't done her job and was trying to reason things out?

He didn't like it. Had a bad feeling that something else had underscored her words.

He wanted to tell Tess he'd be right there and couldn't. Gwen was napping on the chair. He had made a fire and the warmth had lulled his sister into closing her eyes. There was no way he could leave her alone.

"Explain," he silently sent to Tess, testing the strength of their unusual bond.

He felt her attention turn to him. Though she was quiet and couldn't understand where that idea had come from, the strangeness of this possible open pathway to Tess's thoughts made Jonas's muscles tense. Hunters with an innate ability to connect with Weres would be bad news for his kind.

"Explain about the menace, Tess."

The test worked. After a short time, her reply came. *"Another unwelcome visitor was on my doorstep just now."*

Jonas leaned against the wall by the window, shaking his head. They were talking to each other the way Weres did and having a conversation.

"Who?" he sent, eyeing Gwen, relieved to see that his sister's eyes were still closed. *"Tell me, Tess."*

"I thought it was you."

"Not me. So who?"

No reply came. Whether this conversation was real or imagined, Jonas was starting to get worried. Why he should have cared about what happened to Tess Owens was as much a mystery to him as his sister's behavior had been lately. The big surprise was that he did care—even though it felt like he'd known her for about five seconds.

"Tess?" he sent, hoping to engage with her, struggling to comprehend the reason for this link and how it might have happened. *"You do hear me."*

"I hear you," she replied after a beat. *"And I want you to make this stop."*

"Who was there?" he repeated, ignoring her request.

"Get out of my head, wolf."

"Who was there?"

"No one. Someone. Both of those things at once."

Jonas kept his eyes on his sister. If he wasn't with Tess and Gwen was in the chair, whoever it was that had spooked Tess must have been someone unrelated to them. Somebody else might not like wolf hunters. Tess could have other enemies.

Right after those thoughts, he again remembered Tess's rolling darkness comments and pushed off the wall with his nerves jangling. As quietly as he could, Jonas went to the door, slid the bolt and stepped outside, tuning in to his surroundings utilizing the full package of his extraordinary senses.

He found nothing. No new smells. Not one hint of anything out of the ordinary.

"Tess?"

He wasn't surprised when she didn't reply. This mind link had to be new to her, too. Coming from the kind of being she was used to hunting, it might seem frightening.

The danger of reading thoughts went both ways and changed the whole process of hunter versus hunted. It threatened the secrets everyone kept.

"Tess?" he said out loud.

Whether or not she heard him, Tess had closed down. He wanted to know more about Tess Owens and was determined to see her again.

"Tomorrow, wolf hunter." When he turned around to go inside, Gwen was standing in the doorway with her eyes on him. "I know you didn't hear any of that," he said to her, hoping the statement might be true. But

Gwen merely tilted her head, flashed him her golden-blue gaze, and went back inside the cabin, where waiting had already become a dangerous, but certainly not monotonous, game.

Slender shafts of sunlight filtered through the cracks in the boards on the windows, sending dust motes dancing. Morning had arrived and Tess, still wide-eyed and awake, was thankful.

She was also stiff and very tired.

Daylight meant safety, at least from things that went bump in the night. Townspeople never came here, but if they did, they'd knock on a closed door. Her bed was calling to her now, instead of the damn Lycan. She didn't have to cover her ears.

The shower was hot and divine, and yet scrubbing her skin only lessened the wolf's scent, instead of erasing it. Hair clean, dressed in fresh sleeping clothes, Tess brewed a cup of tea and sat on her bed. Attempts to think of things besides the wolf were useless. She was sure that if she didn't clear her mind and get some sleep, she'd go mad.

Sheets felt cool after the long night. The down comforter helped to keep seal in warmth as she finally laid her head on the pillow. Wondering if the wolf would return tonight in human form took up far too much time and energy, so she went over her weapons and clothing checklist several times before turning her thoughts to her deceased mother and dad.

She liked to dream that her parents were alive and in the other room. That fantasy brought her warmth and a further easing of leftover tension. Tess didn't remember closing her eyes.

Waking to partial darkness was like a kick in the pants until she remembered the shutters and got up to check the time. It was three o'clock in the afternoon. She had slept for several hours and didn't feel rested. Bedcovers were tangled and strewn as if she had spent most of those hours tossing and turning.

Dressing for the day took time. Her plan to break more of her own rules meant that she was going into town in order to occupy herself with things that didn't include knives and silver-tipped arrows. Today she needed normalcy.

Her car was an old Jeep, a gift from her parents when she had turned sixteen. Homeschooling in her youth had assured her parents that her education would be flawless. Two years at a local college had been enough for Tess to see what the outside world was like and return home ready to take over her role as hunter in training.

Her folks had left her enough money to be modestly comfortable in the cabin without an outside job, with no room for indulgence and extravagances. This run to town would be for food and supplies only. A question or two directed to the right person might cough up information about the wolf living next door. His name and where he had come from were information that Tess desperately wanted.

The Jeep fired up easily without coaxing. Driving had always been a pleasure for her, so the long trip to town wasn't a hardship. Hill City was a small place modeled after the towns of the old West. In the summer months, tourists came by in droves and shoot-outs were reenacted by local businessmen dressed as bandits. Since summer was still a couple months away, the place was relatively quiet and tourist free.

Tess parked by the general store. After checking for foot traffic, she got out of the Jeep and headed toward the market.

Glad there weren't many people shopping for groceries that afternoon, she pushed back her hood. These employees knew her and were familiar with her scars. If anyone would know about the big Were, it would be an employee here. Everyone around these parts had a grocery account, which meant the compilation of significant written details.

With a small cart of supplies, Tess went in search of the manager. Rounding a corner, she came up short with her nerves on edge. *He* was there somewhere. His scent was familiar.

She found him in the middle of the far aisle. The Lycan was grocery shopping as if he had a right to act normal and be near normal people. As if he were one of them.

Tess's anger flared over this latest example of the guy invading her space. She held herself back from accusing the Were of following her. Hell, he was even more gorgeous in the daylight.

Breathtakingly gorgeous.

He wore faded jeans and a white long-sleeved shirt that was open one button too many at the neck. Today, he also wore black boots. His hair was shaggy and in need of a trim, and Tess hated to admit it looked good that way.

The fragrance of soap and pine that surrounded him only partially masked his wolfishness. Possibly he had just come from a shower.

Tess quickly erased that thought and the image it presented from her mind because he had also seen her. He walked toward her with a calm, casual gait and no hint of a smile on his brutally handsome face.

They were going to meet in public, and even if she'd had a weapon handy, she couldn't have used it here.

Chapter 11

"**W**hat are you doing here?" were the first words out of Tess's mouth, and spoken breathlessly as Jonas approached her in a purposefully easy, well-gauged manner. He didn't want to scare her. What he did want was quite different. The wolf inside him prodded the man on the surface to take her right there, on the floor if need be, reminding Jonas that he didn't have to give a damn about their differences or the rest of the world. Of course, that kind of prodding was ridiculous. This was a public place, and according to Tess, they were enemies.

He waved at the shelves. "This is a store."

She said testily, "You're nowhere near the meat counter."

Jonas thought he detected a subtle rawness in her tone. "Maybe you can show me to it," he suggested.

"I think not. Are you alone? Didn't you bring your pet with you?"

Jonas lowered his voice. "I'd rather you didn't speak of that here, if you don't mind."

"I mind. So would everyone else if they knew."

"Then maybe we should take this conversation outside."

Tess glanced around to make sure they were alone before returning her attention to him. "We're not having a conversation. There's nothing further to be said."

"It might be a good idea if we went over a few things," he countered.

"The situation is strange enough already, don't you think?"

He nodded in agreement.

"We can't be friends, wolf. Acting like we are doesn't help."

"That situation being your need to kill me?"

After a beat, she said, "Yes."

"No matter what?"

"Yes."

He shifted his weight slightly and watched her back up. "In that case," Jonas said, "I find your hesitation in achieving that goal particularly interesting after last night."

Today, Tess wore the tight jeans he had dreamed about during his all-nighter at the window and a snug black hoodie. Hair the color of honey hung loose to drape over her shoulders, daring him to reach out for a touch. Resisting that urge took almost as much willpower as leaving her last night had.

"I warned you not to assume I'm weak and that I don't know what has to be done," she said.

Jonas nodded again. Speaking to that point would only irritate Tess more. On the outside, she appeared calm enough. But that wasn't the case. Tess was ready to spin out if he lingered in her presence much longer.

He had to go and hated the idea. The lack of color in Tess's face told him she hadn't quite caught up on necessary rest and that she might have anticipated a return visit from him in the night. Her skin seemed gray around the edges. There were dark circles under her eyes, possibly due to the connection they had formed. There was a chance she could have picked up on the way his thoughts ran when they weren't openly communicating, knowing he had wanted that return visit.

"We're sharing thoughts," he said.

She shook her head to negate the idea.

"There's no reasoning to back up how hearing each other's thoughts might have happened," Jonas said. "Whatever is going on here is a mystery."

That mystery needed to be unraveled. He couldn't see any way to do that if he didn't continue to see her.

Tess was having none of this. Backing away farther, she asked, "How did it happen?"

He didn't pretend not to understand what she meant. Tess also wanted to know about the uniqueness of their bond.

"I don't know. That's the truth," Jonas replied. "It's not right or usual. We both get that. I'm at a loss as to how to explain the connection that has snapped into place between us and don't know anymore about it than you do. It's dangerous, uncanny, unprecedented, and makes hiding things more difficult for both of us."

She didn't speak again. Maybe she couldn't. Jonas got that, too. After racking his brain for answers, he had run out of ways to explore the possibility that Tess Owens had to be more than she seemed in order for their thoughts to merge. That little tingle at the base of his neck meant something, surely?

He had to find out what that nebulous something was that had tied them together from the start.

Tess was looking at him strangely with her head tilted to one side. *"You're looking for what, wolf hunter?"* he silently asked to prove his point about how strongly that connection worked.

She blanched visibly. Tess had heard him, all right, and her lips parted for a protest she didn't make.

"I think it's important for us to meet on a civil basis," Jonas said. "If that's around here, in public and in the daylight, I'll roll with it."

Eyeing him intently after the shudder she tried to hide from him, Tess said, "Over my dead body," and stormed out of the store.

Jonas sighed as he watched her go. He had already confessed to himself his preference for feisty females, and this meeting with Tess provided no argument with that.

It wasn't that he tended to like what he couldn't have. Women often found him viable as a possible mate and there were several potential connections for him in the packs around Miami. He was already under pressure to choose one of those females. But none of them had hit him as hard as Tess had, when she was the most unlikely prospect of all.

My sudden interest in you is not a good thing, Tess, any way I look at it. If you want me to stay away, I will honor your wish and hope that you'll honor my need for privacy as well. Will a truce be declared here?

Saying those things to himself should have made him feel better, and didn't. Being near Tess again, so soon, was a ball-buster.

This would be better if you weren't so stubborn or closed-minded, were his final silent thoughts on the matter before Jonas resumed his run for supplies, trying not to think too hard about the woman who had become like an itch he was desperate to scratch with his sharp, six-inch claws.

The damn wolf had succeeded in keeping her from getting what she needed at the store, and Tess was in no mood to go back and force the issue. Her senses went haywire when she was around this guy. He was just too beautiful and unique.

"Looks aren't everything, wolf," Tess muttered as she drove back to the cabin. "Everyone says it's what's on the inside that counts, but if they took a look at what you have on the inside, they'd learn a thing or two about what a nice exterior might hide."

She was on her own here and confronted with a new lesson each time she and this wolf met. His behavior had been civilized in the store. She had to give him that. The Lycan was well-spoken for a being with animal blood in his veins. She was in need of something to boost her immunity against this guy and foster a new sense of distance. She needed help.

Tess stepped on the gas, feeling less than up to par. Tremors were shaking her hands on the wheel. Her knuckles were white. She was at her best when hunting werewolves, and felt like she had just fallen on her face.

It was time for a treatment. Past time. She dreaded

the procedure that helped tie her to wolves and to her goal of getting rid of them. Still, maybe it would help her this time in dealing with the arrogant Were and whatever he would throw her way next.

At the cabin, she took time to remove the shutters from the windows and carefully stored them in the shed. Then she went inside and straight to the weapons room where a locked cooling cabinet held the items she'd need for this treatment.

Opening the cabinet, Tess reached for a vial of liquid and held it up to the light. The medicine in that vial shone like grated diamonds in the sunlight. Silver nitrate mixed with the right amount of silver proteinate and injected into a vein had almost magical healing properties. When applied to her skin, the concoction was a special kind of antiseptic.

For werewolves, who were allergic to silver, sinking their teeth into her after an infusion of silver would cause a violent and instantaneous sickness.

Tess's focus moved from the vial to the hand holding it, noting another of this mixture's side-effects. Over years of regular use, the silver she had injected had turned her skin a light blue color that was more easily seen in direct sunlight. No amount of sun exposure could remedy this effect, though most of the color had gathered in and around her scars.

To most people, she'd look pale, and she had never given anyone the opportunity to find out the truth. Skin discoloration was a small price to pay for the benefits she got.

Tess knew this mixture well, and how to use it. But it was ten times harder to give herself an injection like this than it had been for her mother to do the honors.

The needle went into the vein on the inside of her left elbow with a sharp sting. Tess tried not to shut her eyes. When it was over, there would be part two of this treatment to face, and minutes counted.

That Were would return. He wouldn't give up his quest to tame her hunter instincts.

She opened a box that had been nailed to the floor and removed a few cables. Electrical currents came next. What they did to her wasn't pretty, but it was necessary for heating the silver once it was in her veins. She had managed this dual treatment each time a new werewolf had invaded the South Dakota territory she inhabited.

None of those werewolves had come remotely close to possessing the muscle and power this new guy did. None of them had charm or a mesmerizing stare that made her insides quake. Everything in this room was going to be necessary for her next meeting with the wolf next door. She had doubled the usual dosage as a buffer. Otherwise…

Tess Owens, wolf hunter, was going to be screwed.

Jonas pulled his truck in behind Tess's Jeep and got out. The place looked deserted, but he knew better. Tess was here. He could sense her.

Though he had attempted to put her out of his mind and get on with things, he hadn't managed to stick to that plan. The dark circles beneath Tess's eyes had bothered him, as had the extremes of her skin's paleness. She didn't have to like him coming here. He just had to make sure she was all right.

Jonas walked the perimeter of the cabin, found a

window and peered inside, hoping he wouldn't scare the pants off Tess if she saw him there.

What he saw sent his nerves into overdrive.

The small room he was looking at had been outfitted like a hospital clinic. Doors to cabinets stood open, revealing bottles of what he could only assume were various medicines, as well as a whole host of other things.

In the middle of all that, in the tiny space between the cabinets and the table, his deliciously beautiful wolf hunter lay curled up on the floor.

Chapter 12

The sound of broken glass made Tess open her eyes. She was lying on her side, curled up in a fetal position and wasn't sure how she had ended up on the floor. She felt sick. Moving a finger was tough. Lifting her head would have been impossible for several more minutes.

The rain of shattered glass was loud as it hit the furniture and the floor. The voice she heard was out of place in her home.

"Tess?"

"No," she whispered. "Not you."

Her reaction to the Were was like another snap of electricity. He was kneeling beside her and she dared not look at him. His presence here had taken trespassing to a new level. The werewolf was invading her sacred space, a place no wolf had ever set foot near.

The sacrilege of this horrifying moment stretched on and on. Tess couldn't protect herself or the secrets this room held if he lingered. Right that minute, she was at her most vulnerable.

"Tess?"

His voice was like silk. Like velvet. If she closed her eyes, Tess thought, he might go away.

She prayed he might disappear.

"I'm going to help you up," he said gently. "In order to do that, I'll have to touch you. Are you okay with that?"

"No." The word wasn't more than a whisper.

"Sorry," he said. "It's the only way."

He slid both of his hands beneath her. The warmth in them was incredible, but her mind was making a comeback and quickly progressing toward normal. At the moment, there was nothing she could do and she needed his help. She'd have to get him out of this room before he took a good look around at a wolf hunter's secret stash, though. The things that helped to protect people in her line of work.

"What happened?" he asked, concerned.

She didn't ask him why he should be concerned for her when she had made her intentions about dealing with him clear.

"Sick," she replied.

She was even sicker to have been put on the spot. The room already smelled like him. This guy seemed to fill any space he was around.

"I can see that," he said.

His arms, corded with tension, helped her from a floor that sparkled with broken glass shards. As he helped Tess to her feet, another round of vertigo struck before she found herself balancing her weight against the Were's hard body. Neither of them moved while she took a few deep breaths. The wolf didn't seem to be breathing at all.

"It's probably time we introduced ourselves," he said. "My name is Jonas."

The fact that he had a name made things fifty times more personal. Her head was against his shoulder in a wicked rendition of a damsel being rescued by the big bad wolf. The problem was that she couldn't have pulled away from the incredibly strong arms supporting her if she had wanted to. Her legs were weak, and his hold was like being squeezed in a vise.

A brief glance to the side showed her that the needle was on the table where she had left it. Her forearms were free of the two thin wires that looked like jumper cables for a car battery—a good analogy for what those cables did to her body. She must have pulled them off before hitting the floor.

Setting the electricity too high had been a mistake, in hindsight, and the jolts had been too hot for her to take all at once. The procedure had sent shockwaves through her system before on a few occasions but had never knocked her out.

"Where can I take you?" her unwelcome companion asked.

His broad chest rumbled when he spoke, sending more vibrations charging through Tess's body in a way that was startlingly similar to the recent hit of voltage. Although she had stopped shaking on the outside, her insides were picking up a distant drumbeat that felt absurdly sexual in nature.

"Bedroom?" he asked. "Is it nearby?"

Tess closed her eyes to seal off an acknowledgement of that infernal rising beat. This guy could not be allowed to pick up on her hidden absurdities and couldn't be allowed anywhere near her bedroom.

"All right," he said when she didn't answer his questions. "Someplace for you to lie down without broken glass shouldn't be hard to find. Can you walk?"

"Yes."

There was no way she could walk. Her brain might have made a comeback, but her body hadn't fully recovered from the high dosage of silver and the electricity that sealed it inside her body. With the Were here now, she wasn't just vulnerable, she was as good as dead.

He didn't lift her up this time. Possibly he recalled the night before when she'd held a knife to his neck. Instead, he slid an arm around her waist and turned her toward the doorway. All Tess could think about right then was how her mother and father would have disowned her if they saw this. They'd be rolling over in their graves.

Determined to walk, Tess took a few steps on legs that felt like rubber and stumbled when she tried to free herself from the arm supporting her. The Were whose name was Jonas didn't appear to be in any hurry to let her go.

Jonas.

Named like he was one hundred percent human.

"I think it might be this way," he said, and Tess knew he was scenting her trail through the cabin. Among his kind, scent was the richest form of identification.

She had to say something. At least protest.

Tess glanced up at him without meeting his eyes. "What are you?"

"Lycan," he replied.

"And the white wolf?"

"None of your concern."

They were standing in the doorway to her bedroom in full daylight. The way this Were was observing her was causing Tess's internal drumbeat to become louder and much more significant.

Jonas.

His eyes were large and clear. Nothing of the wolf he carried around danced within them, but there was a gleam she didn't immediately recognize. Was it the gleam of lust she was seeing? Hunger?

His sober expression of concern left her feeling feminine and desirable when those things shouldn't have mattered to her. Yet somehow, and in some way, what she saw in his eyes served to deepen the ridiculous bond with him that she had felt snap into place the first time their eyes had met.

Was this trial by fire, and therefore a big test for a wolf hunter? Survival of the fittest?

Like the trick that hunter's used to match the rhythm of their prey's heartbeat, her pulse jumped to keep time with his, mimicking the smoothness of each stroke. The difference was that she was the one now who was hardly breathing.

The concept of danger didn't begin to describe the situation. Her closeness to this guy was unacceptable and death-defying. Tess fought that warning even while realizing that fighting him was not only hopeless, it was a lost cause. The fact that he was large and muscled wasn't the worst of it. The abnormal attraction they were experiencing was.

Her bed was less than ten feet away and Tess would rather have died than reach it. Walls were closing in. Floorboards undulated. The dose of silver in her veins that was meant to save her from the Were world was pushing her toward it instead of holding her back.

There were stories about the kind of union she was fighting, and dire warnings against them. Weres and werewolf hunters had been created to remain on opposing sides of supernatural teams, though every now and then the sheer magnitude of their knowledge of each other drove them together. Forbidden liaisons like that were shunned by her community and never turned out well.

But the Were beside her was warm and helpful. And she no longer had a knife with which to defend herself…from herself. If they reached that bed, it would be over. There would be no going back.

"Uneven playing field," he remarked in a gravelly voice that made Tess believe he had heard every thought her treacherous mind had kicked up. Was nothing sacred or too personal with these guys?

"I'll just help you, and then I'll be gone," he announced, as if he truly believed that statement, and without mentioning why he had come here in the first place.

Terrible thoughts kept coming to her when Tess needed to staunch them. Thoughts about what sex with a guy like this would be like, and the thrill that would come from having this gorgeous Lycan between her naked thighs. Words like *forbidden* had taken on the rhythm of an ongoing echo.

As he guided her to a first step into the room beyond the threshold, Tess felt the last vestiges of her training begin to wither. For only the second time in her life, she wanted to cry.

Jonas knew he didn't belong here, and that fact wasn't lost on him. He could just set her down somewhere. Leave now and minimize the damage.

Her room was exactly what he would have expected—small and neat, other than the unmade bed in the middle. Personal effects had been kept to a minimum. A few photos in frames sat on a bedside table. Piles of paperback books took up space near a small lamp.

In any other visit to any other woman's bedroom, unless passion had taken him over, he would have paused for a look at those photos and to check out the titles of the books. No time had been left here for curiosity, however. Although they didn't have to be sworn enemies, Tess wouldn't allow them to friends.

Or lovers.

So Jonas made a vow not to prove to Tess Owens how much of an animal he could be at times, in spite of the fact that the mattress was like a black hole for him that beckoned, and that her room's faint fragrance of lavender and lilacs was a kind of exotic aphrodisiac that he hadn't expected. Touching Tess in any way produced pangs of possessiveness in him that were as unexpected as they were unjustified.

Tess would hate him even more than she already did for this transgression, and that was okay. Once she came to her senses, Tess would again be after him, but hopefully not too soon.

Jonas helped her to sit down on the edge of the bed, and then he backed away as soon as he could with his hands raised in surrender. *See? It's all good. No bad stuff is going to happen.*

She was staring at him and regaining her strength minute by minute, and yet Jonas didn't understand what had happened to strip that strength from her. If she was ill, that illness had to have set in quickly after he'd seen her at the store in town.

She did look ill.

Her skin was bloodless. Her eyes were bloodshot. He saw the red welts of burn marks on her bare arms, visible beneath the hems of her short sleeves.

What the hell have you done, Tess?

He could have kissed those marks to help them heal. One bite with this teeth or scratch of his claws on Tess's smooth skin and she could become a diluted version of something like him—enough to make them more compatible anyway. And that would end her reason to exist and annihilate the vows and promises she had made to her own kind.

"I'll leave you now," he said to make his intentions clear to her, though his body wanted anything but that.

She said nothing.

"I'd like to make sure you aren't hurt before I go."

"Why?" she replied.

"Maybe for no other reason than I'm a nice guy sometimes."

"You broke my window."

"I'll have it fixed."

"You weren't invited here."

"And yet some folks might agree that it was a good thing I came by."

"We can't be close," she said, getting to the heart of the unsaid stuff swirling between them. "It doesn't work that way and you know it."

"I'm sure we both get that," Jonas agreed.

"You don't get a free pass for being a nice guy sometimes."

"I didn't really expect one."

"Then why are you here?" she demanded.

That question bothered Jonas because he wasn't sure why he had turned the car this way. He'd like to believe it was to speak to her in the daylight, away from any possible public scrutiny. With just the two of them in a place where Tess would feel safe, he had hoped she'd at least listen to his proposal for a truce.

Or maybe he had tuned into Tess's darker emotions and had been worried about her present state of mind.

Now she looked like a fair-haired angel on that bed, when *angel* wasn't anywhere near the term that described Tess Owens. Early on, she had been tuned into the alternate frequencies of the world around her and expected to heed them.

Her role models had been fighting machines. What it took for a human to give up so much was unimaginable, and yet Tess had done just that. However, he hadn't missed the cables or the needle in that other room. God only knew what those burn marks on her arms were from.

"You were leaving," she reminded him. She hadn't moved from the edge of the bed.

"Yes. I did say that, didn't I?" Jonas returned.

"One foot in front of the other will do, and you might want to use a door this time."

Jonas had to smile in relief when he heard the cynicism in her tone.

"Don't come back," she warned. But Jonas heard the wobble that backed Tess's tone and recognized what it meant.

Heat streaked in from nowhere to engulf him. Alerted to a newly emerging wave of emotion, Jonas's inner beast quivered. His skin rippled as Tess's bloodshot eyes found his with a challenge in them that overrode her arguments.

Contrary to everything she had said, Tess was waiting for him to do the wrong thing. The bad thing. The incident they might never live down or live to tell about.

Tess Owens was experiencing the same kind of heat he was and fighting her own inner battles about believing him to be a good guy.

Tess wasn't used to civility between their species. Actually, she was part animal herself. A being apart from the norm. A fighter with a one-track mind.

But her eyes told another story that Jonas chose not to ignore…

So it took him just three steps to reach her.

Chapter 13

When the Were leaned down to look into her eyes, Tess pushed him back, holding her breath, head and heart pounding. In the back of her mind and in the split second it took for him to press her onto her back on the bed, she knew it was impossible to stop this and couldn't understand why.

The silver in her system now seemed useless and more like a magnet calling to the silver particles swimming inside her. The veins carrying the silver solution felt molten. The rest of her was feverish. And Jonas, her Lycan nemesis, was volcanic.

Up close, he was a nightmare of golden skin, sky-colored eyes and chiseled perfection. No scars. No hint of past battles or having just won one here without having to lift a finger.

"Are you trying to kill yourself?" he asked with his attention on the marks on her arms.

Each word he spoke was a puff of warm air on her bloodless face that made Tess despise him for his ability to make her feel anything at all.

"Haven't you gotten the memo? I've been trying to kill *you*," she replied sharply.

"And yet you haven't," he reminded her, leaning over her with his hands on the mattress in a way that turned the dry afternoon air sultry.

"A slipup I won't make again," Tess promised.

"After today, you mean."

"Starting right now."

He smiled. The bastard was having fun at her expense.

"As soon as I recover," she added.

"How much time do I have until that happens, Tess?"

"About five seconds."

She was already reaching for the knife hidden under her pillow, put there for nightmares and emergencies.

His hand stopped her.

"I take it one of the beasts you attribute to being of my kind did this?" His fingers traced the ridges on the wrist he held with a touch that felt extremely intimate.

Tess caught her breath. "He got the worst end of the deal," she said, damning this creature for taking unnatural liberties with a temporarily sidelined opponent.

"Then you do believe me." His observation intensified. "You believe I'm not like those other guys."

"I can't afford to believe you. That's a fact."

"Tell me this, Tess. Are you attracted to all of the werewolves you hunt?"

"Stupid question." *And far too insightful*, Tess added to herself.

"Then it's just me? I'm the only Were you've given the benefit of the doubt to? I'm the only one who has come here looking for answers, rather than a fight?"

Tess shook her head. "When we meet again, you'll know how much I appreciate the fact that you stopped by."

His smile remained fixed. A real smile. Nothing fake about it. The corners of his eyes crinkled becomingly. There was a mischievous sparkle in his eyes that didn't bode well for her current position. If he hadn't been a monster, she would have given that smile an award.

"Get out," she said.

"All right."

He didn't move.

Her strength was slowly returning now that the silver had spread, and thanks to the electrodes that enhanced its effects. Tess raised a knee to gut this Were and found his reflexes faster. He stopped her with a raised thigh that served to pin her to the mattress in a compromising position. Like a cat on its back with its legs in the air, she was far too exposed.

More heat flooded Tess's neck and face. Breathing was a chore. How many ways could this guy trip her up and point to her repeatedly inept performance? Why him? Why was this werewolf so special?

"What do you want?" she asked.

"I want you to listen to what I've been saying."

"What else?"

"That's all."

"You're lying," she said.

"Not lying. But if I added anything more, you might forget the other more important stuff, when that's the reason I'm here."

Tess met his blue-eyed gaze with defiance, even as her insides swirled.

"I came to this area because you were here," he said. "And because other Weres wouldn't be here after knowing about you. I came hoping to cheat Death, rather than inspire you to seek me out for a similar result. Only it wouldn't be a similar result, Tess. Taking a silver blade to the chest would be infinitely easier than what I will eventually face, if not here, then somewhere else in the near future."

Tess heard herself ask, "What could be worse?"

The smile he offered her this time was a faded version of the earlier one, but no less intriguing.

"There are other things in this world besides humans and Weres," he said.

"And you've come here to avoid one of those other things?"

"Yes."

"You need me off your back in order to do that?"

"I do."

"Then you'll leave?"

"If I'm alive, yes, I will leave you in peace."

That last bit was a stretch for Tess, due to the fact that she was sure the concept of peace would elude her from now on. In letting a Lycan go, a new precedent would be set. After meeting this guy, was she going to have to take the time to pose questions to all of the werewolves crossing her path, giving them the benefit of the doubt as to whether or not they were good guys in disguise?

Nothing was going to be the same after this.

Nothing at all.

"You knew I wasn't one of those creatures," he said, as if reading her mind was an ongoing skill that he had perfected. "Somehow you knew it."

She chose not to address that remark since it was true.

"We can speak to each other in a way reserved for Weres," he continued. "How do you suppose that's possible?"

There was no way Tess was going to mention that the silver was supposed to enhance performance in dealing with werewolves, while also bringing hunters closer to wolves in ways no one understood.

Each dose of silver was like ingesting some of the same moonlight that affected wolves, Weres and Lycans. It gave hunters a leg-up on the Were species by helping to equalize their powers.

And here now in her bedroom, Tess had nearly forgotten every damn thing she had learned that might have gotten her out of this mess. She was torn. Confused.

Right then, all she wanted was for this incredibly chiseled wolf to stop looking at her in that particular way he had of making her seem like prey. His eyes on her sparked internal vibrations that made Tess consider crossing another boundary that would condemn her to werewolf hunter hell for even thinking of it.

The Lycan...and her...naked on this bed.

Had he heard those thoughts as well? His face got closer. The smile was gone and all she could see were those haunting blue eyes. The full lips...

Before his mouth rested on hers.

*   *   *

Jonas found himself propelled forward and into a dream world where actions didn't have to be analyzed, nothing was forbidden, and old enemies found common ground.

His mouth was on Tess's and she tasted like a lush and dangerous cocktail of the senses.

Neither of them moved. Possibly she was as stunned by this as he was, but Jonas refused to regret acting on instinct. He had wanted this all along, deep down, when anything having to do with Tess Owens should have been off-limits. His desire for her was inexplicable, as if an outside force was propelling them toward each other at high speed for no other reason than to watch the impact.

Tess's lips were a soft contrast to the tautness of her body. Her eyes were closed. With his hands on the sides of her face, Jonas traced the faint lines of her scars beneath his palms, knowing this would anger her. The kiss was bad enough. Bringing attention to her scars would be, for her, a heinous act, especially when those scars had been caused by werewolves.

Neither of them dared to take a breath as Jonas waited for Tess to strike out. Surely, she would have to. He spoke to her with his mind, sending messages along those forbidden channels while trying to decide what she tasted like and how bad her reaction to a personal space violation would be when she decided to show him one.

"We don't have to be enemies, Tess."

No slap came. No shove. He might have finally pushed her over the edge. And what the hell. If this was a dream, he was all in.

He added pressure to this crazy meeting of their mouths, though the lips beneath his remained closed and unresponsive. Tess would have to do something soon or she'd realize he might take her silence as a green light of acquiescence. He doubted she would allow things to get that far.

His own warning signals were flashing, urging him to back off, ease the pressure, forget the thrill that being so close to Tess produced. He couldn't afford to anger her to the point of no return and make her extra intent on hunting him down for the transgression.

Then again, it was probably already too late to stop that.

"This thing between us..." His lips moved over hers to form the words, planning to say something useful to ease the situation. But then she moved. Her lips parted. And the taste of something metallic soared through his senses with an effect similar to having just sucked on a bolt of lightning.

Jonas drew back, blinked his eyes. In seconds, Tess was in his face in a very different manner—smooth expression, eyes like steel.

"Dream on, wolf."

Her hands were on his chest. She pushed him back using a good example of the strength she had lacked moments before and said, "I'm not into your tricks and not into you."

She was on her feet and had him backing to the window where sunlight bathed her in an afternoon glow. It was then that Jonas saw the detail he had missed before.

Tess's skin wasn't white or a light tinted gray. It was, in fact, a very pale blue when seen in direct light.

Blue skin surrounded her big blue eyes, with a slight variation of the color lining her lips.

Along with his notice of those things came a terrible sudden awareness of what that meant and what Tess had done in that other room.

Tess was torturing her system in order to enhance her healing powers and her strength in much the same way that some athletes used steroids to up their games.

She supposed that silver was the bane of all werewolves and the equivalent of deadly nightshade or a plant aptly known as Wolf's Bane. Silver bullets, silver-tipped arrows and silver blades could take a wolf down when others modes of execution couldn't, she would suppose, as most hunters did. This information was a hunter's bread and butter. Basic werewolf hunting 101.

But it wasn't always true.

It was an ingenious idea, he had to admit, for dealing with werewolves whose blood had been diluted. What Tess had done to herself could in some instances give her an edge if a pair of fangs or claws drew blood. Not here, however. He had been trained to deal with silver.

"Sorry," Jonas said as Tess quickly produced another blade from the table behind her. He wondered how many she had stashed around the cabin and if he wasn't her first unwelcome guest. He added, "In this case, your secrets won't be of much use to you."

She stared back defiantly. "We'll have to see about that, won't we?"

"Lycan," he repeated, as if either she didn't remember he had already told her this, or she truly was lacking a few specifics about his species in general.

"All the same to me," she snapped a bit too breathlessly to have the impact she might have wished for.

Shaking his head, Jonas strode forward to stand beside her. When she raised the knife, he clearly saw that using the weapon wasn't what she really wanted to do and that Tess didn't trust herself where he was concerned. Why had she held back on the kiss if her overall intent was to hurt him? Was her hesitancy due to the fact that she hadn't wanted him to feel the detrimental effects of the silver that would by now have saturated every membrane in her body? She had saved him from that?

He took the blade from her calmly. "We have evolved," he explained. "Some of us have, anyway. If a species continues long enough, the basic details about us get blurred."

Tess was breathing hard. The mysterious attraction between them had been cranked up a notch by coming here today. Tess knew this. So did he. They both wished someone could tell them why.

What if it turned out that she might have been willing to use that mattress if it hadn't been for a round of fresh thoughts on protecting him from the silver in her body?

Jonas took hold of her shoulders. Though she put up a decent effort to resist, Tess showed nothing of the strength she now possessed.

He swung her toward the bed, threw her on top of it and looked down at her with new insight. Fires were blazing between them and the flames were growing. For him, this latest round of attraction was dangerously close to the emotions he had been trying to avoid. Imprinting wasn't possible for him with a human female, he reminded himself. Imprinting was the Were equivalent of placing a ring on a female's finger.

Tess's eyes didn't meet his. Perhaps she imagined the game was over and he was about to prove that to her. Maybe she didn't fear her own death and had seen it coming. If that was true, she hadn't believed a word he had said.

"Lycans have developed a tolerance to all sorts of things," he explained with his face close to hers, leaving out the part about how the silver still sat sourly on his tongue. "Enough for some Weres to get past the pain of silver and other metals touching our skin."

He failed to mention how the buildup of those tolerances had nothing to do with getting past feisty female wolf hunters.

"That makes monsters unstoppable," she said.

Jonas shook his head. "I will again say how sorry I am that you haven't met many of the good guys. Weres who patrol the streets on the lookout for monsters. Weres who go after the criminal element so decent folks of all species can stay safe."

Witnessing the skepticism in her expression, he went on.

"You don't need to electrocute yourself in order to deal with me, Tess. A simple truce between us will do."

The fact that Tess dared to again close her eyes gave him hope about building trust that didn't last long. With a stupendous burst of refueled muscle and speed that must have been gathering inside her, she was out from beneath him and reaching for him from behind.

"Damn it," Jonas muttered, catching her in both

hands and following her to the wooden floorboards. Straddling her writhing body, he added, "Are you deaf? So completely brainwashed that you can't listen to reason?"

Christ. He mentally backpedaled. Maybe he was the one being brainwashed, because they were in a unique position for Tess to rub him in all the right ways and in all the right places. And he was aroused.

As if Tess sensed this, she stopped moving her hips. Her cheeks flushed pink. Thoughts of what he'd like to do with her on this floor returned. Although Tess was human, Jonas was sure they'd be a good fit. They could make this work if they tried.

Yep. He had gone completely insane.

"I want you, wolf hunter," he whispered to her. "How's that for a confession from the big bad wolf you're so hot to take down?"

Motionless, she appeared to be as stunned as he was by his confession.

"Don't you imagine these strange feelings we're ignoring are equally as tough for me?" he asked.

Her lips moved, daring Jonas to turn his attention there. When Tess spoke, it was to confirm what he had suspected all along.

"Feeling anything for you is a sin and against everything I stand for, wolf."

Jonas nodded. "Then you do feel it."

"In this position, I'm able to feel everything you've got."

Yes, he supposed she could.

"Then you see the truth in what I've said about this attraction having nothing to do with fighting," he said.

Her jaw was tight. "If I let down my guard, all will be lost and you will be to blame."

"Conversely, if I were to follow up on the look in your eyes when they meet mine, I'd be distracted from doing what I came to this area to do, all this hunting business aside."

"I'm all for you walking out that door, wolf. Both my reputation and my sanity depend on it."

She was right. He had to let the promise of the moment go. He'd have to do that willingly. Reluctantly. Nodding to Tess while curbing his appetite for her, Jonas got to his feet. Before offering her a hand, he asked, "Do I get that truce?"

"Only until I come to my senses," she replied without getting up off the floor. "And for the short time it takes you to use that door."

It wasn't an actual agreement to his terms, but Jonas supposed it was a small step in that direction. Sweeping his gaze over Tess's lovely long limbs, her expressionless face and the burn marks on her arms that were still livid, he took note of all the details. Nothing of the telling blue cast to her skin was evident without the sunlight. On that floor, looking vulnerable without actually being vulnerable, Tess just looked like a really attractive woman who was undecided about what her future might bring.

She was extraordinary.

And she was his sworn enemy.

Yes, he desired her too much and too badly. He didn't really get that or how these feelings had come on so strongly, and his regret over having to leave her was like nothing he could recall.

"For now," he said without extending his hand.

Either he'd be back, or she would come to him.

This would be a very wild ride when the time came. And all the silver in the world wasn't going to stop him from taking it.

Chapter 14

"Don't come back." Tess called after the Were before stopping to think how mundane that statement was in light of what had almost transpired in her bedroom.

Hearing the front door close, she got up. Satisfied to be alone again with her new dilemma of what to do about Jonas, she looked around. The sun was still shining. Light from the window crossed the floorboards, rendering her mood dark by comparison. The house was quiet again, except for the steady boom of her heartbeat. The room she stood in felt empty without the Lycan's presence to fill it. She felt empty standing in it.

Tess put a hand to her forehead, ran her fingers down the side of her face where he had touched her with gentle hands that hid ten lethal claws. For a large man hiding a beast, this guy's tenderness was a curious anomaly. So was his offer of a truce.

The sound of an engine revving drew her to the window. Jonas had started up a dusty green Jeep. After putting the car in gear, he sat idling in the yard.

"No," Tess said out loud with a firm head shake. "Go now. You have to leave."

She put the full force of her willpower behind that directive and waited to see if their connection was as mind-blowing as she had imagined. *"Do you hear me, wolf?"*

Finally, the Jeep backed up, turned and drove off at a pace slow enough for her to have caught up with it at an easy jog. Did her Lycan want to turn back? Humiliate her some more? Why else had he turned up at her home, if not to test her?

She stared after him, thinking back, mulling over the things he had told her.

I'm here to keep something bad from happening, he had said. *My reason for being in the area is important to people other than myself.*

Those remembered words rang with the promise of being backed by truth. Instinct wasn't always right though, so could she trust her gut this time and believe him?

As for his remarks, what was going to happen and to whom?

Unlike other challengers, it seemed to her that Jonas hadn't come here to go against the local anti-werewolf enforcer. However, the reason for his relocation remained unclear. It was time for this guy to fill in a few blanks. But first, more time was necessary for her to get her breath back and allow the silver concoction to be fully absorbed into her system.

The infusions had always given her confidence and would do so now if she waited it out. Silver particles shored up her backbone and would point her in the right direction to solve this mystery. "Hopefully."

By the time she had finished talking to herself, the afternoon sun had dropped lower in the sky. This was fine with her. Outside and without the loneliness of the cabin, she didn't feel so alone.

Tess closed her eyes.

The big Were next door might have discovered a couple of her secrets, but not nearly all of them.

There were other reasons for taking silver into her body. The instructions her parents had left her were perfectly clear about that, without actually explaining why. Ultimately, Tess would have to discover this for herself. Each time she applied those electrodes, she prayed that kind of enlightenment would come.

What she hadn't planned for was how each new infusion also deepened the hole inside her that had begun to feel bottomless.

Her isolation wasn't just about being different from other people. This was something else. Something deeper. Her sense of being alone got worse each time a full moon rolled around.

"Enough!" Tess shouted, listening to the fading sounds of the Jeep. "We'll need to unravel your secrets first, my fine wolf."

Glad to have a direction that would take her mind off of herself, Tess went to the weapons room to begin preparations for the night ahead and whatever the damn werewolf's secrets might turn out to be.

This was not good and in no way acceptable, Jonas admitted to himself in the darkness-cloaked yard of his cabin. Feelings of unease hadn't left him.

He turned to Gwen. "Did you behave yourself today?"

Jonas would have given a lot to have his sister answer him.

"All day?" he pressed.

Gwen might have been smiling. He liked to believe she was. She was also fidgeting. Darkness always made Gwen restless. She wouldn't sit down, needing to burn off excess energy that increased day by day. Her need to pace was wearing out the carpet and the porch floorboards.

"I'll go with you out there," he said, observing his sister carefully and imagining what this must be like for her. She needed a break from being cooped up.

She stopped pacing.

"One hour only, and then we come back here. Do we have a deal, Gwen?"

She was already starting that hour of freedom. Her arms were twitching. Her eyes were bright. "One hour, Gwen," he repeated, determined to keep up if she bolted away. "And we stay away from the neighbors." Jonas placed himself squarely in the center of the porch archway. "Especially that neighbor. You know who I mean."

Gwen pushed past him as if he had just let her off a leash and as if she wouldn't be able to breathe until she got away from the cabin. One minute she was standing on the porch. Seconds after that, Gwen was on all fours and running for the hills like a bolt of white lightning.

"Hell," Jonas muttered as he sprinted after her. "I might never get used to that."

He ran easily once his legs caught up with his desire

to stick close to Gwen, but he wished he'd had time to remove his boots. Bare feet to the bare ground was another way werewolves tested their surroundings.

Gwen moved in large circles that expanded with each pass, pretending to heed his warning about Tess, though Jonas still feared some sort of rebellion. Now and then, Gwen slowed to look back at him.

When she stopped near the base of the hillside, he stopped beside her, his skin prickling when Gwen turned her head to sniff the air. Catching a whiff of a scent she didn't like, Gwen crouched down the way wolves did in the wild when either the smell of their prey or a disturbance in the distance reached them. She was so still, so intent on whatever she had locked onto, that the back of Jonas's neck chilled.

The scent he noticed soon after needed no processing.

"Wolf," he said. "More than one of them."

Can't be, Jonas inwardly added. Surely Tess would have known if there were more werewolves in the area. Wouldn't she have mentioned it? Then again, why would she have mentioned it to him?

Wait. Was that why she had indulged in a silver infusion? She had been expecting more company?

Gwen brushed up against his legs, seeking permission to do the very thing Jonas had feared she might do, which was to go after these intruders. She was shaking, barely able to hold herself back and growling fiercely. Rogue wolves had hurt her. She wanted payback for that.

"No, Gwen," Jonas said. "There's no moon to shift them. Maybe these guys will be on their way."

The odor of the Weres was like catnip to Gwen,

only in a really bad way. It had been a wily pack of half-crazed werewolves that had attacked her and her friends in that Miami park. Here, now, Gwen recognized the foul odor of an oncoming threat. Her muzzle had drawn back, exposing a mouthful of needle-sharp teeth. The feral sounds she made got louder.

He had to get Gwen out of here and safely back to the cabin. He had to hope that the guys in the trees were just passing through and wouldn't pick up Gwen's scent in return.

Whispering for Gwen to follow him home, Jonas's stomach clenched when she didn't obey. Her blood was up. The pure white fur on her back was raised. She had gone too far into her wolf to listen to anything he had to say. The anguish she had recently suffered had not been forgotten.

Gwen wanted to savage all other Weres that came her way, whether they turned out to be friendly or not. And she was going to do so here if he couldn't find a way to stop her.

Before he could make a move, Gwen had taken off, leaving him standing with his hands outstretched. The harrowing howl she issued echoed in the night with a refrain that broke his heart.

Unfortunately, that howl would also have alerted both of these new guys to her presence, while also possibly inviting a wolf hunter to the party.

He had been a fool for letting Gwen out, but couldn't have helped it. How could anyone have kept someone they loved trapped in a makeshift prison, even if it was for their own good?

In honor of the degree of danger they faced, Jonas's

claws extended. He swiped at his jeans as he sprinted after his sister, and heard the denim rip.

It was a neat trick to be able to call his wolf to the surface without a full moon present. Not many others knew about his ability to shift one more time after a full moon phase had come and gone. His family had always been unusual and this was one more secret in a world already full of them. This particular secret came in handy at times.

Maintaining a tight hold on himself was rough going. However, if the newcomers didn't notice Gwen, they sure as hell didn't need the shock of seeing her big brother partially transformed.

An extra kick of power surged through Jonas to lighten the load of running on purely human legs. His sense of smell tripled as he moved, as if his claws were sending him in the right direction—the path Gwen had taken.

"Stop, Gwen," he sent to her over and over, ignoring the fear that was growing inside him. *"Please stop."*

Rounding piles of rock as if they were part of a slalom course, Jonas crashed through the low-lying branches of the forest with his head pounding and his lungs ready to burst.

"Gwen!"

And then he heard Gwen bark a warning, and the repeat of a rifle shot.

"God. No."

Beneath the helplessness of that internal shout, Jonas perceived another sound and sprinted toward it, slowing only when he heard a voice he recognized call out.

"What's up, boys? Are you lost?" a female voice demanded in the manner of a professional taunt.

Tess was here and had caught up with those Weres first.

Chapter 15

One of the two hiding among the rocks spoke back.

"Why would we need to hide from a tasty morsel like you?"

"Maybe not quite so tasty," Tess said. "Come out. Show yourself."

"With pleasure," the Were said.

A tall humanlike form climbed down from the rocks. This guy was broad in the shoulders, with uncommonly long legs and arms. His thin face was bearded with red stubble and his attitude was familiar to her.

This was a rogue who believed his strength and cunning could get him out of any jam he was confronted with. Of more concern to Tess was the rifle he carried. She had heard the shot.

His partner appeared—another male, smaller, bulkier, younger by some years and dressed in fatigues.

Both sets of dark eyes flashed with animosity for anyone who dared to get in their way. What they were doing here was the question in need of an answer.

"This isn't the right area for hunting," Tess said, watching for and anticipating a move in her direction.

"Isn't that a bow in your hand?" the big guy returned with a sarcastic tone.

"I own the ground you're standing on, which pretty much means that I can do as I please. And I don't recall inviting guests."

"Really? Your dirt? I heard a rumor that a wolf slayer lives here."

"Slayer?" Tess repeated.

"I'm told she wears the pelts of the wolves she has killed and carries their teeth on a string."

This was always the way with rumors, Tess supposed. Facts tended to be blown way out of proportion.

"And if she does live here?" Tess asked.

"Then we might be in the market for some wolf slayer skin," the Were replied. "That would be sort of fitting, wouldn't it? A pelt for a pelt, like that old thing of an eye for an eye. We'd be heroes."

Tess nodded. "You came here for that reason?"

"Why else would we come to a godforsaken place like this? Then again, I wouldn't mind a little detour of the pleasurable kind if you're not the person we seek."

His eyes were on her, but they were human eyes. Tess had a bad feeling about taking down a rogue who looked like everyone else, and yet she saw no problem with defending herself.

The tension was palpable. The air contained a dark, angry vibe. Tess smelled the rabbit they'd killed with that rifle. It wouldn't be long before they were on her, even if they didn't put two and two together about the woman in front of them being the hunter they were after. It was entirely possible these guys didn't know the difference between a wolf hunter and a hole in the ground.

Diluted werewolf blood often left the humans it had infected angry and aggressive. If the blood of a werewolf infected a bad guy, chances were that person would be an even worse version than the original, with five times the strength.

"That wouldn't be you, would it? Does the term wolf slayer fit?" the visitor across from Tess asked.

"I don't care much for fur or necklaces," she replied. "But yes, if it's a wolf hunter you're after, I'm afraid that would be me."

The tall Were glanced at his friend, then turned back to her, licking his lips. Tess slowly raised her bow. A silver-tipped arrow was ready. All she had to do was aim.

"You're so small," the tall Were observed. Disappointment shone in his eyes about the possibility of this taking less time than he had imagined it would.

"Size isn't everything. But then, I'm sure you've heard that before," Tess returned drily.

Angered by her taunt, the tall Were took a step forward. He checked out the bow she was raising and smiled. His partner did a shuffling sidestep that was meant to be a distraction. However, it was obvious that neither of these guys had taken those slayer rumors to heart.

As the rifle lifted to the larger Were's hip and a black metal blade appeared in the other Were's hand, Tess was about to take aim when another sound echoed through the night to steal the attention of both of her wolfish opponents.

It was a howl. A haunting, harrowing howl, the likes of which Tess had never heard before.

From the periphery came a white streak of movement that glowed like a specter in the moonlight raining down through overhead branches. The white wolf was here. Jonas's pet.

Before Tess could loose her arrow, the white wolf lunged for the larger of the two Weres. The sheer force of its attack toppled him to the ground.

Sharp teeth nipped at the downed Were's face without actually touching skin. The wolf's growls were truly disturbing and rumbled continuously, warning the rogue Were to stay down. Although the white wolf was outweighed by over a hundred pounds, the rogue's face registered fear. Everyone here knew that wolf meant business.

In an attempt to defend himself, the Were's hands circled the white wolf's neck—a move the wolf shook off with its snowy muzzle close to the Were's face. One good bite and it would be all over for one of the rogues that had come looking for Tess tonight, hoping to make a name for himself.

Heroes, the Were currently held down by a mouthful of snapping teeth had said.

Seeing his partner in a vulnerable position and seemingly horrified by the sight of the white phantom doing damage to their plans, the Were to Tess's right jumped back. With the black blade temporarily removed from being an immediate threat, Tess turned to face him.

Her heart was racing. She had to determine which

beast was the bigger problem here. The white wolf was monstrously strong, but was only an animal. Werwolves could at least understand the spoken word.

"It's a shame you came here tonight," Tess said.

In the slight lull between her thoughts, the second rogue attacked, coming at her like a madman with his face in a sneer. What Tess lacked in sheer strength, she made up for in speed, knowledge of the Were breed and courage.

Targeting the arm that wielded the black blade, she let an arrow fly. As the arrow found its target, the Were holding the blade shrieked in pain and anger. Silver was a hefty detriment to most Weres whether they were wolfed up or not, despite what the Lycan had said, and this guy had been stung with a healthy dose.

The Were snarled and scratched at the arrow in his arm, hoping to dislodge it. Tess shot forward. Forgetting about the white wolf for the few seconds it took for her to raise a second arrow, she called out another warning. "Even bad plans sometimes go astray."

The guy she faced wasn't about to allow her an even bigger edge. He came at her with his face contorted and Tess's arrow sticking out from his upper arm. The silver the arrow had been dipped in was already showing its effect by slowing the rogue's reflexes down to human levels.

He used his other arm to swing at her and bared his human teeth as if he had forgotten about looking like a human tonight. With his injured arm covered by a blue long-sleeved T-shirt, Tess couldn't witness the spread of the silver that would have looked like a network of spiderwebs on his flesh by now. When it reached his heart, he'd go down.

This guy grunted each time he moved, but kept at it. Tess ducked, rounded and rallied strongly with a boot to his thigh that caused him to utter a curse.

In the forefront of Tess's mind was the question of what she could do with these guys if the white wolf didn't eat them before she could decide what to do in this situation. It wasn't like she could toss these two in jail.

Her attacker's face had taken on a sickly gleam. Though he was wounded, he was determined not to be bested by the hunter he had come here to kill.

Anger filled Tess, chasing everything away but the need to defend herself. This guy was a lot stronger than he looked and used what was left of his strength aggressively by turning, lunging, ready to do anything to rectify the way this was going down.

Tess fought him off, her concern growing about what was happening behind her. She heard a shout and thought she might have imaged it until she recognized the voice.

Jonas was here.

His familiar scent filled her lungs with each breath of air. Her heart continued to thunder. She should have known Jonas might have been in the area if the white wolf was. If two rogue Weres weren't enough, there were now three werewolves in their human guises and a real, white-pelted wolf invading her space.

Would Jonas be on her side, or defend those of his kind?

How about the white wolf with the big teeth? Would that animal come for her next?

The answers to those questions didn't matter at

the moment, because she had to deal. She had to see this through.

I have this, Tess chanted inwardly, fully intending to back that promise up somehow.

The scene was something Jonas feared, and he didn't know where to go first.

Gwen had a guy on the ground. Luckily for the idiot lying on his back, his sister was showing some restraint. The lucky bastard still had a face, as well as all four limbs. He wasn't putting up much of a struggle since Gwen's teeth were inches from his nose. But it was just a matter of time until Gwen's restraint wore off. She was toying with her prey before taking that bite. She might have been enjoying it.

He raced toward Tess, who was grappling with another rogue that she had wounded. Tess hadn't shot that arrow to kill, Jonas saw. She had winged the rogue in order to level the playing field.

Tess was outfitted in her leather hunter garb and in black from head to boot, and she looked every bit the part of what she was.

These guys might have been the monsters she had been trained to take on, and yet they had human eyes tonight. Tess's job was to protect humans from this very thing, but in the Were world, the line separating human from wolf was fuzzy. Without a full moon to strip the word *human* from them, Tess was clearly torn.

On the other hand, Jonas knew what had to be done and who had to do it. There was no way to redeem a bad Were and these two badasses had recently been indoctrinated into the species. They smelled rank and like the blood of the animals they had recently eaten.

Jonas slid his hands between Tess and the rogue and followed that move with his body. Having observed Tess in action and after having been up close and personal with her in a situation similar to this one, he knew she carried a small length of rope on her belt that he could use to hogtie this guy. With one down, he'd then pull Gwen off the other bastard.

Tess tried to shove him aside until her eyes met his. Seeing her determination waver, Jonas spoke to her quietly.

"This is what I do for a living, Tess, and these guys have wolf blood in their veins. Let me take it from here."

She didn't immediately respond. Like Gwen, her blood was up. Silver had bolstered her strength and her courage to do her duty here, and yet her reluctance to truly harm these guys wouldn't add anything to her reputation.

"Let me deal with them," he repeated, taking the arrow protruding from the Were's arm in his fingers and yanking it out, while blocking the Were and Tess from going at each other.

"Out of my way," Tess shouted, trying to shove him aside. She was abnormally strong now, but even with her silver infusion, his Lycan talents would have included besting this hunter in more ways than one.

The rogue wasn't sure what to think about this. He'd be smelling wolf on this new opponent and trying to decide who was in charge. Jonas backed him into the rock and spoke directly to Tess. "This guy is mine."

Jonas pushed that idea with the practiced power of persuasion most Lycans with old blood in their veins knew how to use.

When Tess's eyes softened slightly, Jonas added the magic word *"Please"* silently.

That did the trick. Tess stepped aside to allow him some space. And yet before Jonas could take full charge of the situation, he heard a bloodcurdling scream and knew it had come from the rogue that Gwen had pinned to the ground.

He whirled with a tight hold on the werewolf he'd been confronting. Tess spun with him. While the sight he witnessed made his stomach turn over, Jonas didn't dare close his eyes to block it out.

Gwendolyn Dale had just done a very bad thing.

Chapter 16

Tess's hands froze on her bow. Uncertainty about how to react to the sight in front of her took over her thought process.

The white wolf was standing over the body of the big rogue the wolf had been fighting with, and the snowy white fur was speckled with blood. When the animal glanced up from the devastation beneath it, its muzzle was bright, pure red.

The scene was surreal, as if somehow removed from time.

"No," Tess heard Jonas whisper, and the word echoed inside her head.

The white wolf stared back without moving. Its light eyes were focused on the rogue that Jonas had a hold of as if it would go for that guy next.

"Rope," Jonas said, holding tightly to the wounded Were by his side that, though alive, didn't look so good. Her silver-tipped arrow was doing irreparable damage to this poor bastard's body, and she felt some regret.

Jonas said, "On your belt, Tess. Pass me the rope."

Tess wasn't sure she should lower the bow after what she was witnessing. That white wolf had chewed on the downed rogue, taking his face right off. She couldn't fathom why the vicious animal hadn't gone after her at her cabin the day before.

"Rope," Jonas repeated, and this time Tess got the picture. Without dropping the bow altogether, she tossed a length of rope to Jonas.

The whole situation was weird. Jonas was helping her. He was relieving her of her duties, when she wasn't in need of a partner and hadn't asked for one.

"Relatives of yours?" she snapped, though her heart wasn't in the jibe. Her pulse was pounding with adrenaline. Spikes of anxiousness chilled the skin beneath her ears.

The look Jonas gave her was one of understanding, which riled her all the more and dredged up feelings for him that she had taken most of the evening to unsuccessfully avoid.

"Bad guys," he finally said, wrapping the wrists of the Were that was showing signs of further weakness.

"You think?" Tess muttered.

"My province, not yours," he continued, glancing at her and waiting until her eyes again met his.

Tess looked away quickly.

There was just something about those eyes…

His blue eyes looked golden in the shadows. The fire in them made her fingers curl. Jonas's body was virile and sexy. His commanding presence made her press her leather-clad thighs together.

She got a short reprieve from the look on his face when Jonas turned back to the blood-drenched white wolf to soberly assess the damage the wolf had done to the rogue.

"It's all right now," he said calmly, as if the wolf actually did possess the ability to understand what he was talking about.

Tess sucked in a breath. The stern beauty of Jonas's face, combined with the heady mixture of the danger she had faced and the silver particles swimming in her bloodstream, served to twist her emotions into new knotted threads. Instead of hating this Lycan, the look on his face made Tess want to jump his bones.

She had an urge to drop the bow, forget about the Were that had tried to kill her and have Jonas all to herself. Get down and dirty. Get this crazy attraction over with.

Shaking her head didn't rid her of those thoughts. Watching Jonas's muscles ripple and dance made her want him all the more.

"Crazy," she muttered.

The smile Jonas offered her was a sad one. In order to preserve the thinnest thread of her dignity and enhance her self-restraint, Tess had to believe he hadn't read those last thoughts. *"Because if you have, it will set the clock back to the beginning of time, before there were either of our species,"* she silently sent to him.

He had the graciousness to pretend he hadn't heard that last remark. Graciousness. In a werewolf. Where was there any mention of that in the damn rule book?

Where was it written that werewolves could tap into private thoughts and mess with a person's equilibrium?

That kind of connection was unfair and unruly. She should have hated Jonas. Instead...

Tess felt her face grow warmer. Her hands started to shake as she purposefully avoided the blue gaze that was searching her face. *Have to avoid you, wolf. Must.*

She wasn't sure that thought had been meant for her alone, or if she had openly shared it.

Jonas might be supposing that his charisma would be his ticket to her mattress and that he might single-handedly change the order of the hidden world they lived in. Tess knew better. She could picture what the world would be like if the goals of Weres and those who hunted them collided.

The white wolf moved, forcing Tess's attention there. It had crouched down with its unusually light eyes trained on the remaining rogue.

From beside her, Jonas spoke again, addressing his remarks to the wolf. "Gwen. No."

He tugged the wounded Were into taking a shaky first step. To Tess, he said, "There's nothing I can do to remove the silver from this guy's body, so it's unlikely he will last the night. Was there a large amount of silver on that arrow?"

"Enough to take down two of these guys," Tess said.

He called the blood-drenched white wolf to him with a pat on his thigh. Tess noticed that his jeans were torn and wondered if the white wolf had done that, too, with sharp teeth or claws.

As if nothing untoward had happened here, the

white wolf crept toward Jonas. Just before the animal reached him, it veered toward Tess.

Tess's hand moved to the knife on her belt. She held her breath as the white wolf approached. But the wolf that had just savaged a rogue made no angry growling sounds and didn't bare its teeth.

Steadying herself, Tess withheld a curse as the wolf brushed its bloody face against her right hand, leaving a bright red stripe on her knuckles. In what seemed to Tess like the oddest kind of finale to tonight's surreal scene, she got the distinct impression that this wolf was sending her a message.

"I will take care of this tomorrow," Jonas announced. "There's no more danger out here tonight. Go home, Tess."

When he turned, the white wolf gave Tess a backward glance before following Jonas, keeping close to the wounded rogue's dragging heels. Tess watched them go, equally hating and lamenting each step Jonas took that led him away from her.

The bad guys were gone. Odds tonight had been four to one, and she'd been left standing.

Letting out breath, Tess glanced down at the red stripe on her hand trying to understand what had just transpired, and if she was nuts for believing that the bloodstained white wolf, like its master, had given her a peace offering.

And that, Tess thought, had to be the craziest notion of all.

Jonas spent a couple of hours burying the Were he had dragged toward home. He'd have to do the same for the one Gwen had killed near the rocks. Sharp canines had taken care of one. A silver-tipped arrow had sealed the fate of the other. But for now, the strange and unlikely triangle of him, Gwen and Tess had come through this last attack unscathed.

It took him another hour to get the blood out of Gwen's white coat. With her skin sore from all the scrubbing, his sister had shifted back to her more familiar shape and had wrapped herself in a soft blanket by the fire he had built up for her.

He wanted to hug her, whisper assurances to Gwen that it would be all right, when she didn't seem to acknowledge that kind of closeness.

As usual, Gwen hadn't said a word. Her demeanor was calm, as if what had happened by the rocks was of no real consequence.

It was so damn hard for him to tell what his sister was thinking. No lines of telepathic communication worked with her for reasons Jonas regularly failed to understand. However, those lines were wide open with Tess.

Jonas kept himself from twitching the thread uniting him and the hunter. Filthy from digging, he was in need of a shower. Hot water would rinse away his desire to reach out to Tess. A long shower would occupy his time for several minutes.

"You okay?" he asked Gwen.

His sister was staring at the fire, and that was all right with him. He hoped that her wayward energy had been used up tonight and that they'd both get some rest.

"My turn then," Jonas declared, heading for the bathroom after making sure the front door was bolted and the windows were closed and secure.

He stripped slowly, careful not to drop his dirty jeans on the floor. One look in the mirror told him that the silver Tess had passed to him by way of the meeting of their lips hadn't completely gone away.

He felt sorry for the poor sucker who had been on the receiving end of Tess's arrow, but that was over now and they had to move on. Those guys had been bad news.

Hot water felt good on his neck and shoulders. Raising his face to inhale the steam, Jonas chastised himself for imagining what it would be like to have Tess beside him, and all the things he'd do if she were there.

He'd start with a slick glide of hands over her wet golden hair. He would touch her face, her neck and place a kiss beneath one ear before moving on a downward trajectory to her collarbone and the soft space between her breasts.

He imaged what her breasts would look like. And her hips. He imagined how the curve of her spine would feel if he ran a finger over each bone. He imagined having access to all that smooth, pale skin that would be his for the taking.

The vision of Tess's lush mouth opening beneath the pressure of his lips made him groan.

Stop! he commanded, aroused and aching for the reality of those dreams. He wasn't a fool. Her next arrow might have his name on it. And if that were to happen, who would look after Gwen? Who would be left to see to his sister's needs?

He missed Miami and his job on the police force. He missed his packmates. But going home was not an option, nor was spending time with Tess Owens on a bed or in a shower. He had to get that last part through his thick skull. His objective was to make sure his sister lived long enough to finally and fully heal from the damage that had been done to her, so that Gwen could eventually live a relatively normal Lycan life.

How long it would take for Death to look for her here was the question they faced. How he was going to rein Gwen in until that happened was another.

Though the water was hot, the shower tiles were cool. Tired of going over all the problems they faced, Jonas rested both hands on the wall, surrendering to the almost mystical allure of the steam…until he had to look up, startled by the newest sensation of hearing a voice inside his head.

"This doesn't mean we're on the same team, wolf. Merely that tonight, we were on the same page."

His smile was automatic. Tess had reached out.

"I want to make sure that you won't return, won't come looking for me," she sent to him.

"Not tonight," Jonas sent back. *"You can relax."*

"I don't owe you anything."

"I don't expect any thanks."

There were a few beats of silence before Tess spoke again.

"You gave your wolf pet a name."

Jonas thought back. Had he done that? Said Gwen's name in Tess's presence? If so, he had slipped up mightily.

"Doesn't everyone?" he returned. *"Some people even name their cars."*

"That wolf is lethal."

"Only to those who need to be reminded of the rules."

"Rules?" Tess echoed.

"You suppose we don't have them?"

"The same rules governing the bastards we met up with tonight?" Tess's skepticism danced along the wires of their connection like little electrical jolts.

"I don't suppose they had been Weres long enough to acknowledge the rules. So it ended the only way it could have," Jonas said.

He waited it out another brief lull in the conversation.

"I didn't need help," Tess said.

Jonas turned off the water and reached for a towel, not wanting to miss a single syllable of what Tess was saying. After wrapping himself up, he offered consolation. *"I know that."*

"Is that wolf wild?" she asked. *"Your pet?"*

"Sometimes, yes."

"Why didn't she attack me?"

"She?" Jonas echoed, annoyed with himself all over again.

"Gwen."

Jonas leaned against the sink.

"It's a pretty name for an animal who chews on living things. The point is..."

Jonas finished the sentence for her. *"You have an arrow with her name on it?"*

"If that wolf comes anywhere near me again, she will taste the magic of what an arrow can do."

"That wolf helped you out there tonight."

"Or am I just lucky she found a monster to munch on first?"

Jonas said, *"She is my responsibility."*

"We are talking about the wolf?" Tess sent back.

"I like you, wolf hunter. But don't take that confession too far. Liking you only covers so much territory."

"You're touchy about your pet."

"You have no idea."

Another minute of silence passed before she said, *"Good night, wolf."*

And as if Tess had slammed down a phone receiver, the connection abruptly ended.

Jonas looked to the bathroom door, listening for any evidence that his sister might have picked up on that conversation. After all, he knew so little about anything having to do with his sister.

The fact that Tess knew Gwen's name was troubling. Seeing how Gwen had taken to the hunter bothered him more. If Gwen went back to the Owens house, he had no real inkling of what Tess might do. Would she shoot something so beautiful?

Another touch came—not so light this time, and in the tone of a warning.

"Hell, I think it's back," Tess said.

Jonas thought she whispered when she added, *"And I'm guessing whatever this dark thing is might have something to do with you."*

Before those words had been fully spoken, and although they explained nothing really, Jonas found himself heading for the door.

Chapter 17

Tess closed down communication with Jonas and turned in a slow circle near her front gate, sending her senses outward.

The feeling had returned of having company she couldn't fully sense or see.

Nerves fired up beneath the surface of her skin. Her right cheek twitched. Something was out there, all right.

Behind her, the cabin felt as dark and as empty as she did. Loneliness was one thing. This new feeling of emptiness was different. Jonas had warmed the place up that afternoon and had shown off his fighting skills tonight, but he wasn't anywhere near here at the moment. The warmth of his presence was missing.

She was on her own with whatever was heading her way.

"For the record, I know you're there," she called out, continuing her search of the yard. "There's no need to hide."

A reply would have been a welcome surprise. Tess tried again.

"I've just come from a fight and don't have a tired bone in my body. In fact, if trouble is what you want, I'm ready."

Nothing.

Damn it.

The night had gone misty, with storm clouds rolling in to partially block the moon. It had to be late. Ten o'clock maybe. The mist blowing in seemed unnaturally cold. Tess shivered, waited, watched, with her hands clenched.

The night's temperature dropped by noticeable degrees as the mist fully blotted out the moon. Visibility beyond her fence was hampered by the dark curtain that had fallen over the landscape. As Tess stood rooted in place by the gate, taking in one icy breath after another, fear began to settle in.

The urge to call Jonas came and went. What good would it do when he wasn't close by? Besides, she had no right to go back on her vow of needing no one.

The uncanny mist entered the yard, flowing like a low-lying fog. Tess tried desperately to place what might be driving it. Her fear was close to reaching its zenith. She swayed on her feet, seeing nothing, finding no one, not even the outline of a shape in the mist that was getting closer by the second.

Tess sensed that something hid within the darkness, and she fought the instinct to run. After a painfully icy breath, she said, "What do you want?"

In a move so creepy that Tess almost crossed herself, the darkness drew upward and began to coagulate with a sickening flurry of motion. A face appeared that was unlike any face Tess had ever seen. Black veil. Black eyes. No mouth. There were no real features at all; just a filmy outline that came so close to her, Tess leaned back.

Were there words? Had it spoken when there was no mouth to speak with? In her mind, the word *wolf* appeared as if this thing had put it there.

When the image of what this dark apparition sought flashed through Tess's mind, it was an image she didn't recognize. In her mind was the wavering image of a dark-haired young girl.

Tess's heart rioted against the intrusion, thundering loudly. And yet her relief was instantaneous. This thing wasn't after Jonas, so why was it here? If it wasn't the bad thing Jonas had spoken about vaguely, and the thing he was expecting, the reason he had come to South Dakota, what else could this misty freak be?

It was too much of a coincidence.

The dark, featureless face was now level with hers and only inches away. Hell, it was trying to read her. She felt it probe her mind. If it had been Jonas this thing was after, it could have smelled him here and on her. Given its power to project an image directly to her mind, perhaps it had the ability to retrieve images from hers. In that case, the tiniest slip on her part might send this thing in Jonas's direction—even if the Lycan wasn't on its current to-do list.

"Enough!" she said adamantly, frightened enough

to be near to collapse. "Abominations aren't allowed in this place and it's my job to make sure you know that."

Her next breath hurt like hell. Ice filled her mouth, her throat, her chest. Swallowing was painful. Her breathing had slowed. Unconsciousness hovered like a weakened spark, but she had to keep standing.

"Wolf slayer," Tess whispered with the last full breath she could manage, repeating the name the rogue Weres had called her tonight as her vision began to tunnel and awareness started to drift.

No. That wasn't right. She wasn't drifting. The dark mist was. The face that wasn't a real face had backed away, taking the ice shards with it. Darkness began to recede. Wisps of that filmy black mass separated into ribbons that curled and tangled with the brush as the whole thing, rippling like disturbed waves of water, disappeared beyond the trees.

What the hell?

That question was internal, and the echo went on and on. Fear still gripped her. Sorrow was there as well…for the young girl this spooky thing had been after. Whoever she was.

Maybe Jonas knew?

The dark mist had flowed toward the fields leading to Jonas's cabin again tonight, and she had to warn him.

Could he be hiding a young girl at the cabin?

If so, the black abomination might be calling there next.

Jonas had to be prepared because he had been expecting trouble, even if this wasn't it. That thing she had seen wasn't after him, though. It wanted a girl.

That's what Tess told herself anyway as her feet, no longer so numb, started to move.

* * *

Jonas felt Tess's fear as if it were his own, and it deepened his concern for her. His ears rang with the shout she had sent to him through open channels. Chills on the back of his neck signaled the kind of warning he couldn't afford to ignore.

Tess was trying not to think about him, and by trying so hard, her thoughts came through like waves of static.

What are you afraid of, Tess?

At the window in a flash, he was careful not to let Gwen in on what he was sensing.

Inside his chest, Tess's heartbeats now thundered. She was frightened. Breathless. And she was running.

Tess was coming here.

The clock on the mantel confirmed that he and Gwen had been inside this cabin for less than half an hour. He had left Tess almost an hour before that. If more Weres had shown up in that time, Tess wouldn't have been afraid. After the skirmish with the last two, she would have done her job whether conflicted or not.

"Tess?" He let her name slip out.

Gwen moved in the chair.

"It's probably nothing," Jonas said to his sister. But he wasn't the only one who could feel and sense things. The suddenness of Gwen's attention was like the snap of a whip on his backside.

"I'd better go out just to make sure," he added. "Please wait here."

His skin chilled further when he stepped outside. The sensation of having an ice cube dropped down his shirt was the waving red flag of a premonition. And it was a damn good one.

"Gwen." Jonas spoke over his shoulder. "You must stay inside in case…"

He couldn't finish the statement. There was no doubt in his mind that Gwen was aware of his anxiousness. Thankfully, Gwen hadn't ignored this suggestion. But she was alert. For the first time since she'd been attacked, Jonas could have sworn he heard her silently mumble words that he didn't quite grasp.

"I'm going to the edge of the driveway," he told her. "Just need some air."

It was a lame excuse, but he didn't have another one handy. He kept hearing those waves of static originating in Tess's mind. Fully attuned to her and more than a little concerned, Jonas was aware of how close she was getting. She had passed the rocks where he had left her earlier and had paused for a quick look at the body of the rogue Were on the ground.

"What do you see, Tess?" Jonas sent to her. *"What's here?"*

This time, she replied, *"Black mist."*

She was breathing hard, and the breathlessness affected her thoughts similarly to having spoken those words aloud.

"A face that isn't a face. You know this thing?"

Jonas didn't immediately reply since he wasn't really sure what Tess had seen. However, her fright had been real and she carried it with her as she ran to warn them of a larger danger than the two werewolves they'd encountered earlier.

Jonas closed the door behind him after making sure

Gwen hadn't left the chair. Instead of using the steps, he jumped to the grass and strode toward the driveway, praying that this wasn't the danger he had been expecting and that his sister would have more time to heal and more time to live before facing everyone's arch nemesis and life-stealer.

The plan had always been to seeing to that objective, when no one could actually know what to expect from Death's minions. Not one person he knew of had lived long enough after being tagged by Death to tell their tale.

"Cold."

Tess had sent another message. Cold? What did it mean?

His senses told him she was in the field, sprinting near the base of the big pines, though he couldn't see her. There was no sign of anything else. He detected no sensory notification of danger, which would have been strange with Tess so riled up. Even with exceptional Lycan vision, he saw no black mist.

That didn't mean he couldn't picture such a creature. On the contrary, Tess's brief description pulled things from his mental databanks that he had been hoping to avoid. Terrible things. Very bad news.

Behind him, the door opened.

Gwen stood there. Her intent gaze swept past him, but she remained in the open doorway, probably having locked onto his buzzing nerves. Jonas spoke to her in a soft voice reserved for his sister. "Do you sense anything out there?"

Her gaze transferred to him. As usual, she didn't speak. Only her eyes told the stories that Gwen kept tucked away inside her. Right at that moment, those eyes were shining like the stars overhead…which didn't help Jonas much since the rest of her was so visibly calm.

Still, no one knew his sister like he did. He had found her that bloody night in Miami and had picked up the pieces. He had carried her to the pack surgeons and held her hand while they went to work. He loved Gwen more than life itself, but she hadn't come through that event unscathed.

Her wolf had been unleashed that night, as if the monsters had beaten it out of her, and Gwen's wolf was a truly wild rendition of Lycan four-legged beasts. No one had been able to tame her really. It was a miracle she behaved as well as she had, having been uprooted.

When Gwen advanced one step, Jonas's nerves fired up. When her gaze again bypassed him, there was little information for him to go by to dissect what she was feeling, other than the far-off look on her face.

"What is it?" he asked, mentally going over how long it had taken to scrub the blood from Gwen's face.

Blocking her wouldn't have made any difference, so Jonas didn't try. It was a beautiful thing he witnessed, and he'd never get used to it. Her abilities were either pure life-altering magic or a descent into madness, depending on how one chose to look at what his sister did next.

From the porch, she jumped to the ground, avoiding the steps like he had. But her leap had Gwen airborne. And in a graceful, soaring arc, Gwen shape-shifted from girl to wolf in the space of a blink, as if she were made of liquid mercury instead of flesh and bone.

Landing on snowy white paws that still held a few leftover traces of the blood of tonight's victim, Gwen was again on the move.

"Damn it," Jonas swore.

Some guardian he had turned out to be.

Chapter 18

Tracking her prey was a talent Tess excelled at usually, and yet she had failed to find the misty creature that had stirred up so many self-doubts about the kinds of knowledge she lacked. She had never heard of a thing as abhorrent as the ghostly apparition that had blown icy breaths in her face. Fear still coated her skin with chills.

She couldn't have stopped running if she had tried. Odd situations were framing her night one after the other, and after a long hiatus, as if Jonas's presence here had attracted the supernatural.

This last disgusting creature had left a pointer for her as to the reason for its visit. *Wolf,* it had said, and there just happened to be one nearby. Two of them, if she counted the white-furred animal that sometimes accompanied Jonas and liked to sink its teeth into others.

The red stripe on her hand, left there by that animal, was a strong reminder of Were and wolf ties. Maybe animals often had kindred spirits in species sharing their DNA.

"Tess."

It was *him* calling, and her mind was an open book of thoughts and mismatched patterns.

"We're heading toward you," Jonas sent through the airwaves. *"I don't see anything abnormal."*

Tess almost told him to look down at himself if he wanted the definition of abnormal but restrained herself. Jonas, she had come to believe, was a different animal altogether. He seemed quite normal at times…which, she supposed, was the secret weapon he wielded.

Then again, beauty wasn't everything.

That realization tied her stomach into more knots. Knots on top of knots. Jonas had said *we*, and Tess understood what that meant. Jonas and his vicious pet were coming.

Hell, she could kiss the damn rulebook goodbye and write a new one. The whole wolf-versus-wolf-hunter scenario was being tested here and she felt like a human guinea pig.

"If you come east, toward the rocks, we'll trap it in the field beyond the trees," she sent back to Jonas.

In spite of her job, that nasty black misty apparition seemed like the bigger danger here. Beneath her chills, Jonas's fragrant masculine scent lingered on her clothes, and that had to be what had interested whatever hid in the foggy folds of this black mist.

"Do you see it, Tess?"

"Lost it. But that doesn't mean it's not here."

"Further description of what to look for?"

"I've got nothing more to offer you."

Jonas had more to say. *"Keep back if you find it again. It's likely this thing isn't after you, and we wouldn't want it to change its mind."*

"It isn't after you either, Jonas. I got the impression it might be seeking someone you might know."

"Explain."

"It's looking for a girl. A young girl."

The connection filled with a string of raw, emotional curses before Jonas returned. *"How do you know this?"*

"I saw her. Saw her picture in that thing's mind."

Having gained more experience with the inexplicable connection she and Jonas shared, Tess knew when the mind-thought channel between them closed.

She had reached the edge of the field and still saw nothing of the encroaching mist. In the distance, she located Jonas, who had stopped to glance around. From her vantage point, Tess also saw the white animal as it darted into the trees more than half an acre in front of its Lycan master. Jonas had named that wolf Gwen. A better choice might have been to name it Killer.

There was no slithering layer of ground fog in the field between Jonas and where she stood. The moon was out. So were the stars.

Tess couldn't think of an explanation for why the apparition had disappeared a second time, nor could she see where it had gone. The chills covering every inch of her body suggested that it was still in the area, and could have been watching her and Jonas like an insidious, malignant beast.

Her chills doubled. Her heart thrashed. Something had crept up behind her. Tess whirled around with a tight grip on the handle of the blade to find Jonas's white wolf crouched on a rock above her.

The sounds the wolf was making made Tess's head feel light. Growling low in its throat, its muzzle had drawn back to expose a mouthful of needle-sharp teeth.

Tess gestured for the wolf to take its best shot. "Come on then, if you want a piece of me."

The wolf was trembling as badly as Tess was, but neither of them took the initiative to end the standoff.

"What are you waiting for, Gwen?" Tess taunted. "Take me down, and you can have him all for yourself."

The wolf lunged forward with a bound that should have tackled Tess and dropped her to the ground. Having anticipated this, Tess would have used the blade. But the wolf soared over her head, growling loudly as it landed beyond Tess and then launched itself at the black entity that had sneaked up from behind.

The creepy bastard hiding in the mist hissed like steam escaping from a tea kettle. With no face or visible entity to hurl herself at, the white wolf went for the center of the wavering black mass, snapping her teeth without finding purchase.

And then Jonas was there, appearing suddenly and swiping at the darkness with claws as lethal as the white wolf's canines.

In her mind, Tess heard the raspy voice that she now realized had tricked her into bringing Jonas to her and into the open. Because she had been manipulated, this latest round was partially her fault.

"Wolf," the dark thing whispered as it closed around Jonas.

"You don't want him," Tess shouted angrily. "He's not the one. You as much as told me so."

Jonas was in a life-and-death situation. He pounded the air with his fist and slashed at the misty creature with the claws he seemed able to call up at will. He used his body like a battering ram.

Uttering more oaths and curses than Tess had known existed in the English language, her Lycan fought like a demon.

The dark mass swirled and regrouped repeatedly, as if nothing remotely solid actually existed at its center. But that didn't deter Jonas. He came in and out of Tess's focus, meeting each turn with one of his own. Jonas the fighter. The Lycan with incredible speed and power.

Tess had never seen anything move so fast. Both Jonas's and the white wolf's determination to get at this creature transferred to her. She hurled herself at the fog, stabbing at it with her blade, tearing the fog apart only to see the moonlit field beyond it before the foggy apparition began to gather itself together again in another spot.

When Jonas appeared, Tess cried out his name. None of them were making headway against this foe. How did anyone fight a gathering of misty nothingness and hope to wound or vanquish it? The idea struck Tess that this was a situation of diminishing returns, and yet she and Jonas kept fighting until she heard another haunting howl that slowed things to a halt.

The landscape seemed to freeze. Nothing moved during the space of her next few heartbeats.

Beside her, Jonas was tightly strung and taking in deep breaths of air. And then she saw what he held in his arms. Jonas had the white wolf that was struggling to get free in order to re-enter the fight.

"Over my dead body," Jonas vowed dangerously, speaking to an inky patch of darkness that had gathered between the trees. "And that won't be so easy."

Though Tess didn't have any idea what Jonas meant, she quickly added her two cents. "And over mine."

She was heartened by the way the fog had backed off, a move she found odd since neither side had won this fight or even made much headway against the opposition. Still, Jonas had captured the white wolf.

The more that wolf struggled, the tighter Jonas held her. The fog remained aloof. Hell, did it even have a brain hidden in there somewhere?

Tess imagined that if it did have a brain, the entity might be considering what it would do next. She also was giving that question some serious thought. If no headway was to be made here and there was to be no real victory, what was the point of a face-off?

She waited, puzzled, while Jonas spoke again.

"You have no right to take her," he said, directing that speech to the darkness. "She came back and she's alive. You lost her and there's no going back, so suck up your loss and float off to wherever you came from."

Tess glanced sideways, able to feel in every cell in her body that Jonas was serious. Beyond that, what he had just said let her know that he not only knew who the girl was that this formless entity searched for, but that he had a stake in the outcome of that search.

It again crossed Tess's mind that the Lycan beside

her might be hiding someone at the cabin—the same person this dark faceless thing had come here to find.

Jonas and his wolf pet had to be protecting a young girl from this frightful beast. That was the Lycan's secret and his reason for being here. That was the reason for his brilliantly defiant stand against a creature like the one slithering through the trees.

Jonas was a guardian responsible for someone's life. He had told her this early on in cryptic ways. Could that have only been two days ago?

Tess dragged those questions through her memory until she dug up a string of his words.

I'm not what you think I am, Tess. I'm here, not to mess with you, but to protect a secret of my own. I'm needed. Someone else's life depends on what happens here and what I do.

Gutted by that memory, Tess stepped back. Flashes of heat streaked along cheekbones and slipped under the tight black leather when she had been so sure nothing could reach her there. This heat wasn't anger related. It had to do with Jonas as a protector and what that meant.

Who was the girl he was trying to help? Was that girl a Were or human? Tess had seen a young girl in the image in the monster's mind and supposed her to be human, but looks could be deceiving. Case in point, Jonas. With all that perfectly packaged brawn and bronzed skin, he was the walking equivalent of a female's wet dream. Any female.

Fierce and fighting fit, hazardous to his opponents, Jonas, with the talents and abilities of his full-blooded Lycan heritage, was one hell of a male. The human parts of the package he presented only punctuated that point.

He was perfect. He was beside her. But Jonas could never be hers, however much she might want that to be the outcome here.

The result of the admissions she had just made caused Tess to take another step away from him, as if a few more inches of distance between them might help her get back to reality.

It wasn't really any of her business what he did, as long as he was honest with her about it. And tonight was a further blow to her vow to rid the world of his kind.

Was it too late to change things?

Could she envision more Weres like him?

The answers to those questions were painfully elusive. Something very serious was at stake here and she was witnessing only the tip of whatever that was. She had only scratched the surface of Jonas's secrets.

The white wolf in Jonas's arms kept thrashing. Finally, and in a move so surprising that it made Jonas stumble sideways, the wolf kicked out so forcefully that he lost his grip.

Teeth bared, fur raised, the white wolf barreled forward. As she reached the trees and the darkness between them, the animal Jonas had named Gwen leaped into the air again. And as though that wolf had traveled through a black hole in the universe, the white wolf with her shining coat...vanished.

Chapter 19

"No!"

Jonas froze in place for the few seconds it took for him to fully realize what had just happened. He looked down at his hands in disbelief. Finding them empty, his sluggish synapses began to fire.

White-hot beams of power streaked through his system, rocking his stance on the fine line between human and Were. Prompted by the emotion roiling through him, Jonas's inner wolf soared to the surface. His two sides began to merge with a terrible impact in a desperate attempt to meet the challenge that sent his pulse skyrocketing. The result was a partial shape-shift that nearly sent him to his knees.

This wasn't supposed to happen.

Fires ignited inside him and spread so quickly his head snapped back. Anger, frustration and hurt had fueled this impossible piecemeal shift. The snapping sounds when he turned his head caused a chain reaction. His shoulders broadened. Muscles stretched to accommodate an impossible physical transformation.

He rushed after Gwen, lunging toward the core of a blackness that was slowly receding. Dampness clung to his face. The darkness stole his vision. None of that was going to stop him.

Punching with both hands to clear a path through the mist, Jonas made enough headway to see light on the other side. Moonlight. He couldn't find Gwen.

This unusual shape-shift was flagging in slow-motion, leaving him mostly human, with benefits. His heart was in a state of suspension. He forgot to breathe. His legs were churning on their own, driven by fear and heartbreak. Losing his sister would be like facing the end of the world.

Jonas sensed someone beside him. Tess. The wolf hunter was joining him in the hunt for his sister, despite her animosity for his kind.

He didn't have time to consider how to thank her for that. They were together and on the same page. They were connecting on a level too deep to acknowledge. Tess wasn't questioning his reasons for needing to find the white wolf so badly. She wasn't looking at him. His emotions were carrying her along, sweeping her into his business on a grand scale and spiraling her into unparalleled danger.

Fuck was the first word that came to his mind to describe what was going on tonight, and it was a word he repeated over and over as he strained, hoped, prayed, to see a flash of white.

The foggy mist rolled back each time he and Tess

charged forward, as if the mist was leading them away from the rocks. Jonas just couldn't stop himself from trying to cut his way through that unnatural dark. He couldn't hear anything beyond the beating of his heart.

"Gwen!" He still had a voice. His shout caused Tess to groan.

There was nothing to catch or hang on to with an opponent that had no real form. On the surface, the mist was just that…mist.

"Gwen!" Tess shouted, putting a lot of energy behind the call, as though she also had a stake in the outcome of this chase. Jonas could have loved her for that. But there was no sign of his sister. No damn sign at all. And he could not fathom how that could be true.

The wind that picked up felt cool on Jonas's overheated face. It whipped through loose wayward strands of Tess's golden hair, so that she had to press those strands back in order to see. Like the dark fog floating in it, this was an unnatural wind, since there wasn't an overhead leaf moving.

He had known this would be bad, and yet the probability of this dark entity being only a piece of the will of the master who had sent it was an idea too terrible to face.

"Wolf!" Tess shouted, her voice less forceful now that she also realized they were fighting a losing battle.

Was it a losing battle?

Jonas knew he had to stop fighting. The idea forming in his mind was an idea worth considering. If this dark thing had truly captured Gwen, Death's misty minion wouldn't still be here and leading them on a merry chase, would it?

He dialed in his wolf with a stern reprimand and

felt the wolf retreat. Rocking on his feet as the last of the strange shape-shift dissolved, Jonas stuck out a hand, caught hold of Tess, said, "Wait."

She paused with her muscles on adrenaline overdrive and quaking.

"Wait," he repeated until she looked at him.

To stop her from protesting or speaking...

To keep their opponent from doing further damage by taking up more time and energy when those things might be needed later...

And to steady himself from backtracking on the idea that had taken root...

Jonas pulled Tess to him. Resting his lips on hers briefly, he then bore down on her mouth with a savage ferocity that would either seal their fate or prove a point.

Caught up in a world of sensation that was spinning out of control, this latest surprise stunned Tess senseless. In the midst of chaos, Jonas was kissing her.

It wasn't just a kiss, though. This was also a sample of the level of this fierce Lycan's frustration over losing his pet.

Or was it more than that?

His mouth was both torturous and an unexpected delight. The breath he exhaled was fiery and added to the flames of interest for him that she had already been tamping down. An excruciating electrical current soared through her that wasn't related to the jumper cables she had used to ward him off.

All of that in the midst of danger.

The stiffness of her body thawed beneath Jonas's talented mouth. He was kissing her without letup, leaving no leeway for complaints. She found it strange how her hope for those complaints dissipated when Jonas slipped his tongue between her teeth.

His mouth was incredibly hot. His body was hotter. Pressed tightly to him for the third time in their short acquaintance, Tess felt her own temperature rise. She should have been torn between remembering her vows and the exquisite new pain of wanting this male so very badly, but couldn't think about that either. Lycans, she discovered, had made an art form out of kissing.

Without her consent, her body was surrendering to this meeting of their lips, tongues, chests, hips. The sheer force of Jonas's hunger demanded that she give in. On some level, their mutual attraction was as overpowering as it was irrational. By going down this road and setting a single foot upon this path, some kind of intimacy was bound to happen eventually. But she had hoped he'd be gone before then.

Nothing Tess had ever encountered tasted like he did. His mouth was demanding. Beneath the unrelenting pressure of his lips on hers, new emotions were being pulled to the surface from deep within her.

The depth of this intimate connection with Jonas was stirring up feelings of wildness, as though his wolfishness was contagious and being transferred to her. Visions came, taking over her mind with images of her running through green fields by Jonas's side, while howling at the moon. Wolf thoughts. Wolf pictures. Wolf madness.

That isn't me... Tess's mind protested. But those images also faded as the beast continued to devour her, and her hands, seemingly of their own accord, clung to his wide, supple back.

And then he spoke—silently. Softly.

"Tess..."

The way he silently sent her name was like a further touch.

"I'm sorry, Tess."

The pressure of his lips eased slightly as Tess considered his apology. Sorry for what? The kiss? Bringing that black thing here, if that's what he had done? Maybe the kiss was merely an outlet for easing pains she didn't yet understand.

Struck by that last thought's feeling of rightness, Jonas's kiss suddenly seemed to be full of possibilities that didn't necessarily include her for the reasons Tess had been anticipating. The realization was that she was being used.

"Meet me," he sent. *"Tomorrow."*

With his arms still encircling her, Tess couldn't move.

"Can't speak out loud," he sent. *"Have to use the pathway open to us."*

Those words added to Tess's moment of weakness.

"I don't think that thing can read us, Tess. It can't hear what we say this way."

And there it was...the reason for the kiss and the closeness that had her panting inside and longing for more. Jonas had forced intimacy on her in order to throw that other entity off in some way.

Why? Was it so that in seeing Jonas give up the chase, the dark entity in the mist might leave without getting what it had wanted?

Why would a kiss produce that result? After com-

ing here, surely that dark mass wouldn't give up so
easily.

The closing of Jonas's arms around her brought
her thoughts back. *"All of what you're thinking is partially true, though it explains nothing really and only
touches on the depth of my desire to get close to you."*

"You're using me," Tess sent back, though Jonas's
lips had left hers.

"Yes. But it's not what you think."

"Because you know so well what I'm thinking?"

The heat that had elevated her temperature only
moments before now crept into her face, and Tess
blinked slowly to hide the foolishness she felt for having thought, having believed for a few brief seconds
that this was something else.

"Tomorrow," he repeated, speaking out loud. "I
will explain."

Tess couldn't look at him. She cast a sideways
glance at her surroundings. There was no black mist.
Fields were again visible in the moonlight. Trees were
trees. She wasn't running through those fields or howling because she wasn't anything like the beguiling
male beside her.

The bad news was that she had just been made a
fool of and had been caught in what might turn out to
be the biggest mistake of her life.

When Jonas turned from her, Tess kept quiet. She
watched him take a few steps in the direction of his
cabin before speaking to him again.

"Where did she go, Jonas?"

He turned back.

"Your fierce companion," Tess clarified.

His need to follow up on that question was easy

to see. He wore a worried expression on his finely etched features. Creases lined his brow and his hands were fists. She saw no evidence of the claws he had wielded tonight without the moon's permission. Right then, Jonas looked like an ungodly handsome human being beset by far-reaching problems.

Jonas was anxious to find his white-pelted pet and couldn't hide that fact. Having been groin to groin with this Lycan five minutes ago, Tess felt as though she had developed the ability read him like an open book.

"I can't stay," he said.

"Who asked you to?" Tess returned.

His attention was intense. "The silver in your system won't hurt me."

"We've already discovered that."

"Would you have wanted it to?" he asked.

"That was the plan."

"Was? What about now?"

"Now, you're mocking me, and I don't appreciate it."

He stared at her appraisingly. "She might have been hurt. That hideous thing might have hurt her."

"Then you'd better find her. Find out," Tess said.

His gaze slid to the distant field. "I can't explain to you how important she is to me."

Tess couldn't even nod her head. "I think I got that."

"Tomorrow," he reiterated. Then he turned from her, giving her a ringside view of the ribbonlike string of marks she had scratched into his back with her silver blade in a now regrettable moment of all-consuming, over-the-top passion.

She waited until Jonas had gone before managing

to take a first step. She whispered a final personal lament. "I'm sorry, too, wolfman."

The night had been a long one and wasn't over yet. She started toward home, scouring her surroundings for any hint of either Jonas's white wolf or the dark entity his pet had gone after so viciously. No sign of either turned up.

Her cabin was dark when she reached the front gate. Windows were shutterless, the way she had left them. One of those windows had been broken by Jonas, whose scent would be everywhere inside her home and on most of the things she would touch. She couldn't do anything about his scent but would have to board up that hole before exhaling a breath of relief.

"Damn you, wolf."

At the gate, Tess paused with her senses open, probing the area for a hint of anything out of the ordinary, the way she usually did out of a need for caution. Things would have seemed normal and the way clear if it wasn't for the wave of chills covering the back of her neck. Premonition chills. Warnings. But she was almost too tired to care.

With her knife in one hand and her bow in the other, Tess retraced her steps to the edge of the trees bordering her yard. Nothing jumped out at her. No one spoke or showed up. She got no sense of having more unwelcome company, though the damn chills seemed to have come to stay.

"Overactive imagination due to extreme moral distress," she muttered, unable to face one more odd escapade after so many of them in the days since Jonas's arrival in her area. Promising herself to buck up and be the hunter destiny had predicted she'd be.

So, okay. He had kissed her, and she had liked it. How was that for a confession?

She could almost see other wolf hunters shuddering.

Another hour went by as she stood guard, half-expecting another round of trouble. Eventually, the moon no longer shed enough light for her to see beyond the fence. She had no idea what the time was and never really bothered with the ticks of a watch or wall clock. Out here, day was day and night was night.

Cautiously, she made her way inside the house and locked the door after her. She broke the doors off an old cabinet in the hallway and nailed them over the broken window. Satisfied that things were at least calm for the time being, she fell fully dressed onto her bed, attempting to count all of the rules she had broken in the past forty-eight hours…because in a situation like the one she found herself in, what good was counting sheep?

Chapter 20

Jonas's voice was raw from calling out to Gwen. He was sick, weary and not yet willing to give up the search for his sister.

The cabin was just as he'd left it when he had returned there to look for her the first time, over an hour ago.

The place smelled empty. Felt empty.

All that made him sicker.

Jonas leaned against the porch railing to recalculate the odds of finding a wolf that didn't want to be found, hoping that the god-awful black mist hadn't figured out who that white wolf was. Death himself wouldn't have been so naive, so Jonas supposed that having Death send a lesser minion on this mission had been in the Dale family's favor.

Perhaps this entity had never dealt with werewolves

and couldn't see through the wolf's disguise. If that was the case, Gwen still had to be out there somewhere. And if that unformed beast had taken her, harmed her, surely Gwen's big brother would have known.

Searching the dark, unable to erase the tension spiraling into his neck and shoulders, Jonas listened to the night birds in the distance and prayed that he might see Gwen coming across the field. Every stray bit of light out there made his heart skip a beat.

Going inside was not an option. Retracing his steps on the hillsides would have been a waste of energy. There had been nothing solid enough in that mist for his sister to have plunged her teeth into, which had to mean that Gwen was either chasing that dark devil out of the area or lying in wait for its return.

She wouldn't run away. Not Gwen. She wouldn't hide.

"Damn it, Gwen. Moving to South Dakota might have been a waste when viewed through the lens of hindsight."

How could he have predicted how quickly they would be found?

And then there was Tess. He refused to think about that kiss and hated that she hadn't understood why he had kissed her. His mind had to be taken elsewhere for those seconds, minutes, that the kiss had lasted in case the foggy bastard had the ability to read it.

Allowing his mind to wander back now to the exquisite feel of Tess's mouth and the way she had surrendered to the emotions overtaking them would bring more pain when he wasn't sure he could take anymore. There was no use wallowing in what he could never have.

He was surrounded by two unruly females that were so much more than they appeared to be on surface details alone. He had no real future with one of them and was trying hard to prolong the future of the other so that his sister might someday experience a kiss like the one he and Tess had shared.

The night couldn't last forever, Jonas told himself. Gwen would come back before dawn if she was in any way able to. Until then, he had to wait. He had to offer Gwen his open arms and whisper gentle words to appease whatever fears she harbored.

So he sat down on the steps with his senses trained on the distance. His thoughts kept veering back and forth between the memory of what had happened out there and the image of Tess Owens on the floor of her cabin with two fresh burn marks on her arms.

He had to forget that kiss and the way it had stirred him up.

He had told Tess that he'd explain everything tomorrow, to temporarily appease her. How he was going to do that was another problem. Because Tess was a wolf hunter, he was going to have to lie…about everything.

The sound Tess heard wasn't the thrashing of her heart. Nor was it an animal's mating call. She sat up to listen.

Scratching?

Anxiety over the way things had gone down tonight hadn't eased by much, and now made a curtain call. She was off the bed and leaning against the wall by the window with the silver blade gripped in one hand before the sounds came again—softly, and reminiscent of an animal trying to dig something out of a crack in the wood with its paws.

Doesn't have to mean anything.

Doesn't have to be ominous, Tess told herself.

That was before she caught an idea of what this visitor was and the word *ominous* took on a whole new meaning. One of them was here. Outside. Her senses screamed *wolf*.

Angry to have been right in her prediction of more trouble to come, Tess walked boldly to the front door and shoved back the latch, still dressed in her leather armor and with the knife ready.

A quick scan turned up no one on or near the front step, but it was here, all right. The image in her mind was unmistakably wolf.

"What else could you possibly want?" she asked in a firm voice, purposefully keeping her ongoing reaction to Jonas's kiss out of her main train of thought in case this was him. A replay, or even a visit from Jonas right then, would have been unfortunate for both of them. She was in no mood to deal with hunky, unruly werewolves who looked like God's gift to the species.

The scent got stronger. Tess stepped into the dark, ready to face whatever had shown up. The fact that no one replied to her question or presented their wooly Were self was a further annoyance that undermined her determination not to show fear.

"Come out, wolf," she said.

The next noise sounded like whining and brought with it a trickle of chills that dripped slowly down Tess's back. She turned toward the gate, using her silver-enhanced night vision to search the yard, and saw something. Nerves jangling, Tess waited a while longer before speaking again. In an unsteady voice, she asked, "Gwen?"

More whining sounds reached her that struck Tess as being distress calls for help. Cautiously, Tess crept toward the sounds, calling out to the animal she now knew was out there.

She found the white wolf at the edge of the yard, not lunging or attacking anything this time but lying on its side. As Tess stood over Jonas's pet, its big eyes never left her. She saw pain in those eyes. The beautiful white coat was filthy. Tess had a horrible vision of the wolf dragging itself here.

Upon closer inspection, and without getting too close, Tess saw the wounds that had taken this lovely creature down to its current level of pain. The white coat was matted in several places with dark blood that looked nothing like the earlier werewolf kill. One of the wolf's delicate ears was torn.

The white wolf had come here for something. Was it looking for help? Could wolves know what a human wolf hunter was?

Earlier, this one had left a bloody mark on her hand instead of trying to bite it off. It had shown no attempt to harm her the day before. In that respect, this wolf had acted more like a domesticated dog.

What good was asking this animal anything? Even if it responded to Jonas's commands, the white wolf was just an animal.

The question Tess had to ask herself was why it had come here instead of returning to the Were who so obviously cared for it. For *her,* Tess amended. This was the wolf Jonas had lovingly named Gwen, and an animal he loved.

After sheathing the knife, Tess knelt down beside the animal, careful to remember that wounded animals could be overly aggressive. Tentatively, she touched the white wolf's body. The big eyes that had been trained on her closed.

"Who hurt you?" Tess asked, honestly wanting the answer to that question, along with all of the others, chief among them being how she was supposed to help this creature.

She only knew that she had to help. It was likely that the desire to do so stemmed from the way this wolf had accepted her and then returned here now when help was needed…and also because of the look on Jonas's face when his pet had disappeared. Loss was the emotion that had rearranged the Lycan's chiseled features. Pain had flickered in his light blue eyes.

"You're too large for me to carry," Tess said. "Can you try to get to the house?"

She didn't for one second feel stupid for talking to the wolf as if it understood every damn thing she said. Tone of voice could sometimes soothe an injured soul, Tess had often found in the past.

"I'm afraid to touch you, in case I hurt you more."

Acting as if it did understand, the wolf struggled to get up, managing to get to all fours, barely, with its body shaking hard enough to almost topple the animal again.

"If you can make it to the house, I will do what I can to ease the pain." Tess inched backward, tapping her thigh the way she had seen Jonas do when he wanted the wolf to follow him. "I won't purposefully hurt you. I'll swear to that."

The wolf took a staggering step and followed it with another.

"That's right," Tess encouraged. The front door wasn't too far away, but she wasn't sure the animal was going to make it in the shape it was in.

"Do it, Gwen," she said, backing up again. "I've seen what you're capable of. You can do this."

This was the same magnificent animal that had growled fiercely a couple of hours ago. It had gone after a werewolf disguised as a human when that Were had threatened Tess, as if this wolf's intent had been to protect her. Now, it made faint whining sounds with every move it made. Nevertheless, the wolf did move forward.

What was she going to do with the animal once she got it inside?

Tess wondered if Jonas allowed Gwen inside his cabin and if any wolf that had been born in the wild could have been domesticated that much.

It took a while to get the white wolf to the door. Once all four paws were inside, the wolf could go no farther.

"I'll get some salve and warm towels," Tess said, used to talking to herself, thinking that more conversation to soak up some of the shock of the situation wouldn't be so bad here.

The wolf lay on the floor with its head between its paws, seemingly content to be inside, though Tess figured she could have made that part up. Because who the hell knew what a real animal thought, or even if they did think things out?

She went to the room housing medical and silver supplies and turned on the light. She hadn't yet bothered to clean up the broken glass on the floor but did a quick check to make sure the boards she had nailed to the window were secure.

The cabinet was filled with bottles of concoctions her mother had made from local plants and more secret sources. Tess removed two bottles and returned to the front room. The wolf hadn't moved from that spot by the door.

"Hot towels first," Tess said. "We have to clean up those wounds. I'll be right back."

The kitchen was a place where she had never spent much time. A kettle was already on the stove from her afternoon cup of tea. She filled the kettle with water from the tap and adjusted the valve that turned on the burner. Then she circled back to the wolf on her floor without glancing at the framed photo of her parents on the table beside it.

Wolf hunters weren't animal haters. Her mother and father would have approved of helping this wolf, Tess preferred to believe.

"The medicine will sting," she explained. "I know this because I've used it many times and uttered some very bad words right after."

She returned to the kitchen to fetch the hot water and poured it over a clean hand towel at the sink. The white wolf's eyes followed her comings and goings. Its whining sounds had ceased.

Tess again knelt down beside her new four-legged guest. "If you try to bite me, I'll have to kick you out."

With gentle strokes of the hot towel, she began the process of cleaning blood and matted fur from the wounds she found on Gwen's neck and back. The wounds were strange and more like deep burn marks than injuries a sharp weapon might have made. They were bright red and raw.

The animal let Tess tend to its wounds and kept the lethal teeth Tess had twice seen in action to itself.

"Gwen, is it?" Tess said as she worked. "Why Gwen, I wonder?"

The minute the question was out of her mouth, Tess felt a foreign thought drop in.

"Gwen."

The urgency in his tone made Tess rock back. She put a hand to her mouth, able to feel the lingering imprint of Jonas's mouth there.

Jonas had heard her speak Gwen's name and, with palpable relief, was already on his way.

Chapter 21

Jonas covered ground that he barely felt beneath him. Tess had seen Gwen and therefore had to know where his sister was. Tess's thoughts led him to believe his sister was alive. He owed Tess big-time for letting him in on that.

He sprinted through the fields and up to the rocky hillside leading to Tess's home, going over what he'd say and what he'd do when he got there. Throwing Tess against a wall and kissing her to within an inch of her life was not an option. Finding Gwen was. But man, he wanted to get close to Tess, who could very well be teetering on the cusp of understanding both him and his priorities.

There were lights in her cabin, though the yard around it was dark. The wolf hunter's scent layered over the place like its own telling fog. Over that hovered the scent he sought.

Without concern, he ran right up to the front door and pushed it open. What he saw inside stopped him in his tracks. Gwen was there, all right. So was Tess. The mighty wolf hunter that so many other Weres feared sat on the floor beside his sister, with Gwen's white wolfish head on her lap.

Tess looked up at him, showing no surprise over seeing him there. "She's hurt, but I don't think her injuries are life-threatening."

Jonas almost slid to the floor in relief, having been in a similar situation once before when the news about his sister's outcome wasn't so positive. In fact, no one had expected Gwen to make it through that night.

"What happened?" he asked.

Tess shook her head. "I was going to ask you."

"I couldn't find her. Looked everywhere."

"Everywhere but here," Tess said.

He squatted down to run a hand over Gwen's muzzle, glad to have her make the kind of sound that told him she was happy to see him. His gaze slipped to the bottles next to Tess, then to Tess herself. She averted her eyes.

"It's good medicine," she said.

As he had expected, Tess was still tightly wrapped in black leather. She had expected the return of some kind of trouble, and here it was, in her lap.

Luckily, Gwen had stayed in wolf form and was the kind of special Lycan she was. Tess had no idea what kind of secrets that white furry form hid. No one other than Jonas did. That was the beauty of Gwen's uniqueness and one reason why his sister was so important to the future of the Lycan race.

Werewolf hunter talents couldn't break through

Gwendolyn Dale's defenses to see what the outer shape disguised. To Tess, a talented hunter, his sister was just an unusual wolf. The promise of passing along that particular trait to other Lycans would set wolf hunting back hundreds of years.

And here, now, Tess Owens was coming to the aid of that special being due to the fact that inside Tess's leather-clad chest, a sentimental heart beat.

Jonas rested both of his hands on Gwen's neck, careful to avoid his sister's wounds but wanting a closer look at them.

"I'm doing what I can," Tess said as his gaze roamed over Gwen's white coat.

She was doing just that, Jonas saw. Trying to help. Again, though, he wondered why Gwen had come here, and what had made his sister so attracted to Tess when their relationship was anything but symbiotic.

Then again, hadn't he reacted to this wolf hunter in a similar fashion and been more or less smitten by her from the start? From the first sighting?

What is it about you, Tess Owens?

Jonas kept that thought behind a closed door in his mind, but the question was an intriguing one and the problem was in need of a solution.

He wanted to show his gratitude to this mesmerizing wolf hunter for helping Gwen, and yet with Gwen watching, Jonas kept his hands to himself. His sister missed nothing, it seemed to him. Possibly his feelings for Tess were what drove Gwen to form a similar kind of reaction. Possibly his sister could read him after all and had fooled him completely on that score.

"Will you take her?" Tess asked with her eyes downcast.

Jonas perceived how, inside her chest, Tess's heart was now revving to chase the same dreams he was running after. The small hands stroking Gwen's coat had been on him once and had burned him the way the fire in her eyes did.

He could have counted each of the beats of Tess's pulse by the rise of the smooth skin beneath her ears. By the dappled light of one table lamp, Tess, with her pale skin, her lacing of lavender scars and her big gleaming eyes, looked more like a Were than most of the wolves he had met.

Maybe hunting Weres had over the millennia truly changed hunter chemistry in more ways than anyone could have imagined. All Jonas knew for sure was that in that moment, which was somehow removed from time, she was the thing he desired most in the world and also the one thing he couldn't have.

And that if he couldn't have her…

If he could never breach or break down the barriers keeping them apart…

His life would never be the same again, and he'd be left with nothing but years of unrequited longing and loss.

As if she had followed that thought, Tess's eyes finally met his. The expression on her beautiful face was blank. Her eyes flashed in the lamplight as if inlaid with gold fire.

"I want you, Tess."

He had confessed this to her before while knowing those kinds of needs were a lost cause.

"Can't happen," Tess said aloud. "We both know that, and why."

Before he could respond to her remark, she fired

off a question. "What was that dark entity, and what did it want here?"

On the tail end of that query, she asked another. "Did it do this to Gwen?"

While making an attempt to maintain eye contact with Tess, Jonas felt his sister's attention snap to him. He had to be extra careful now so as not to frighten Gwen.

She knew nothing about Death being on her trail. As his younger sibling, Gwen had to follow his lead and go wherever he went without question. He had led her to believe, without explicitly saying so, that coming here was so that she could rest and recover from her injuries. Only that, and nothing more. He was her legal guardian, as far as Gwen and the rest of the world were concerned, and as such, would have her best interest in mind.

"I don't know if it could have done this," he replied truthfully. "Or how it could have caused these injuries."

Tess wasn't appeased. "But you do know what that thing was."

Glancing at Gwen, Jonas said, "I can make a good guess."

"And?"

"I'd rather not say until I know for sure."

"That's no answer at all, wolf, and gets us nowhere," Tess said.

Jonas was glad she hadn't said his name. If she had, he might have closed the short distance whether or not his sister had been watching. Tess's voice had a certain power over him that was disconcerting. When he looked into her eyes, it was like falling into a bottomless well. Every cell in his body was reaching out to Tess. Instead of acting on that, he alluded to Gwen with another long stroke over her coat and said, "She must really like you, Tess. It took a lot of courage for a wolf to show up on this particular doorstep."

"Maybe this was the closest place," Tess suggested. Neither of them really bought that explanation, however. They had lost sight of Gwen quite a distance from here.

Jonas shook his head. "I think there's more to her coming to you than a matter of distance. What that is escapes me. Perhaps you can explain?"

"A real wolf wouldn't know about me and what I do. Nor would this wolf or any other animal need to be afraid."

"Just Weres."

After a beat, she said, "Yes. Just Weres."

Gwen's attention on him felt like hot sparks. His sister was following this conversation in spite of the pain she had to be experiencing. Small quakes rippled her coat.

"Don't," he sent to his sister, locking Tess out of the personal message and hoping Gwen actually heard it. *"Do not show this woman how the world could be shaped in the future by changing back."*

When he turned to Tess, it was to find that she had more to say.

"Did that dark entity come for you? At least tell me that."

"I don't believe it came for me," Jonas replied.

"If it appeared randomly and was every bit the evil bastard I thought it was, it could have harmed me the first time it came around. But this entity didn't seem to have me on its radar." She looked at Gwen. "Your wolf here seemed to believe that entity was a threat."

"Yes," was all that Jonas could say without telling Tess everything. Answering her questions would mean letting Gwen know everything, too, when he had avoided that conversation for weeks.

As if sensing his reticence, Tess leaned closer to him. She laid a hand on his arm, causing the muscles under his shirt to dance.

"We'll get nowhere without the truth," she said. "And if that thing comes back, who will need the most help, you or me?"

Jonas closed his eyes to absorb the current flowing through him that made him consider taking Tess right here on this floor to end the strained tension standoff. Hell, she might even have let him. Only Gwen, whose injured body lay between him and the realization of his true desires, kept him from taking that kind of liberty.

Tess had gone too damn far down a bumpy road. Without claws, she had snared him in a dangerous, deceitful web of revolving species. This wasn't her fault or his. They were what they were. However, it all made a mad kind of sense to Jonas and others like him. They got it. Werewolves were not welcome among the human population. So most of the time, Weres successfully blended in with the human population. And yet there were hunters who would put an end to that kind of existence, and one of them sat across from him with the future hope of the Lycan species' head in her lap.

"I'll take her home," Jonas said.

Tess's eyes again found his. "Which home?"

"This one won't do us much good for much longer," he replied.

She wouldn't let up. "Because the thing you said you came here to avoid found you tonight? Because it's here now?"

Jonas smiled wearily, feeling so damn tired of the secrets entrusted to him. "I can carry her home, but maybe you'd be kind enough to give us a lift in your car so that Gwen won't be hurt anymore than she has been?"

"She can stay here," Tess said.

Jonas shook his head. "That wouldn't be wise."

"Are you expecting that dark misty bastard to make a comeback?"

"Tending to an injured wolf will keep you from resting, and Gwen is my responsibility."

The woman across from him had no right to argue with that. She clearly swallowed back a retort before finally saying, "I'll get the Jeep."

"Thank you," Jonas said. "Thanks for everything you've done for Gwen tonight."

After carefully moving Gwen's head, Tess got to her feet and reached for the latch on the front door. Halfway outside, she turned back.

"If that thing does return, will you be safe?"

Jonas shrugged.

"When will you leave South Dakota?" she asked.

"Tomorrow."

He saw Tess sway on her feet. But she nodded to him, took a set of keys from the table near the door and headed into the dark.

Gwen whined. Jonas brought his face close to hers.

"I know you like her, but she's not for us. She isn't one of us."

Gwen knew a human being when she saw one. She had lived in a city filled with humans all of her life. What she didn't know was how hard he worked to avoid letting her in on the specifics of the situation they were in and that staying here longer would not only put Gwen in jeopardy, but drag Tess toward peril as well.

Wants were nothing when it came to maintaining everyone's safety. Possibly things would be different someday. Once Gwen was out of trouble, he might come back for Tess. With his sister safe, he could tell Tess everything and it wouldn't matter.

The sound of the Jeep's engine turning over was the green light for his departure, and Jonas was as reluctant to leave as his sister was. Gwen whined again when he stood, and growled when he bent to pick her up.

"She's not like us," he repeated. "And she never will be."

Lifting his sister had to hurt her tremendously, and yet she made no more sounds. He really hoped she wouldn't change shape in the time it took for them to reach their cabin, giving Tess the surprise of her life. As talented as Tess was at discerning man from werewolf, it was clear she didn't have the slightest notion about Gwen.

With Gwen in his arms, he walked toward Tess's Jeep. He climbed onto the seat, holding Gwen tight.

Tess didn't look at him as she drove, but the things left unsaid were piling up. The air in the Jeep crackled with tension. Jonas counted the inches between them and watched Tess from the corner of his eye.

Tess drove the route in the dark like she knew it well. When she pulled up in front of the cabin, she waited without speaking while he slammed the Jeep's door with a light kick of his foot. She waited until he had mounted the steps before breaking the silence.

"Catch," she said, tossing a small bottle to him that he caught even with his hands full of white wolf. It was the medicine for Gwen's wounds. A parting gift.

Then, in a whirl of kicked up dirt and dried grass, the woman he craved in so many impossible ways was gone. Leaving her and South Dakota was going to be the hardest thing he'd ever done.

Chapter 22

Turn around, Tess's inner self urged as she drove. *Go back. Talk this out.* But really, what was to be gained by doing any of those things? Jonas was going to leave the area and she would get on with her life, be back on track, do her job the way she was supposed to.

He would leave and she'd start over.

"Yes. That's the plan," Tess muttered, slapping the wheel with both hands. "It's a good plan."

The only problem was how much she didn't actually believe that. Her life had radically changed. The wolf hunter had crossed a line drawn by a werewolf whose magnificent presence had sucked her into his orbit, only to leave her spinning out of control.

Her speed on the road rivaled the speed of her heart rate at the moment. She felt every damn beat and took the web of tight turns like a race car driver, needing to get home so there'd be no option for turning around. Her mentors hadn't stressed the finer points about the kind of physical voodoo Lycans wielded and how effective it might be. Any self-respecting wolf hunter in her position should have felt ashamed for having succumbed to that sort of power.

If she turned around, she'd tell this Lycan a thing or two. "Go to hell" would have been a good way to start.

Tess kept up her inner monologue until her home came into view. By then, it really was too late to switch gears. She pulled up and parked in the driveway, noting that the front door was open. Jonas had left it that way. His hands had been full.

Tess sat in silence, staring at the house. After a while, she went inside and straight to her room, tired, bone-weary, mentally fatigued and in need of a few moments of peaceful oblivion. She stripped off the leather that carried Jonas's musky male scent and climbed onto the bed without thinking about anything other than how to stop the ceaseless chatter going in her mind. She almost succeeded.

"Tess?"

"Oh, hell, no," she sputtered, covering her ears. "There's no point, wolf."

"I'm sorry, Tess."

Flipping onto her back, Tess stared up at the ceiling.

"You asked if that dark thing was after me, and I lied when I told you I didn't know. It's a truly dark being, Tess, and I came here hoping to stall the inevitability of meeting with it. If Gwen and I leave, that thing will also leave. You won't have to worry about what it is and what it can do. Trust me when I say that you wouldn't want to know anything more."

His thoughts came in waves of remembered warmth. Tess heard those thoughts as clearly as if he was here in her room, sitting on the side of her bed.

"I've never been good at guessing games," she sent back to Jonas, since it was either talk back to him or go mad.

"I can't leave Gwen alone now," he said. *"If it was any other way, I'd be with you."*

"Your white wolf will be all right. Use the salve. Let her heal."

"If only she could heal."

"It's good medicine."

"Can it work on the inside, Tess? Do you have a salve for that?"

They were no longer speaking about Jonas's pet. The point of Jonas's comments had shifted as quickly as he had shape-shifted in the moonlight.

"Tess?"

"What is it you want, Jonas? To make an even bigger fool of me?"

"I want to hold you."

Tess's insides were churning. She blinked slowly to get a grip, touched by the sentiment Jonas had just offered. How long had it been since anyone had held her and offered comfort? It had been over a year since her parents' death, but her parents had never coddled their grown-up offspring.

Hold her? Jonas's simple statement and the emotion it represented brought tears to her eyes. Either he had her number and knew about her loneliness, or holding her was something they both truly wanted. Closeness. Comfort. Understanding. Truce.

As powerful as Jonas was, the wolf wasn't crude,

arrogant or pushy. He hadn't mentioned taking her to bed or offered up pornographic innuendos. She would have given a lot to have been able to feel his arms wrapping around her. To breathe easily, rest her head against his chest, and feel like she belonged to someone, even if the feeling was to be short-lived.

All of the loneliness she had filed away as being unimportant came rushing back. But the simple truth here was that the male of her fantasies was not someone. He was a werewolf. Allowing any sort of closeness with a werewolf would demean the work her family had done. In loving a werewolf, desiring a werewolf, her life would be over.

"Come back, Tess," he sent to her. Possibly he sensed her turmoil. *"Get in the car and come back here. Come now. Let's finish this."*

"Too late," Tess argued. *"It's already finished."*

"You're wrong. What's between us won't be over no matter what happens or how far away from you I go."

Tess exhaled a long breath before addressing that remark, wishing for a second wind to help her deal with this situation.

"We'll see about that, won't we, when you leave tomorrow?" she said.

"Come here, Tess. Come now."

This was the time to say the words she had rehearsed in the car. Go to hell, Jonas. The command sat on her tongue, begging to be spoken. The words filled her mouth. But Jonas spoke first.

"Please, Tess," he sent over the channels that inexplicably connected them. *"Please get here."*

And damn it, that polite little phrase trumped any argument she could have made.

It was time to end this. Past time. Jonas had to stop talking to her the way Weres talked among themselves. He had to be made to leave her alone if he wouldn't do so willingly.

She had to demand this in person.

Forgoing the leather, pulling on her jeans and an old sweatshirt, Tess grabbed her key, closed the front door and got into the Jeep, thinking that morning couldn't be more than a couple of hours away and that when that sun appeared, Jonas would be gone.

That was a good thing. The only way out of this dilemma.

Right?

With Gwen curled up by the fire, Jonas again stood in the open doorway, waiting. Tess was coming. She had accepted his invitation and before she got here, he had to decide how much to tell her.

Speaking to her had been a bad call that he hadn't been able to avoid. As a wolf hunter, Tess had access to other hunters around the globe. If Were secrets were to be disclosed because of one Lycan's need to appease one of those hunters, he'd be responsible for the trouble all Weres might be in if any of those disclosures got out.

Asking Tess to keep those secrets wasn't any more of a viable option than making love to her would have been. Although Tess wore her loneliness openly and had possibly been ripe for a connection of any kind, he might have unwittingly taken advantage of that.

He really was sorry, kind of. On the other hand, waiting for Tess to arrive made Jonas question his one motive for asking her here. A motive she might not like. An idea that had presented itself when he had kissed her and had hounded him ever since.

It read like this: Tess Owens wasn't one hundred percent human, after all. She couldn't be.

The sound of the Jeep's engine brought him up from the inward search for a way to tell Tess about his theory. Maybe she would simply head back home, glad to be rid of him, kicking herself for having agreed to this meeting when he explained. Why should she even consider what he'd have to say?

She was here and turning down the dirt driveway. When she reached the cabin, there was no hesitation on her part or playing coy in the car. After slamming the door, she walked toward him with a dark expression on her beautiful face. Swear to God, it was the most beautiful face Jonas had ever seen.

He was off the steps before she had reached them. She stopped to face him when she was no more than three feet away, without speaking. Jonas found his own tongue tied.

Her eyes were bright spots in her pale face. She looked much softer in a gray sweatshirt and jeans, and much more human than Jonas would have liked. Her hair was loose and hung over her shoulders, slightly tangled. Her scars were hidden by the messy golden strands. Tess was tense, but there were no weapons in her hands. He didn't smell the presence of weapons in her car. Tess was trusting him and he was about to break that trust.

When their eyes met, she sighed.

And then she was in his arms.

His hunger for Tess took over, guiding his actions without leaving room for regret. With his lips on hers and their bodies pressed tight, she was the focus, the need, the way to satisfy his cravings.

He kissed her as if there would be no tomorrow, because there wasn't going to be one. Jonas devoured her, using sight, sense, taste and touch. Without hesitation or protest, Tess responded in kind. She kissed him back with fury, offering herself to him, asking for more, with him all the way.

The meeting of their mouths was excruciatingly divine. Tess's breath was hot. Her mouth was like fire. Hell, he wanted to climb inside her and find a way to access her soul. *You need me. Need this*, he would say as he wrapped his claws around that soul. *Because you are more like me than you think.*

Her arms were around his neck. Her hips were against his, and he had to have more. He slid his hands under her sweatshirt, ran his greedy palms slowly upward and over her spine to discover each lean, graceful curve.

Growling with pleasure, Jonas gripped her shirt, broke the contact with her mouth and swung Tess around so that they would be out of view from the open doorway. He pressed her against the only available thing he could find, the solid concrete base of the porch railing above their heads.

She made a sound as her back met with the concrete. And then she looked up at him with wide blue eyes that expressed the hint of wildness that Jonas not only had seen before but that had led him to the recent conclusion of Tess's true nature.

"Do you think this is normal?" he asked her, his voice hoarse with longing.

"No." She was breathless.

"Why do you suppose you can hear me in your mind?"

She shook her head.

Now wasn't the time to talk about this. The truth would ruin the only moment like this he was likely to have.

Her lips parted as though she had more to say, but the truth he had formulated about the strength of their bond kept him from letting her speak.

Kissing Tess produced a feeling similar to the kiss of the moon. The silver in her system had no lingering taste but made his lips tingle. He was hard, aroused and aching. For her.

This second kiss was lighter than the first. Possibly he had left the way open for Tess to consider what he had said to her. In fact, there had to be so much more to this attraction than two kinds of beings colliding in a small space.

His fingers found the waistband of her jeans. Tess laid her hand on his as if she'd stop him from moving but instead, began to guide his fingers beneath the fitted denim.

Jonas withheld a groan. The naked skin his fingers glided over was smooth, warm, taut, ultrafeminine, and made him question how he could possibly have gotten this far.

He breathed in the essence of Tess Owens, feeling through touch the rise of that wildness she kept hidden inside. As if his fingers had beckoned it to come forth, the wildness she housed roared toward the surface, causing Tess to shake.

He popped the button on her jeans. The sound of the zipper sliding on metallic tracks was unconscionably loud in an otherwise quiet night. Tess held her breath as his fingers moved over the lower portion of her abdomen and as he briefly detoured to note the sharpness of her hip bones before continuing to drop downward.

All of this had taken seconds...

She drew back when he found the place he had been seeking in the deep V between her thighs, but she had nowhere to go. Her breath came in soft, irregular hisses that Jonas breathed in. His heart was racing.

The place he found with his fingertips was soft and moist. Jonas thought he might go crazy if he didn't find out more of what Tess's body had to offer, but the tight fit of her jeans limited his access.

He ran a fingertip over her sensitive folds, then applied more pressure there. Tess gasped. Her arms fell away from his neck. Jonas's mouth demanded the same kind of pressure from the lush lips he was kissing. Tess made little sounds that might have been protests, without backing them up.

He was searching for her soul and had made headway. If he could just find that soul, he would know if he was right about Tess. Tess had to be open to this.

She squirmed when he paused at the gateway to her womanhood. The beat of her pulse met Jonas there as he waited for her to calm down. Suddenly, she stilled as if she feared what the next step between them might be.

Tess Owens was no damsel and couldn't be treated like one again after his last attempt to carry her. Nevertheless, Jonas's hunger for her demanded that he tear away anything barring him from the soul he wanted so desperately.

The rapidly escalating level of his need to possess her dictated what his next move had to be. Withdrawing his fingers, leaving her mouth, Jonas took hold of Tess's hand. He led her toward the Jeep and sat her on top of the hood. He pulled off her boots, too riled up to explore the option of taking his time to get her undressed.

Slowly, he ran both of his hands up the outside of her long legs until he again found her waistband. One good tug of his arms, and her jeans slipped off. It all seemed too good to be true.

His hunger raged as Tess's fires called to his. And suddenly, riotously, he was the one being led down the path toward carnal closeness, with Tess directing the show.

She was sleek and silky, her skin ivory in the darkness. Tess was everything a she-wolf should have been and didn't even know it. Jonas couldn't hold on, couldn't stave off the degree of his hunger for her much longer. The urge to have her, mind, body and soul was almost more than he could take. The fact that she wore nothing under those jeans was not only a surprise, it was a turn-on.

It was also his way in.

Jonas pressed his cock to her soft folds and held there without breathing for the right second to finalize this. In another minute, he'd start to sweat. His body was quaking with need.

The buzz of Tess's tense muscles against his was an added turn-on. The way he was hesitating made her shake more. They'd have to breathe sometime.

When she exhaled a long, slow stream of warm air, relaxing slightly, he was inside her with a stroke that made her seize. But he was unable to move after that. Tess didn't just have fire at her beck and call, she was fire. And that fire was going to burn him alive.

Chapter 23

Tess refused to give in to the need to be taken by this Were without giving back. Time stopped when he entered her with a thrust that made her insides burst with white-hot explosions of sensation. Pain came and went in a flash. Heat rushed in. She gasped as too many new feelings struck simultaneously.

There was no feeling anywhere else, beyond the point of the intersection of their bodies. Jonas's move seemed to have had a similar effect on him. He stood with his feet on the ground and his weight balanced on the hands he had placed on either side of her. Shudders ripped through him before he acted again.

He backed off and out of her, his body rigid with pent-up tension. She would have killed him if he had changed his mind and stopped this now, after coming this far.

His second thrust came with a shockwave that tore through Tess with the force of a hurricane and threatened to tear her apart. For the first time in years, she was feeling gloriously alive, and because of this sudden awakening, she wanted more. She wanted it all.

Taking hold of Jonas's shoulders, she leaned back on the Jeep's warm hood. Tall enough to accommodate this position, her Were lover growled deep in his throat with pleasure before he moved again and again, entering her as if he was already in possession of her body and would prove that to her.

Slowly at first, he worked his magic. After a few more strokes, he began to build up speed, and the delicious physical attack took on a rhythm that threatened to knock her senseless.

Tess wrapped her legs around him so that he didn't have much room to move, and still he managed to make one sweet thrust after another, each one better than the last. With a firm hold on her hips, Jonas slid her closer to him. Locked together, she met him with a molten moistness, lifting her hips, taking him in, massaging him in ways that were primal and instinctual.

Her pleasure came in waves that bordered on ecstasy. He'd attack and retreat. Tess moved to accept and accommodate the pressure and friction of their bodies melding in perfect harmony.

Oh yes, he knew how to pleasure her, though that might not have been so very difficult since he was her first talented partner and the first male she had wanted inside her this badly. Hunters conserved their energy by forgoing the rituals that came with sex and physical gratification with others. More often than not, she had pleasured herself after a good hunt that ended well and left it at that. But this…

You…

The energy they were exuding bordered on insane. Faster. Deeper. God, this was so incredibly good.

When it seemed as though he couldn't possibly do more or do it better, he did.

She was sitting up now, with her arms around him and her head thrown back. Her legs were open and he stood between them, buried to the hilt. Heat came from everywhere at once—his body, his moves, his breath. They were joining like this as if they both had become possessed. Or mad.

Or both.

The height of sensation he provided her was like running, screaming and chasing her destiny all at once. Each fresh rush of feeling was almost too much to handle and at the same time not nearly enough.

Tess dug into her lover with her nails, wanting to hurt him for changing things for her, and needing him to feel what she was feeling. She nipped at his mouth each time he came in for a kiss and still was left needing more, already addicted to the level of pleasure he was showing her.

More.

There was more. She knew this.

And when he reached her core, the place with a direct link to her soul, the world tipped on its axis. The surrounding darkness lightened with fireworks that went off like the Fourth of July.

Tess finally let go of the cries that had been building, and Jonas, with one final, perfect thrust, joined her with a cry of his own.

Their sounds merged, mingled. Hers was an orgasm that continued endlessly without letup. Waves of pleasure and streaks of light hit over and over until finally Tess was able to draw a much-needed breath. Even then, she couldn't open her eyes. This was what sex was supposed to be like—fierce, powerful, masterful, perfect.

But there was something wrong; some little hitch in the afterglow.

Wrapped tightly in Jonas's arms, Tess began to spiral back to awareness with a new flutter inside her that felt as though it didn't belong. It was fear, and it quickly took over where pleasure had reigned, because there had been a mistake.

The cries of ecstasy she had heard had not been cries. The sounds Jonas had made were growls, but there had been more than one voice making them... and one of those voices had been hers.

Jonas was afraid to move. He felt the sudden spikes in Tess's heart rate and didn't want to let her go.

Tess had growled. And she had just realized this.

The moment was one of confusion and mental backtracking. They were still on the downside of an orgasm that had shaken him to his boots, and the necessity of their coupling and what they had done had stunned him completely.

Still, the bigger issue of note here was he had been right about the female in his arms. Tess was not the human she had always assumed she was. Not even close.

It had taken sex with a Were to unlock the secret of what lay hidden in Tess's blood and DNA. That secret was so large and startling, Jonas couldn't wrap his mind around it.

How was it possible that her family could have neglected to tell Tess something this important? That she belonged, not to the human race, but to the species she hunted so fervently?

Possibly a secret like this was the reason the Owens clan had preferred to live in so remote an area. It was obvious to him that they hadn't wanted their daughter to know anything about her real heritage since Tess's secret beat out all other secrets combined.

She had no clue that she was a Were. How could she?

Those scars she bore might have been the wounds that had indoctrinated Tess into the moon's clan. Still, how could she not have known about this after so many full moons had passed...enough of them to have turned those old wounds into scars?

Jonas was at a loss as to how to explain this. If things had gone according to Tess's plans and she had managed to take him down, or if he hadn't come here in the first place, there was a chance she might never have known what she actually was.

But she had an idea about that now. She'd just had her first look at the real Tess Owens, whether she liked what she had found or not.

She was a wolf, all right. And this explained a lot. It made sense out of their immediate attraction and their need to be with each other. They actually had imprinted with the first look into each other's eyes, and had just sealed their fate as a couple on the hood of this car without any prior knowledge of what would happen.

The wolf hunter was one of the creatures she hunted. About that, there was no mistake. The only mistake had been to cover all that up and let her go on believing she was above all that.

"It's the reason for the immediate attraction I felt for you," Jonas explained, holding her, waiting for her pulse to slow. "And it's the reason you're here with me now, I suppose."

He understood that there was no way Tess could speak, let alone get a grip on this kind of news. For her, it would be the worst of all outcomes and totally unbelievable. Discovering the truth was momentous in terms of her future.

"Imprinting is a state that only happens between two of us who are meant to mate."

"You mean meant to fuck," she said.

"No. Anyone can fuck. Imprinting is the way we find our true mates. It starts and ends with our needs. Weres mate for life."

Who could blame her for not fully accepting what had happened tonight? After a shock like this, Jonas didn't see how she was going to recover, but as the key to this momentous discovery, he planned to be with her until she did.

She sat on the edge of the hood of her Jeep, naked from the waist down, with a shocked expression on her beautiful face. He had done this to her. He had inadvertently hurt her by wanting her so badly.

Selfish idiot.

Now what?

How many times could he tell Tess how sorry he was when his own wish was to keep her with him? Had he just lost her because of that wish?

Gradually, she began to pull away from him. Without asking him for her pants and without getting off the car, Tess just sat there, looking at him as if she was in a trance.

Then she said, "It's a lie," shoved him back and jumped down. She bent over to pick up her jeans and boots and, putting them on, turned from him and walked toward the cabin like nothing had happened.

Tough Tess. Strong Tess. When will you crack?

He observed the way she climbed the steps, using the railing with both hands and placing each foot carefully above the next. He should have stopped her, kept her from going inside where more secrets awaited. But those were his secrets, and it was too late for stopping Tess now.

If the daughter of Tamsen and Marcus Owens was going to go after werewolves in the future, Tess was going to have to start with herself.

Tess's world was no longer recognizable. Each step she took was a chore that required a concerted effort. All of this was a dream, a nightmare. Any minute now, she'd wake up. *Please.*

Tess didn't recognize the cabin she was about to enter. Her current objective was to reach the front door. By going inside, her wits would return and she'd be able to think straight. The night had become a pressure squeezing her into an unfamiliar shape. Her body felt heavy and unreal. The air she breathed was thick.

The wolf was watching her, his focus blisteringly hot on her backside. She had let him in, brought him close and been alarmingly intimate. The blurring of the images of what had taken place between them was due to guilt, shock, shame.

She had mated with a Lycan...and it had been like nothing in her experience. She had been lost inside his wolfish aura, where desire had its own set of claws.

But that was all. That was it. He had hinted at so much more, yet imagining she was like him was an overindulgent fantasy on Jonas's part. He had lied to her about that. He had to be lying. Besides having sex with the enemy, this wolf had to be into mind games.

The latch felt cold on her hand. The heavy wood door swung inward quietly. Tess stepped into a room that wasn't vastly different from her own front room, except that this one was warmer, with a roaring fire in the grate.

Two leather chairs had been placed near the tall stone fireplace. Between them, a braided rug covered the floor. All of this would have been well and fine, homey even, if it hadn't been for the ghostly appearance of the young girl curled up in one of those chairs.

This, Tess's senses told her, was the secret Jonas had kept to himself. This was the girl he had been protecting and the reason he was in South Dakota. Here was the girl that she had seen projected in the evil entity's thoughts. The one she had assumed Jonas might be hiding.

Small, fragile, rail thin and with a whitish glow on her young, skeletal face, the girl in that chair had platinum hair, instead of brown, and wore no clothes. Seemingly at home with being stark naked, the girl eyed Tess with an unsettling blue-eyed stare.

"Shit," Tess whispered as the door swung closed behind her.

Chapter 24

Tess could see that the girl Jonas was protecting was more otherworldly than almost anything she had seen—with the exception of the entity hidden in the dark mist. The appearance of two strange creatures in one scarcely populated area was rare and not to be underestimated.

Tess didn't know whether to speak or turn around and leave when Jonas would be outside the door. This was a young girl, however ethereal she looked. The fact that the girl was naked at the moment was bothersome. She had to have been at least fifteen or sixteen years old.

"You're the reason Jonas is here," Tess said, testing the waters of forced social skills and wanting desperately to retreat.

The girl didn't respond to that statement. She continued to stare. Maybe she couldn't talk. Due to the extremes of her thinness, it was possible she didn't have the energy to speak. Chances were, this girl could be ill.

"I didn't mean to disturb you," Tess went on. "I..."

She looked around for Jonas.

"I'll go," she added, turning for the door.

A cool hand stopped her. The girl was beside her, having moved so quickly, Tess hadn't caught any movement at all. The hand on her arm was a nonverbal request for Tess to wait.

Tess turned back. Deep inside her, a noticeable flicker of fear returned. Wolves were a species she could deal with, for the most part. This girl was different. Although the cabin smelled like Were, the female in it carried no particular scent at all. She was like a white-skinned black hole for details pertaining to who she was and what she could have been doing here with Jonas.

Hadn't he told her a couple of times that Tess's education had been lacking?

Tess didn't look at the door. Jonas was standing on the other side of it, biding his time, waiting for the right moment to enter. She felt him there. In her mind, she saw him place his hand on the latch.

"Can I help you?" Tess asked the girl. "Do you need help?"

The girl's face was expressionless, but the blue eyes weren't. Her eyes were a light sky blue like Jonas's and like her own, and they were the eyes of someone who was smiling.

Questions like "where are your clothes?" and "what

are you to Jonas?" went unsaid. Intrinsically, Tess sensed that this girl wanted her here despite the awkward nakedness. She just couldn't get a handle on why.

Everything surrounding Jonas was a mystery and had been from the beginning. Meeting this girl was just one more layer of that mystery. Saying the whole thing was strange would have been an understatement.

"I have to go now," Tess said.

She'd have to get the hell out of there. Tension was again mounting. Maybe the cabin had a back door she could use to avoid Jonas as well as the mysterious female he associated with.

And where was the wounded white wolf that Jonas had strong feelings for?

The hand on her arm was firm and much stronger than Tess would have guessed. The girl's eyes never left her. This pale creature wanted something. What?

"Can you speak?" Tess asked. "Can you tell me who you are?"

That got a reaction in the form of a slight shake of the girl's head, proving that Jonas's young friend had understood at least one of those last questions.

"I'm sorry," Tess said, growing more uncomfortable with each passing minute. There was a residual ache between her thighs. Deeper than that and tucked away inside her was a sensation of emptiness that demanded to be filled. And there was only one way to do that. Damn if she would satisfy that urge again. Mistakes were piling up.

"I'm sorry," she repeated, again going for the door. The hand on her arm loosened and fell to the girl's side. Tess looked back as she pulled on the door.

The mysterious girl had sunk to a crouch, a position

that needled Tess's mind as being uncannily familiar. Still, there was no time to reflect or dig into memory. Jonas was blocking her exit and looking past her, his eyes on the girl.

"Tess, wait." Jonas moved his gaze back and forth between Tess and Gwen, who was now in human form but crouched like a wolf ready to spring into action. Gwen was also buck naked. Seeing a human like that had to have further messed with Tess's equilibrium.

"Out of my way, wolf," Tess said.

"It's important that you don't mention her to anyone. If I had the power to erase minds, I'd use it now, on you," Jonas said.

"If you had that kind of power, I'd beg you to erase what happened here tonight," she snapped.

"This isn't between you and me, Tess. What's at stake here is so much larger than that."

"Thanks for the overview."

"You don't have to believe me about what you are. You do have to believe that trouble is looking for her and has already arrived."

Her eyes blazed. "Have you forgotten that I've seen that thing, and also who it's looking for? I know this girl might be the one on its radar."

He nodded. "Then you realize how important it is for that thing not to find her."

Jonas saw that Tess got that without being privy to any of the particulars, though her mind wasn't going to allow her to let the details go for long. Their sexual liaison had tainted the moment and left a bad taste in Tess's mouth for mysteries. He had led her toward enlightenment about her true spirit, and she was fighting that.

But it was too late for changing paths. They had imprinted. Sex had sealed the deal. Tess would eventually have to come to terms with that, as well as the reasons underlining why it had happened. Sooner or later, she would have to believe.

Imprinting meant that they would crave each other from now on and demand that they satisfy those cravings. The animal inside each of them would push those urges to the limits. Physical and mental closeness was the way this worked. Wolf to wolf. No exceptions.

He stepped out of the doorway.

Tess hesitated briefly, as if about to say something, and then breezed past him with the kind of speed all wolves possessed without stopping to wonder how she had found that ability.

Jonas's heart ached to keep her there. He wanted to explain things. But, he thought as she got into the Jeep, that the hunter parts of Tess were going to be difficult to dislodge in order to make room for the truth, because her parents had kept that truth from her.

"Silver," Jonas said in afterthought. "It's the silver, and how you've been using it. That has to be the key."

"Good luck with your pale friends," Tess called back over the rev of the engine. "And with whatever dark things are lurking."

In a flurry of kicked up dirt and pine needles, Tess was gone…and Gwen was limping toward the steps, intending to go after her.

"No, hun," Jonas said gently. "Let her go. If she has

any reason to believe why we need her and what we see in her, she will be back."

He laid a hand on Gwen's head. "That's what you sensed, isn't it? That Tess is like us? It's the reason you went to her?"

Gwen made a sound that was half growl, half protest. Still, it was a response after so many weeks without one. Heartened by that, Jonas faced her.

"Is it also because Tess is a female? You crave her company because of that?"

Gwen's gaze strayed to the trees in the distance. Jonas supposed his sister might be straining for a sight of the Jeep.

"We're close now," he said. "You know that thing is here. You've seen it. I can no longer keep that from you. What I didn't realize was that it couldn't see you in the wolf form you presented to it. That's invaluable information. It might be safer for you to be a wolf until it arrives on our doorstep. What do you think about that? Can you manage it? Maintain it?"

She had heard him, but maybe his sister wasn't quite ready to do as he asked, since she fit better like this in the chair by the fire. Giving Gwen any kind of comfort now, with the dark entity so close, was worth a few more moments of risk.

Just not too many of those moments.

What had Jonas meant about the silver?

That question plagued Tess all the way home, but it had to stand in line with all the others.

If she could have found another werewolf on the prowl tonight, some of her useless, wayward energy could have been used up. As it was, her body had become a nagging, treacherous backstabber, compelling her to turn back and sample more of what Jonas had to offer. He was so damn good at screwing, and she was a sucker for the high.

Still, what they had done hadn't fit the term *screwing*. There was more to what their bodies had expected from that session on the hood of her car. Jonas had called it *mating*. He had used the word *imprinting*. But Jonas was nuts, and told her she was a wolf. The only word to describe her now was *idiot*, and Tess was fully prepared to own it.

As she drove, Tess searched the dark, looking for a blacker piece of night that might hide a lurker. That thing was after the girl Jonas kept hidden away, and no one would have wanted it to find her.

That girl was...unusual. Meeting her produced pangs of jealousy that were as outrageous as they were unwarranted. Jonas wouldn't have touched that girl. She knew this. So had he been hired to hide her, or were those two related?

Those blue eyes might point to the latter idea. Nevertheless, lots of people had blue eyes. So did she.

Her cabin seemed forlorn when compared to the one Jonas had filled with a comforting fire. And yet there was nothing comforting about the vibes that girl had given out. There was something disturbing about her, something Tess couldn't pinpoint. Those eyes still seemed familiar. The way the girl had dropped to one knee was familiar.

If only she could think straight.

If she could go back there and demand answers, she

would have felt better…until Tess remembered what Jonas had told her.

"Wolf? In your dreams," she muttered as she got out of the Jeep. She felt compelled to add, "There will be silver waiting for you if you show up here again without an invitation."

But her body wasn't one with her on that threat. She was throbbing in all the wrong places when danger was all around them…and there was nothing she could do about that.

She had made a stand and had to stick by it.

Getting out of the Jeep was tough. Her stomach was tight. Her legs felt weak. And there was that leftover emptiness, still demanding to be satisfied.

"I'll deal," she said with determination. "I will get over it."

She had been well used tonight, and mating like that, with a male like Jonas, required the one kind of stamina she didn't have in her repertoire. A warm bath to ease the aches and a cup of her mother's special tea would be a good start to a full recovery. She would sleep tonight. The silver infusion was already wearing off, burned away by all the chasing and…*mating*.

Putting Jonas out of her mind was going to be a harder chore if he could break in whenever he wanted to. The echo of his last words were with her still.

It's the silver, and how you've been using it. That has to be the key.

Key to what?

"Don't go there, Tess," she said aloud to set the remark in stone. "It doesn't matter."

Getting Jonas's scent off her was what mattered.

Catching up on sleep mattered.

She was not going to be tainted by the words of a werewolf, a Lycan, hoping to turn her head with nonsense.

Looking at the floor by the front door and the drop of blood she hadn't stopped to clean up earlier, Tess's vow crumbled.

"So where is the white wolf, Jonas?" she asked, hopefully keeping that question from the airwaves connecting her to the Lycan who believed she had to be like him in order to explain what had transpired between them tonight.

Tess stared at the floor. Thoughts nagged. Chills cascaded down her back.

Suddenly, strange feelings of having just put two and two together arrived with the force of a physical blow. The girl at Jonas's cabin had looked at her with the same expression of need that his pet had exhibited on the floor in this hallway.

"No." Tess shook her head to negate the absurdity of the thought. However—and hell—if a Lycan was hiding both a girl and a white wolf, what if those two things were one and the same?

"No. Can't be true."

The girl didn't smell like a wolf, but she had been naked, with pale skin and hair. That girl had the look of someone who was ill and in need of warmth. Could a Lycan change into a four-legged animal? Jonas hadn't, and besides, she had never heard of such a thing.

The thought persisted.

Was there a chance the girl in Jonas's cabin had done that—changed into a four-legged wolf with no Were scent attached to the transition? Had that girl sustained injuries tonight after attacking a dark evil entity in the mist?

Tess sat down on the nearest chair, stunned by the revelation.

"You bastard," she sent to Jonas.

reached up over Jonas's arm and made the ring
come up off the floor.

Tess reached for the device that cloaked her in
radiation.

"How many do you think we have left?" Jonas

Chapter 25

Jonas's body was throbbing with need for Tess, and
the reason for that had been made clear.

He'd have to use more caution now. The plan to get
away was a good one. Still, an imprinted pair couldn't
be separated for long. Any prolonged distance would
tear a mated pair apart both mentally and physically.
The only way to cheat that kind of pairing would be
if one half of the imprinted pair died, and he wasn't
going to allow anything to happen to Tess.

She had been…

Tess had been sheer bliss tonight, both beside him
in the fight with that damn dark entity and beneath
him on the hood of that car. Her body was as warm
and pliant as the leather clothes she wore. Her mind
was another matter.

He looked at Gwen, who was standing near the fire

covered in the blanket he had tossed her. His sister had to know what he and Tess had done.

"Yes. Okay. The mighty hunter next door is one of us," he said to his sister.

Gwen was looking at him the way she always did—expressionless face, wide eyes. Jonas now realized he had begun to see a pattern there, however slight, that provided hints of what his sister might be thinking. As he had already surmised, he wasn't the only one in this family who was seriously attracted to Tess.

"I'm afraid she will now know about you after this," he continued. "Tess is smart and savvy. The problem is that I just don't know what she will do with the information. And anyway, that dark thing hovering around here is too close for comfort. We will have to go."

Jonas heard the ache of regret in his voice. Leaving Tess was going to be one hell of a cross to bear.

Gwen's gaze moved to the window, which was his sister's way of asking a question without having to use her voice.

"I didn't tell you about that dark thing on our trail. I didn't want you to worry about anything other than the road to a full recovery."

Her gaze slid back to him.

"I won't tell you more about that now, other than to say that leaving would be in our best interest and as soon as possible. Tonight, if you're well enough to manage it. I'll start packing up while you rest. It won't take long. We didn't bring much."

Gwen shook her head, a response that came as another surprise.

"We can't stay. Not now," Jonas explained.

In his heart, though, he already knew that the dark

thing out there would find them wherever they went and that leaving here would only prolong the next meeting, as well as the one after that.

He also realized that Gwen hadn't recovered enough in her human form to be able to constantly travel from place to place without spending most of her time as a wolf. It was tough to hide a white wolf, as they had recently found out. And Gwen's behavior was still unpredictable.

"We can come back here later," he said, meaning that. For him, there would be no other option. He'd have to be with Tess again no matter what Tess's thoughts about it were.

"Bastard."

The word Tess sent arrived to punctuate his last thought. Jonas whipped around to hide his expression from his sister. He had been right. Tess now knew that Gwen was the white wolf and he couldn't wait around to see what she planned to do about it.

Man, he hated that. He felt the loss deeply, and already.

He found a much bigger problem when he turned back to find Gwen on the floor, gasping for breath. No curse he had ever heard was sufficient to describe the pain that struck him as he rushed to gather his sister in his arms.

"Gwen? Hun?" His voice was hoarse with worry. "Can you open your eyes? Slow your breathing the way we've been taught to do? Gwen, can you hear me? Don't panic. There's no need to be afraid."

That was a lie, of course. The dark thing might not have been able to find Gwen in the wolf's outline, but it was here nonetheless. This could be what Gwen was sensing and the reason for this latest panic attack.

"Breathe," Jonas directed, thinking he'd never get used to seeing his sister affected like this, gladdened by the fact that he and others in the strong Miami pack had caught the bastards that had hurt her so gravely.

Hell, compared to what Gwen had faced, Tess didn't know what a real bastard looked like.

As Gwen's shaking began to calm, Jonas revisited his vow to do anything to keep his sister safe, even if that meant tearing himself away from Tess for as long as was physically possible so that he and Gwen could hit the road.

He studied Gwen's face as she drew in a few deep breaths, heartened when her white lashes fluttered. In a minor mind disturbance that called for his attention, he heard Tess ask a question. *"Why have you ruined everything?"*

Hearing her voice brought back each blissful moment he had shared with her when they had made love...though making love didn't accurately describe the way they had gone at each other in his front yard. Hearing her voice in his mind, without having her beside him, was making him hard all over again.

He had it bad for this wolf hunter.

"The truth is the truth," Jonas sent back to her. *"There is no getting around it. You might never have found out what you are, but that doesn't change the facts."*

Gwen's lashes fluttered again. Her shaking had ceased. The lines on her young forehead had smoothed out.

"I need you out of my head, wolf," Tess sent.

"Won't happen, Tess."

"Make it happen."

"Disconnecting with you is beyond my abilities. We have mated. For me, that's a strong, enduring link."

Gwen's eyes opened, blinked slowly, remained open.

"What does silver have to do with anything?" Tess asked.

"Now isn't the time to explain, Tess."

"You're with the girl?"

"Yes."

"That girl is the wolf."

"I will protect her with my life, whatever she might or might not be. The question I now have is whether I will have to protect her from you."

Gwen was looking at him in a way that made Jonas believe she could hear the silent conversation taking place between him and his lover. He didn't really care about that if hearing Tess's thoughts was the trick that had eased Gwen's tremors.

"Why is that dark creep after her?" Tess sent.

"It's not the time for discussions like that," Jonas replied.

"You will go? Leave here?"

"I think we have to."

"I won't hurt her. Would never hurt her. I wanted to tell you that," Tess sent.

Jonas closed his eyes. When he reopened them, it was to find Gwen smiling.

Tess stopped herself from thinking about Jonas and the wolf girl by telling herself that her sanity depended on her taking a break.

Jonas was going to leave here, leave her.

All around her and in each direction Tess looked, there were signs of the parents that had taught her to hate his breed. Her father's chair was by a fireplace where no cozy fire burned. Her mother's dishes lined the shelves, and her mother's favorite tea mug was in Tess's hand.

Those were the parents she had loved. This was the family she had given everything else up to emulate, including the hopes of having her own family some-day. And her life had been a lie? That's what Jonas was suggesting?

Somehow, according to Jonas, she had become one of the creatures whose numbers she had been trained to cull. He had good reason to wonder about that, she had to admit. How else could she speak across chan-nels only open to his species? There was no other way to explain the sound she had made while in the throes of ecstasy in Jonas's arms.

She had growled. And that wasn't all. A new kind of wildness had been born when Jonas's erection had been buried inside her. It was as if Jonas's skillful penetration of her body had shaken loose some new part of her, and that thing had clawed its way to her throat. She felt that wildness now, more distantly, but still there. The feeling was of having swallowed some-thing alive that now wanted out.

There. Inside her. A fistful of foreign sensations roused by Jonas's touch. His goddamn werewolf Lycan touch.

Tess found herself at the medicine cabinet without actually knowing how she got there. She had replaced her mother's mug with the bottle of liquefied silver, and as she held the bottle, Jonas's words regarding the silver and how she'd been using it rang over and over in her mind.

Tess fingered the bottle, trying to recall the first time the contents of this particular bottle and others like it had been used to shore up her energy levels. She struggled to recall if she had seen either of her parents dip into this cabinet for themselves and couldn't picture it.

Werewolves were allergic to silver and various other metals. That was one of the first rules she had learned. There was enough silver in this cabinet to take down an entire pack of werewolves. Ten packs. So if Jonas's beliefs were founded in fact and she harbored latent Were tendencies, the injections she had endured would have killed her long ago.

Yet here she was.

"Explain that, wolf," she whispered. "And go to hell for making me think for one second that you could be right."

Nevertheless, she wasn't quite right inside. Not after being with Jonas. She hadn't been on track since meeting him. Part of her gravitated to him easily. Part of her wanted another session with Jonas's physical talent and sexual prowess. He alone had made her feel like she could be someone else. Like she might actually be someone else, other than the woman she had grown up believing herself to be.

Would that be such a bad thing?

Hell, yes.

She thought hard, digging up another possible explanation for the way she was feeling. Maybe being intimate with a Were meant that Were virus had been passed to her as a type of transmittable contagion. Maybe Jonas had put it there with each pulse and thrust he had made into her open-legged, willing body and sealed it inside her with an orgasm that had rocked her world and everything in it.

She'd damn him to hell if that turned out to be true. She would hunt him down and show no mercy.

Or else, damn it, maybe a growl was just a growl and nothing more...and she was being played.

Tess put the bottle back on the shelf and closed the cabinet. If it was all a game with Jonas and she was imagining things, he'd take those games with him when he left.

In the hallway, Tess paused to look into the mirror. Due to the darkness of the hallway, all she saw was her outline. But it was her outline, and familiar.

"Bastard," she muttered for the tenth time. Because the only real way to find out if Jonas had spoken the truth was to wait for the next full moon, ditch the silver infusion and see what happened. And there were a lot of nights to get through between now and then.

Gwen wasn't happy with his decision to pack up and leave, and neither was Jonas. He had to constantly remind himself that a sprint to Tess's house would be a bad idea and that he couldn't leave Gwen alone.

His sister hadn't gotten up off the floor. She sat cross-legged on the rug with her back to the fire. Her eyes tracked his moves. She was better now. Gwen's latest panic attack was over. It had taken a toll, though. A light film of sweat dampened the pale hair at her temples.

He looked at her over his shoulder. "If we stay, there's no way to determine the outcome. We can't really be sure how strong that creature is. You do see that?"

Gwen would go after Death's dark emissary again if it showed up here, and he couldn't stand the thought. Besides being necessary to him, his sister was necessary to every other wolf on the planet. Jonas didn't see how he could go on if he couldn't live up to his vow to protect his sister.

However, running from place to place and dragging Gwen along wasn't good for his sister either. It would have been better if he had been able to keep her in Miami without bringing attention to her and how special she was, and that hadn't been possible.

If they stayed, he might lose Gwen. If he ran, he'd lose Tess. The only way to reason that kind of dilemma out was to simply realize that the world was screwed up sometimes.

On the periphery of his mind, he felt Tess thinking about him. It made him want her all the more. Everybody needed answers. He wasn't the only one with gaps to fill. But the fact staring him in the face was that he wasn't the only one here with a desire to be near Tess.

"Gwen," he said, turning slowly. "Let's get you dressed. We're going to pay a call on our neighbor."

Gwen was way ahead of him, which confirmed more of his guesses about her. She was already heading for her room to make herself more presentable to the only wolf hunter in this part of the state...meaning that Gwen might stay in human form for a while longer. Plus, Jonas couldn't contain his own enthusiasm over the thought of seeing his lover again so soon.

"*Tess,*" he sent to the newest, if reluctant, she-wolf on the block. "*Heads up. We're coming. Don't shoot.*"

Chapter 26

The sun would chase the moon away soon, and for once, Tess was happy about that. Sleep was a nonissue. Tea didn't help either her nerves or her anxious state. How did a person comb back through a life, looking for clues that might suggest their life had been built upon a shaky foundation when she didn't even truly believe the reasoning behind such a search?

This was the Lycan's fault. Jonas had infected her with more chilling ideas than she could handle all at once. He had also taken advantage of her detestable state, although she had to share the blame for their session on the hood of her car.

She had mated with a Lycan. His word, *mated*.

They were forever linked, he had told her.

"Bullshit." Allowing that to happen had been a slipup, nothing more.

The tea in her mug had grown cold and she was too tired to reheat it. Tess couldn't be concerned about the last time she'd had a meal since there were more important issues on the table. The silver infusion hadn't worn off yet and it was easy for her to see the shapes of furniture and other objects in the dark room. She wished the silver had properties that would make thinking easier, too. That would have been a neat trick.

Her head still hurt. The ache between her thighs hadn't quite already dissipated the way other aches and pains usually did. Seems that what she felt on the inside wasn't open to negotiation. Even when measured by the leftover aches of their lovemaking, the damn Lycan scored high.

Tess set her mug down when Jonas's message arrived to break up her thoughts about inventing a way to turn off those messages.

"We're coming," he sent.

We.

He was coming here? So soon? And he might bring along the girl with the unusual talent for shape-shifting into an animal. Shifts like that fell into the category of myth for wolf hunters. Legend. Hearsay.

This information was yet another loose end adding to the discomfort building up behind Tess's eyes. Still, it was obvious to her that Jonas was protecting that girl, and that the thing inside the black mist was the dreaded enemy. Not the hunter. Not this time.

"Don't," Tess said aloud. "Don't come."

She hadn't sent that message over the ether so that Jonas would get it faster. Why? Because her sense of justice had been tampered with and she needed to figure out how that had happened. She had to understand Jonas and get to the bottom of his reasons for suggesting she might be like him when that was so obviously untrue.

Why was she even thinking about this? She had growled. So what? Plenty of people probably had no idea what kind of sounds resulted from an orgasm like the one she'd had tonight. The orgasm Jonas had given her. The act itself, as well as the memories and lingering physical aches associated with it, was a sacrilege.

But Tess felt him getting closer. His oncoming presence was like a desert wind heading her way. There was no way for her to escape.

If that Lycan bastard assumed she would cower and bend to his will, he had another think coming.

Tess found herself at the door, mindless about how she got there. She was opening the door when she didn't want to. She had a knife in her hand, but no weapon she could have chosen to defend herself against Jonas would have had any leverage when facing him again.

She stepped out of the cabin, hoping to cut through the bullshit if that knife found no other use.

He was there—Jonas, in all his wildly beautiful sculpted glory. He had donned a blue shirt in honor of this visit and the soft fabric hugged his perfectly muscled torso. Absurdly, the ache between her thighs seemed to recognize the male who had caused them. Her insides were quaking again. Lust for this Lycan was making a swift comeback.

Tess warned herself to keep her wits intact and her eyes off the well-honed body she had been intimate with. Jonas's looks were nothing but a distraction now.

"I thought you were leaving," she said.

"I can't seem to make up my mind about that, and I think you know why," he returned, his voice low and like the brush of a warm hand across her private parts.

Refusing to let Jonas see the effect he had on her and despite the fact that her heart was in her throat, making speech difficult, she said, "Is this where we spill our guts about our various jobs and attempt to comprehend our feelings?"

Beat after beat of her racing pulse slammed against her neck. Jonas, tall, broad-shouldered, and looking in that moment like some kind of werewolf god, stood near the gate with one of his arms draped across Gwen's shoulders. His shaggy hair fell becomingly across his brow. The jeans he wore were torn in several places, exposing stripes of his smooth, bronze skin.

Beside him, Gwen looked like the ghost of a teen from some unknown distant gene pool.

"Coming here like this is unprecedented and dangerous," Jonas said.

"Yet you're here. So I have to wonder how dangerous this meeting could be, and for whom."

Okay. She had lied about not knowing how dangerous it was and what might be out there beyond the trees. Tess swung her gaze to Gwen and kept it there, sensing the girl Were's desire to advance. She-wolf was the term used to describe a female werewolf, but at the moment, this one looked like a strong wind could have knocked her over.

The danger they were in also had to do with appearances. To say that looks could be deceiving was a massive understatement on both accounts when staring at Jonas and his ward.

Another kind of danger lay in their submerged strength and in the way their eyes were fastened on her. Hunger was there, in those blue eyes. Need was there. As if that same kind of need mirrored her own tumultuous emotions, Tess fought the impulse to invite them inside.

She said, "The dark bastard is still out there."

Jonas nodded. "Yes. It could be anywhere."

"Will it follow you wherever you go?"

He nodded again. "Relentlessly. Until tonight, Gwen didn't know that. I have attempted to keep things from her so that she could heal. Since she has now seen what's out there, there's no sense in holding things back."

Tess spoke to Gwen. "You're ill?"

The girl said nothing, just stared.

Tess had heard the white wolf's haunting howl, but the girl hadn't uttered a sound. That silence wasn't broken now. In the girl's big eyes, seen from a distance, Tess saw more emotion than she was prepared to handle. This delicate she-wolf was after something and that had to be part of the reason she and Jonas were here.

"What do you want?" Tess asked, getting right to the point.

"We're not going away. This was a joint decision between Gwen and me. We'd rather stay and fight than continue to hide," Jonas said.

Those words added to the buildup of Tess's internal quakes. He wasn't going anywhere...

"I think you will give us the leeway we need to

stay and face that dark thing again. Am I right, Tess?" he asked.

"How stupid is this entity if it doesn't always know how to find what it's after?" she asked.

"Oh it's not stupid or mindless. It isn't as savvy as its master, perhaps, in dealing with Weres, and we might have been able to trick the abomination so far, but it will find the shape it's been missing any time now and it will come calling."

"Does this entity have a name?"

"It does."

"And that name is…?"

Jonas first looked to his sister, then back to Tess. "Reaper."

Hearing his answer made Tess's stomach churn. Grim Reapers were supposed to be strange creatures that came to collect the souls of the departed. Neither ghosts or gods, they were synonymous with Death.

Were they real? Was one of them here?

So many mysteries surrounded Jonas, it boggled the mind. Tess processed this news, looking for a loophole but sensing that Jonas was telling the truth. That truth pointed to this Reaper having come here for the girl standing by Jonas's side. Gwen. A dark shadow had fallen over this young Were and Jonas had been hoping to postpone a final showdown by coming to South Dakota.

Bad luck there.

Tess looked up from the ground, where her focus had slipped. She spoke to Jonas while looking with fresh eyes at Gwen. "Is she family?"

"My sister," he replied warily.

More chills piled up. Tess saw no resemblance between the two Weres across from her. Gwen was so much smaller and years younger. If Gwen was Jonas's sister, this girl with the ability to become a real wolf also was a full-blooded Lycan.

Jonas's transformation had been strange, too, Tess now recalled. He didn't turn furry when the full moon bloomed. Jonas merely became more of everything that faced her now.

She had to speak. Her upbringing demanded it.

"I will let you get on with whatever it is you need to do," she said.

Jonas nodded, but none of the tension she had sensed left him. When Gwen stepped forward, he stopped her with a light tug of his arm. The fact that the white wolf had come to her after being injured, coupled with the way this girl who wasn't really a girl at all had looked at Jonas's cabin and was looking at her now, caused more chills to drip down Tess's back.

What was this she-wolf trying to say, and why couldn't she say it?

Why wouldn't Gwen shun a wolf hunter the way most werewolves did?

Had Tess Owens lost her edge?

"I've never met anyone like either of you," Tess said, shaking off her own internal reactions to this pair. "You have set the art of wolf hunting back a hundred or more years."

Jonas nodded. "We will leave you now and will remain next door until Death comes."

"Comes for her. For Gwen," Tess said.

"Yes."

"I have to know why. I won't rest until I do."

"Some things aren't meant for the ears of old enemies," Jonas returned.

"I thought maybe we were beyond the whole old-enemies scenario," Tess said. "What does Gwen want here?"

Gwen's movement stole Tess's attention again. Jonas's hold was successful in keeping his sister from getting closer to the front steps.

Jonas said, "I would have thought that was obvious by now. She wants you."

Tess swallowed hard. Flashes of recent memory again brought images of the white wolf attacking the Were that had been intending to come after Tess near the rocks, as well as images of the white wolf on Tess's hallway floor, and the blue eyes so intent upon her now.

This she-wolf didn't plan to harm her. Gwen desired to be close to her for other reasons that Tess couldn't fathom.

Unless...

"I'm not like you," Tess said. "Don't you get that?"

Jonas smiled sadly as Gwen tried to take another step. He said, "You keep believing that, Tess. Believe it for as long as you can and for however long you need to."

Damn right she would.

However, Tess wondered what would happen if Jonas let Gwen go. Would Gwen curl up on Tess's floor, with no fire to warm her delicate bones? Could Jonas's condemnation of Tess's human status have incited Gwen's behavior?

"Time is ticking away," Tess said. "Will that Reaper return in the minutes left between darkness and dawn?"

"I don't think so," Jonas replied. "It needs darkness to travel in and blend with."

"You've met one of them before?"

"No. Only this one."

"Before this?" Tess pressed.

"Once before."

"When, Jonas?"

He said solemnly, "On the night my sister nearly died."

The news startled Tess into a kind of information-saturated silence. Gwen had been hurt at one time or another, and that's why she looked so ill in human form. As a wolf, though, Gwen had showed no hint of weakness.

Ideas began to coagulate into a more cohesive whole, and went like this: in a wolf's shape, Gwen was better able to tolerate the weaknesses that might otherwise plague her. The wolf was stronger than its other half, and Tess had witnessed this.

Hell, as far as anomalies went, she was staring at one of them now.

She had just one more question to ask as she looked out and saw it growing lighter. "What about the silver?"

Unexpectedly, Jonas replied, "Silver doesn't give you added strength and power, Tess, contrary to what you might think and what you've been told. It actually has the exact opposite effect."

"Sorry I asked if all I'm going to get from you is a bunch of cryptic gibberish," Tess snapped.

"What it does," Jonas said slowly and with the kind of precision it took to get his point across. "What it does is keep your wolf—the wolf curled up inside you—in check. Tamped down. Hidden not only from others, but from you."

Before Tess could shout the expletives that remark deserved, Jonas and his sister had disappeared...much like the wraith that was chasing them.

Chapter 27

So now she knew, Jonas told himself. Tess had information that no one else had been privy to, minus a few key specifics. What she did with that information would determine her character and whether she would test his hypothesis about her. He had just blown the wolf hunter issue to smithereens. She just had to trust in what he had said.

They were walking back to the cabin. He and Gwen. Side by side. Once in a while, Gwen glanced back in the direction of Tess's home. Jonas kept a tight leash on himself to keep from doing the same thing. "I've won this game before and can do it again," he said to Gwen. "There has to be a more permanent way to keep that misty bastard off our asses, and if given the time, I'll find it."

His insides fluttered when Gwen tucked her hand

inside his the way she used to do. She didn't give off any of the vibes of fear and frustration he was experiencing. This last panic attack was behind her, and it appeared to him that tonight's episode had little to do with a Reaper.

"It has been weeks, hun," he said to her. "Isn't it time to tell me what's on your mind and what you're feeling? We used to talk. I miss that."

He squeezed her hand, found it so very frail and unlike her wolf's paws.

"Tess can't be involved any more than she already is," he continued. "She has her own issues to deal with. We have to leave her alone and hope she honors my request for distance."

After sliding a sideways glance at him, Gwen again stared straight ahead.

"You do understand, right?" he asked.

When Gwen nodded her head, providing a direct acknowledgment of his question, Jonas's world suddenly changed for the better in spite of what else the future might bring. Gwen was healing. She was getting better and she was listening. If there was nothing more, he'd have been happy with that.

Or he would have been happy with that if his senses hadn't sent up a silent warning about having company.

"Prove it."

That statement hadn't come from Gwen and wasn't in his mind. Every cell in his body reacted riotously, the way they did each time he faced this same problem. Tess had followed them. Jonas turned around to find her standing a few paces away.

Gwen's fingers slid from his.

"Prove it, if there's any way to actually do that.

Prove to me that I'm more like you than the people in town," Tess said.

"I believe we've already done that tonight."

"What we did proves nothing other than we have the hots for each other."

"That isn't good enough to shake your foundation of beliefs?"

"Not nearly enough," she said.

"Then stop."

"Stop what?" she asked.

"Stop using the silver."

"I only use it when…"

Jonas finished that sentence for her. "When there are werewolves around."

Through tight lips, Tess said, "Yes."

He had to be careful now and choose his words wisely. "You know that silver messes with our systems, shutting down certain functions. If you've had twenty doses over your lifetime, in measured amounts, your tolerance to the stuff would be similar to mine."

"It makes me feel…" She didn't complete that thought.

"No," he said. "That's just it. Those infusions keep you from feeling what you're supposed to be feeling. They don't tie you to Weres, they merely tone down your natural reactions to your own kind."

"BS. Prove it," she repeated, showing signs of restless agitation.

Jonas shook his head. "You need time to come to terms with this. I have provided you with a way to test the truth."

"My mother and father were human. Therefore, I'm human," she said.

"I can't explain that, unless you were scratched badly enough to cause the change."

"My parents would have disowned me."

"Would they? Would they have turned you out for the price you might have paid for doing your job?" Jonas asked.

He raised his hand and traced a pattern in the air, as if he were touching the side of her face. "So many old wounds, Tess."

She put a hand to her scars.

"You might have lost those if you hadn't taken your silver pills. We heal quickly, you know, with little or no intervention."

He observed how Tess's eyes landed warily on Gwen. "Then why hasn't your sister healed?" she demanded without the kind of inflection that might have made her question sound offensive or mean.

He said, "Some things take more time than others."

Her face showed that Tess was thinking that over. Worry lines had gathered on her brow.

"She's not like you," Tess pointed out.

"Or like you," he said.

"But she is your sister."

"She is."

"So you intend to kick that Reaper's backside because it wants her soul?"

"It wants her life, and that is unacceptable," Jonas replied. "She might have been slated to die, but she didn't die, so all bets are off. In my way of thinking, Death can't have what he doesn't deserve to have."

He had not told Tess about what had happened to Gwen, and she didn't ask about it now.

"And you know the secret for beating a Reaper?" she pressed.

"I found it tonight."

He saw more worry lines gather above Tess's calculating blue eyes.

"That thing didn't see Gwen in the wolf," she said. "It didn't know Gwen was right there."

Jonas nodded.

"So the longer she stays in wolf form, the longer you can avoid what's coming?" she asked.

"Remaining a wolf also means the longer route to her full recovery," he replied. "We maintain a human shape most of the time and must let that part heal."

All of this was said in front of his sister, but most of it wouldn't be news to her. Jonas had already considered the possibility that Gwen had already figured some of these things out for herself anyway. His sister was sharp-minded and incredibly tuned in to her surroundings.

Tess looked at Gwen. "Do you hurt?"

Jonas didn't fail to notice the change in Tess's beautiful face when she addressed his sister. Tess's expression became softer. Her voice was lower, gentler. Among humans, this would have meant that she cared about the person that question had been addressed to. Was it so with a hunter? Could Tess change tack in two days? She was moving through her own transitions so quickly, Jonas had to think hard in order to keep up.

Gwen looked to him for permission to move. This time, Jonas nodded, needing to find out exactly what Tess might do.

Walking slowly, Gwen approached Tess without making a sound, almost as though her feet didn't touch the ground. Taking several steps in her wake, Jonas followed his sister, ready for who-the-hell-knew what might happen next. It was easy to sniff out the knife in Tess's hand. After promising to leave them alone, would Tess change her mind and use it?

He didn't actually believe that any more than he believed Tess would refuse to look at her past with fresh eyes after all of this. And when Tess settled the knife in her belt, Gwen closed the remaining distance between them.

His sister was shorter than Tess, and though both females were small-boned, Gwen was frail by comparison. Tess's hair fell loose over her shoulders, golden under the last remnants of starlight. Gwen's hair was also loose, and much paler. Still, they were both she-wolves, and their courage to meet like this was just a sampling of the fortitude of the breed.

Gwen had to look up to peer into Tess's face. What Jonas now saw in Tess was a wide-eyed expression of curiosity that he jealously wanted turned his way. He could love this hunter if given the chance. Part of him already did.

"Was it a hunter that hurt you?" Tess asked Gwen seriously.

When Gwen shook her head, Tess exhaled in relief.

Gwen inched closer to Tess. With her hands laced behind her back, his sister leaned forward to place her head against Tess's shoulder. There was only that smallest of telling connections, and yet it said so much. His sister had recognized a kindred spirit in Tess before he had, and Gwen was finding solace in being close to the wolf hunter housing wolf particles in her blood.

No one moved for a long time. So long, the pink hue of the sun's rebirth cast long shadows on the trees. It was Tess who eventually broke the spell. Easing herself back, waiting until Gwen was solid on her feet, Tess gave him one long last look of forlorn agony before she hustled off with a rustle of fallen leaves.

When Gwen turned to him, he put on a smile. Seeing Gwen smile in return made everything that was going on seem doable and not quite so hard. They truly were in accord about liking Tess, and Tess would give them room to face what was coming.

Now, they just had to survive another night in the fight with a Reaper who wouldn't fail to recognize Gwen for long.

Tess's mind was sluggish and on full system overload. Thinking was like wading through mud. Jonas, Gwen, Reapers... How much trouble could land within her borders on any given day?

She wasn't sure what to do next. Jonas wanted space, but dealing with an entity like the one she had seen wasn't going to be easy. Odds were against him having a positive outcome because Death was Death, right? And this version was incorporeal.

Could someone actually cheat Death and get away with it? After having witnessed the gentleness the girl carried inside her, the fierceness of the white wolf in action seemed distant. Also strange were Tess's growing feelings for Jonas's sister. Then again, maybe she was just a sucker for any show of tenderness.

Wondering what that Reaper would do to Gwen when he found her wasn't going to help Tess assess the situation. And why did Death send a Reaper to collect the souls of the departed? Why not send an angel. Someone pretty, with wings?

Tess sat down on a rock with her head in her hands. Then she rolled up her sleeves to take a good look at her arms. Hardly any indication of the burn marks was visible. Rapid healing was also supposed to be part of the beauty of working with silver.

But Jonas had proposed a new idea, and that idea had spread through her mind like an insidious plague. Werewolves had the whole rapid healing thing down. So what were her markless arms an example of—the magic of silver or the possibility of having wolf in her DNA?

The dawn was quiet. Only a few bugs and early birds sang. There was no scent of wolf in the air. No coyotes yipped in the distance. A cool breeze rippled through the pine needles in the trees beside her. Two rabbits scurried near her feet. All of that would have been normal if it hadn't been for the fact that somewhere out there, a Reaper roamed, searching for its next victim. Gwen.

Tess raised her hand, sniffed her wrist, just to make doubly sure that Jonas had been wrong about her. But that wasn't a good test. Jonas's scent still saturated her skin, a stubborn reminder that no kind of soap or shampoo was going to erase him.

The main problem here was that she no longer wanted to be rid of the handsome Lycan. Things had changed, big-time. So where did that leave her?

And what was she going to do about it?

Chapter 28

Jonas couldn't shake the feeling that darkness hovered over the breaking dawn of a new day. At his post in the open doorway of the cabin, he searched with tired eyes for any sign of a Reaper being able to move around in the light.

Gwen had fallen asleep on the rug after eating the biscuit and some of the chicken he had warmed up for her. He hadn't been able to swallow a morsel. The countdown was on. In his mind, he heard the clock ticking.

He didn't like the way he had left things with Tess, but there was no changing that now. She would either believe the things he had told her or not. In her place, he'd have been laughing at his theories. It was too bad for the wolf hunter that those theories were true, and yet maybe not so bad for him.

Gwen had demonstrated her approval of his unlikely choice for a mate and was as smitten with Tess as he was. None of this would amount to anything if he couldn't find a way to trick this Reaper a second time.

How could he face a Reaper and tell it to back off?

Did Reapers have reasoning skills?

Could he negotiate with this one?

This round was on him. Gwen's life was in his hands.

The morning air was cool. As usual, the cabin was quiet, which was the new norm. Gwen's silence was expected. Tess's silence was excruciating. Lately, his reaction to hearing her voice, even in his mind, was second only to making love to her.

Each sentence she spoke brought him to a peak where lust and blistering heat reigned. He would have given anything for a replay of having her long legs wrapped around him and her sweet breath on his face. He wanted to make her moan. He wanted to hear her growl.

Was he destined to experience those things only once?

His right eye twitched. He rolled his shoulders to ease the buildup of muscular tension that came from standing up all night and spat out the last of his thoughts.

"Damn Reaper."

At two o'clock in the afternoon, he finally sat down in a chair. Gwen hadn't stirred. He sipped coffee and thought his mind would explode before presenting him with a way to deal with Death's servant.

At five o'clock, he got up again and began to pace. For the hundredth time, he thought about going to see Tess and nixed that idea equally as quickly.

If he were to die tonight, their imprinting would be null and void. With Weres, "Until death do us part" actually meant what it sounded like. There was no way to undo an imprint. Tess would be free of the bonds tying her to him only if he died. After that, if she preferred to go on believing herself to be human, no one would be there to argue with her. Tess would again be alone. Tess and her silver-tipped arrows.

Jonas looked up suddenly, struck by an idea exposed in that last thought. If he were to die...

He was so lost in thought that he bumped into the doorframe. He closed his eyes. The way to deal with this Reaper had just presented itself to him. The answer to his dilemma was wrapped in the word *sacrifice*. All he had to do was offer himself up to this Reaper in Gwen's place, trading one life for another.

Christ! He couldn't open his eyes, but he could do this. He could save his sister, and along with Gwen, the future of their breed.

Then what?

What would happen to Gwen if the Reaper took him up on this offer? She also would be alone, without her protector and so very far from home.

He felt his eyes blink open as a new idea floated in that centered on Tess.

He'd have to convince Tess to take over the guardianship of his sister until Gwen was fully healed. At that time, Tess would have to take Gwen home to Miami, where the rest of the pack and his sister's future waited.

A wolf hunter wouldn't be able to comprehend such a thing, but Tess was so much more than a hunter. The Miami pack would have to allow Tess's help in getting his precious sister there because Tess was one of them. Maybe she never had been human.

How to break this idea to Tess was the next obstacle. She had to listen. She had to care. He wouldn't have to tell her everything, only part of it. The ifs. *If* anything were to happen to him… *If* Tess felt anything for the white wolf that so openly felt something for her.

He had a good handle on Tess's mind and what was in her heart. He'd had her breath in his lungs and her tongue in his mouth. He heard her thoughts and he had been inside her in both body and spirit.

He wouldn't only be sacrificing his life, he'd be cutting Tess loose from his wolfish tethers. Both she-wolves would go on without him. Tess would do this, if not for him, for Gwen. He would have to ask Tess to do this when she owed him nothing, when he had dramatically complicated her life. But if Tess agreed… then Gwen would at last find peace.

Hell, the answer to this problem was as brilliant as it was horrifying. It made his heart sink.

Opening up a channel to Tess, he sent her a message.

"Tess. One last thing. I'll only ask one more thing of you, I swear, if you will hear me out."

Her reply was swift, as though she had been waiting for him to reach out to her.

"You'd dare to ask me anything, wolf?"

"Not for me, Tess. This isn't about me."

Tess sensed a change in Jonas's voice and thoughts. A storm system surrounded those thoughts, protecting the images that usually accompanied his messages.

He was in a hurry to speak his mind and was truly in need of help.

She sat up on the bed that had offered no comfort for the last couple of hours she had spent on it. *"Is Gwen all right?"*

The next message rode on the tail of her question. *"Do you want her to be well, Tess?"*

She'd be damned if she answered that question, and damned if she didn't, so Tess decided to be truthful. *"Yes. Okay. I care."*

"Will you help her if I can't?" he sent.

"Are you asking me to speak to her?"

"No. I'm asking a hell of a lot more than that from you."

"Then spit it out, Jonas."

"I'd like you to help her. Watch over her and eventually take her home to Miami."

Tess's insides stirred uncomfortably. Underscoring these messages was a dark ulterior motive that required Jonas to bring up such a thing, and she didn't have time to ponder that.

She said, *"Where will you be when I do those things?"*

When he didn't answer the question, Tess's nerves began to dance the way they always did when trouble was brewing.

"Jonas?"

His reply was slow in coming. *"I have to face this Reaper and find a way to get it off Gwen's back. There's no way to predict the outcome of a meeting like that. You do see this?"*

Tess felt a sickness rise to her throat that would have made it impossible to speak out loud.

"It's what we do, you once told me, Jonas. We fight and hope to win."

That was true, and yet it wasn't the full picture here, Tess realized with the suddenness of her well-honed insight. Jonas wasn't planning on coming back from his appointment with the Reaper. Because of that, he was asking her to take over the guardianship of his sister.

She got to her feet and reached for her sweatshirt. She hadn't stripped for her useless session with sleep, somehow understanding that she had to be ready for the next stage of this story to happen and whatever the finale would be.

"You won't face this beast alone," she sent to Jonas.

He had a protest ready for that statement. *"Someone has to be here for my sister in case this goes wrong. You've seen her and what Gwen can and will try to do, Tess. She can't be there tonight. You have to make sure she isn't. Can you do that? Will you do that, if not for me..."* He let that sentence dangle and started over. *"Not for me. For Gwen, and for the life that's ahead of her."*

Secrets were tied up in knots inside of Jonas's plea. He wasn't telling her everything. He wasn't telling her anything, actually, hoping she wouldn't demand those secrets in order to do as he asked.

Did those unspoken reasons center on Gwen and her unique abilities? How special was Gwen, aside from being a full-blooded Lycan's younger sister?

Tess wished there really was a rule book that she could consult. The Owenses had been simple people who didn't believe in computers and other modern gadgets and didn't believe in polluting the mind with unnecessary bites of information irrelevant to their vows. She wasn't sure what she could have looked up here anyway when her gut was telling her that Jonas was going to do everything he could to make sure Gwen survived tonight.

The werewolf was asking her for help.

She fought the desire to run to Jonas. Fear had raised its ugly head and wasn't to be dismissed. She had to admit to herself how much she wanted him to stay, and how greatly she wanted to be with him in spite of their differences. And if it turned out that she was...

She closed her eyes before completing the thought.

If it turned out that Jonas was telling the truth and she was like him, then she did owe him something, didn't she? She owed him her own enlightened future.

"What do you want me to do, Jonas?"

"Come and get her. Stay here or take Gwen to your place...whichever is easier for you. Let me do what I have to do to ensure not only my sister's safety, but yours as well."

"I can take care of myself, wolf."

"This isn't your problem."

"You have made it my problem."

"Then consider the pledge I'll make you now, Tess. It goes like this—in watching over Gwen and taking her back to Miami, you will never be alone again. And you will, I promise, find happiness among your own kind."

Tess's thoughts were tangled. Her own kind? Weres was what Jonas meant. She would find other Weres in Miami.

It was important not to concentrate on that now.

Mentally, she rasped, *"All right. I'll be there before nightfall."*

His relief washed over her as if it were her own and could fly through the air.

"Thank you," he sent to her as the direct channel between them closed.

When his voice had gone, Tess felt more alone that ever. The great emptiness carved out inside her pulsed with the need to reconnect and to hear more of Jonas's words. Her body reacted in kind, aching for him, hungering for Jonas and longing to be touched by his hand.

Only his hand.

But her feelings for him didn't have to be the result of being like him. She would probably have been attracted to his looks, his power and the kindness he showed his sibling anyway.

And when he was gone? If he was killed by this Reaper while trying to protect his sibling...what would be left to fill the emptiness inside her the way his love-making had?

Sunlight streamed in from the window in her room, sending dust motes twirling. She pulled on her sweat-shirt and knotted her long hair at the nape of her neck. There were several hours to kill before she'd work up the courage to see Jonas again, and she planned to use those hours wisely.

Courage is what she would need, having agreed to Jonas's request. Courage to further defy her vows where he was concerned. Courage to let him go when the time came for that. But she didn't plan to take any of this lightly. She had agreed to help him with-out fully committing herself to what he'd need her to do. She hadn't lied, exactly. She just hadn't spelled things out.

Would she follow his wishes?

Would she find a way to prove him wrong about her having wolf blood in her veins?

First though, she would find out more of his secrets. They would fight the dark beast and save Gwen from the fate that beast had in mind for her. And when that was done, she and Jonas would hopefully, maybe, thrillingly, make love on a bed instead of the hood of her Jeep. For hours. Naked.

To hell with species.

She got that plans didn't always work out the way they were supposed to, but this one had to work. Jonas had to live to fight another day. Gwen had to be liberated from a Reaper's clutches. And Tess had to find out who and what she really was or die trying.

So Tess headed for the armory down the hall to get things ready for whatever horrors nightfall might bring, certain there would be plenty.

Chapter 29

Jonas didn't feel good about this. Tess's acceptance of his proposal had been too easy and too quick. Still, she had agreed.

He had to keep his hands busy and his mind occupied until then. Making the most of the hours left to him was paramount, and he still had to speak with Gwen. His eyes strayed to the window, to the door and back to his sister who was starting to wake up.

One more time, he told himself. He just wanted to be inside of Tess's body one more time. He might even die a happy Lycan if granted that opportunity. He'd have one more good thing to hang on to when the curtain fell.

Gwen was sitting up. She rubbed her eyes the way innocent youngsters did when they were sleepy. Yet she was far from innocent, and too damn smart.

"I love you," Jonas said. "I will always love you, Gwen."

She slid her attention to him and tilted her head so that long tangles of white-blonde hair curtained the sides of her narrow face. Curious blue eyes peeked out from beneath lowered lashes.

Jonas remembered how she used to like it when their mother had brushed those tangles from her hair. He supposed that no one had given his sister that kind of pleasure after their parents had died in the aftermath of the attack on their daughter. He wondered if Gwen blamed herself for their deaths, though he had no way to know.

Gwen had a bead on the fact that he was antsy. He hadn't really hoped to be able to keep that from her.

"Tess will come over," he said. "I won't lie to you. I'm going out to look for that Reaper, alone. Tess will either stay here with you or take you to her place. She wants to be with you."

Gwen's eyes tracked each twitch of his shoulders that threatened to give away the things he didn't say. She discerned too much and had developed senses like no other Were he had ever known. How those things had gotten inside her was an unanswered puzzle. Just a throwback to the DNA of old? A mistaken turn in her genes?

"It's time to tell you a few things," he continued. "You already know how special you are, I think."

Big eyes. No other response.

"Your uniqueness makes you valuable to our species. Therefore, all avenues toward protecting you have to be taken into consideration. Do you understand?"

The blue eyes blinked.

"She wants to help," he repeated, thinking in this terribly awkward moment about the way Tess had looked at him when they had made love.

"You can teach her, Gwen," he coached softly. "Tess doesn't know what she is. Doesn't believe it. You can be her guide. She assumes that you need her, but it's the other way around."

Gwen was getting all of this. Chills of recognition having to do with his sister's powers covered Jonas's back.

"Therefore, you must keep her safe, Gwen. You have to be present to do that. No retreating inside yourself. No getting around the fact that you know exactly what has to be done. It's time to move forward, leave the past. You're stronger than all of us and can no longer have the luxury of hiding that."

Her eyes met his. His sister nodded.

Jonas sat down in the chair. "Tess will want to fight on your behalf tonight. She has an innate sense of justice that's refreshing, but this isn't her fight. We can't afford to let that Reaper see you, so you must promise me that you'll stay away while I search the woods. Can you do that? Will you?"

"No," Gwen said. "No promises."

The shock of hearing her speak made Jonas's heart skip beats.

"Damn if I'll let anything happen to Gwen," Tess affirmed to herself. "After that, all bets are off."

The Jeep would get her to Jonas's cabin faster than her feet would, though she would have liked to comb the area between the two properties for anything out of the ordinary. Like a Grim Reaper.

That monster hadn't come after her, so possibly she wouldn't have to worry overmuch about meeting it again. It had three opportunities to harass her and hadn't dug in. So she was worried about Jonas and what he planned to do. Who the hell knew how to fight a creature that acted as Death's right hand? Did Jonas?

Although the sun was about to set, his cabin was already lit up like a Christmas tree when she pulled into the yard. Lights were on inside the cabin and on the porch. Red and green bulbs edged the roof, leftover from December cabin rentals, providing an out of season glow and leaving Tess to wonder if perhaps Reapers had an aversion to holidays.

Jonas was already in the yard. It was likely that he had sensed her arrival, but seeing him near the spot where their bodies had entwined made Tess's insides ripple with excitement.

She didn't get out of the car after shutting off the engine. Her courage wouldn't stretch that far. She had to look at him first, take it all in and manage the intensity of her longing for him. She had to settle her restlessness and catch the breaths he had a habit of stealing from her.

He was so unbelievably gorgeous.

At her open window, and before she got a grip on any of those things she promised herself to do, Jonas tugged at the door handle. Yanking open the door, he took hold of her shoulders before Tess could come up with an argument to combat the flash of emotion in his eyes, and pulled her out of the Jeep.

Who was she kidding? Deep down, she had secretly hoped for this kind of reception.

She was in his arms and looking up at him. The

meeting of their eyes was full of lightning strikes and forbidden fireworks. As if one look was all it took for her to completely forget her vows, the flames of passion rose to overtake her.

He tilted her chin more so that he had easy access to her mouth. He ran his thumb over her lower lip as his eyes roamed over her face.

Tess could not breathe. Could not speak. Her pulse soared. Her muscles fluttered. It didn't matter if this was wrong, or if the timing sucked. Having a scary opponent wasn't an issue right then. Only Jonas mattered, and the expectation of what would come next.

Jonas's face came close—all those elegant angles and planes that made him seem so perfect. He wasn't smiling. There was no sign of condescension. He whispered her name as if it was a personal form of torture for him to utter it and rested his hungry lips on hers.

Everything else was lost.

Hunger ruled Jonas's actions, and it was a hunger like no other. She was his focus. Tess was the center of the universe and the personification of his need.

Merging heartbeats fueled Jonas's desire. This was a physical attack of the senses and more like a tryst between two souls destined to join in an otherworldly dance than just two beings meeting for a brief liaison.

He savaged Tess's mouth. Drank her in. Couldn't get enough. He felt Tess's wolf rise to the occasion with its own fiery burst of yearning. He was tugging her sleepy wolf awake and untying its tethers. This kiss was serving to set her wolf free.

Tess wasn't motionless. Her muscles moved beneath his touch as he swept his hands over her, searching for a way to reach bare skin.

Finding the edge of her shirt behind her back, he slipped his fingers under the hem. Tess's skin was smooth, taut and very hot. She was, for him, a form of liquid desire.

Her hands were on his hips, holding him close. There wasn't one spare inch of space between them, and yet that wasn't close enough. He had to be inside her. All the way inside her. Now.

There was no time for undressing or for him to honor the pact he had made with himself after the last time they had met like this about doing things better and taking their time if they were to meet up a second time. Soft beds were out of the picture. The Jeep wasn't an option and would have been redundant as a makeshift mattress. Hell, they couldn't even go indoors.

He sensed Gwen moving around in the cabin, and she didn't need to see what he was planning to do with the she-wolf in his arms. Gwen was too young to understand what real need was and how it could rule even the sharpest of beings.

When he lifted Tess up, she wrapped her legs around his hips. Her arms encircled his neck. Jonas stepped forward with Tess clinging to the front of his body. The spot of her body that he longed to enter, and that was now covered in jeans, was rubbing him the right way.

Now was a concept that was just too damn long, and there were too many clothes in the way to settle this particular score.

Turning, he carried her toward the trees without

losing one single second of the kiss that was sealing their date with the fates. Jonas felt feverish and half mad. The world was not a safe place at the moment, and he had to ignore that.

Tess's back hit the bark of the closest tree with a soft thud that she didn't acknowledge. There wasn't even a hitch in her breath. Like the rest of her, her mouth was volcanic. She was an inferno that burned him to the core, and possessing her was the only goal. He couldn't have been harder or more turned-on.

Peeling her body from his was both a pleasure and a pain, but he could not access her like this. When she slipped to her feet, Jonas leaned in. When his lips left hers, she drew them back to her with her fingers knotted in his hair.

There was no room, no space to find the zipper on her jeans, and yet he had to gain access to what lay beneath all that denim. His mind looped with commands... Be inside her. Get there. Feel her. Taste her. Show her what this could really be like.

Neither of them made a sound as Jonas pushed himself back far enough to slide the metal zipper down its track. Tess's chest rose and fell. She gasped as he dipped his fingers into the opening the zipper had created. She gasped again when he worked his way downward to the soft spot he craved more than life itself, and then she sighed and widened her stance.

Jonas couldn't resist her eyes, which were half closed. Already, thin ribbons of shadow were crossing Tess's face. Night was coming. There was little time left for indulgences.

These were going to be his last hours on earth if

his plan worked. He would love Tess Owens, and then he'd be gone. He would show her the depths of his love for her, show her what being a werewolf felt like, and then take all that away.

Yes, he loved her. For others, this would have been hard to understand, but this was how it worked with Weres—lightning fast, absolute, sure. Two souls connecting without the time commitment necessary for many other species to get to know each other. Two bodies and two minds in sync after one meeting of the eyes. The Were way was a beautiful thing, and yet he was going to lose her. Lose Tess.

His fingers paused in their search. Tess's eyes opened as if she'd ask for a reason. What he wanted most was right here and within reach. All he had to do was to take it. And yet a sudden rush of conscience reared up. He was going to die and Tess would remember this night. He would unleash her wolf, expose her for what she was, and she'd remember every last thing they did.

Although the bonds chaining them together would be broken when he died, Tess's wolf would be in stasis, neither here nor there, but no longer buried deep. She wouldn't cope on her own, wouldn't be able to face who she really was without help, and he had asked a wolf hunter to deliver Gwen to Miami, to one of the strongest wolf packs in the world.

Christ, he had never been a fan of loose ends. Love Tess or not, by mating with her again things would be worse for her. Calling to her wolf, demanding that the wolf show itself and then abandoning Tess when she might need him the most was selfish and self-defeating when he was all about justice.

Hating the part of him that required this level of analysis, Jonas, with one brief brush of his fingers over Tess's softness, pulled his hand free...and closed his eyes.

Hating the part of him that couldn't be less of
a monster, Trace, with one final brush of his lips
to her jaw and breast, pulled his head free... and open
his eyes.

Chapter 30

He had withdrawn...leaving Tess with a myriad of
emotions. Chief among them was anger over the suddenness of his change of heart. Next came the urge
to punch Jonas somewhere crucial and make it hurt.
Those things flitted quickly though her mind as she
regrouped enough to look him in the face.

She saw immediately that this had not been his
plan. Though Jonas had not shape-shifted, his face
morphed from one expression to another, landing
somewhere between sadness and determination.

He hadn't meant this half-assed attempt at having sex as a test of her willpower and his. Jonas was
breathing hard and working to contain needs that had
to rival hers. Jonas had stopped this for a reason, and
only that reason could have stalled the inevitable.

His voice was hoarse. His eyes were bright. "Listen, Tess. You can choose to be what you believe you have been for all this time, or you accept your true nature. If I…if *we* do this again, there won't be a choice."

Her voice, and the effort it took to speak, made Tess's comeback sound jagged and staccato. "You're good, Jonas, but not good enough to make me lose my mind."

He shook his head. "It's not your mind you'd have to worry about."

She thought about daring him, taunting him, goading Jonas into proving any of this nebulous wolf crap. The air was charged with electricity that had nowhere to land and filled with the scent of arousal.

Arguing with him about this issue would have been redundant.

"Take care of Gwen," he said so solemnly that Tess felt her small gathering of anger crumble.

She shook her head. "I'm going to help you find this Reaper whether or not we run with our desires. We can't have a beast like that around here."

"Gwen needs a guard," he said. "That Reaper can't find her yet, without seeing her in human shape. I'm trusting you with private information, Tess, because it's so important that you listen."

He gave her a few seconds to wait for the rest of what he had to say.

"If you haven't believed anything I've said to you so far, please believe this. My sister is the future of the Lycan race, and that future is in your hands. You can end it here by allowing the Reaper to take her, or else you can protect her if anything were to happen to me. If you're the wolf hunter, that choice will be easy.

If you're a wolf, your way will be more difficult than anything you have encountered in your life so far."

Protests rose in Tess's mind like whirlwinds of words that remained unspoken. Her life, for the past three days, played like a movie in her mind.

She lowered her chin to break contact with Jonas and said, "I asked you to prove it. Prove what you're implying. Make a real case for confusing me with your species."

He said calmly, "I think we've already done the groundwork. And I think you know it."

What if she did? Tess wanted to shout. What if she had started to believe him? A charge like that required proof, and she was in no state to demand that they get on with their exchange of body fluids in order to find out who was right.

"I'd be an unusual guardian for her, Jonas," she said. "So you need to make sure nothing happens to you."

"I..." he started to say, but was interrupted.

A guttural growl came from behind them that added to the tension of the moment. Hearing it, Jonas whirled.

The white wolf was there with her eyes trained on a growing bit of darkness pooling behind the trees where she and Jonas stood.

Tess strained to see what had upset Gwen. She hadn't been trained to sense Reapers. Before recent events, she had never come across one.

Now she wondered if someone had to have already come close to death in order to truly feel a Reaper's presence, and that possibly the Reaper's target's name was on some kind of list.

Was Gwen's name on such a list?

Had the young she-wolf already battled either this Reaper or another one like it in the past…and could the frail state of Jonas's sister be due to something that had happened to her recently, incurring the attention of this Reaper and whoever it served?

Tess's entire body, so feverish just seconds before, chilled. She zipped up her jeans and stepped forward, placing herself shoulder to shoulder with Jonas. She lamented the loss of her weapons, realizing that silver-tipped arrows and daggers were useless against a being composed of true darkness. Reapers, she supposed, had to reflect the nothingness they represented.

There was no time for more guesses as to why Gwen was this entity's target. But she hoped to God that this wasn't what everyone could expect to see when their time was up.

Gwen, formidable in wolf form, circled them before coming up alongside. Like a first line of defense bridging the gap between life and death, the three of them stood there, anxiously awaiting what was to come.

Jonas cursed the way this was playing out. He actually had expected Gwen to respect his wishes this time. Having her here was going to make things immeasurably worse. Hell, his sister was here to warn him. She probably thought he'd need help with the misty bastard on their trail.

No one spoke.

The surrounding trees were live with sounds, none of which gave any indication of a Reaper's slithery approach. Gwen knew it, though. Of all of them gathered here, she alone had been touched by Death's talon. Though Jonas had taken his share of bullets and wounds, and Tess had the scars to prove her worth as a fighter, only Gwen had gone far enough into the Dark Beyond to call forth a Reaper.

Tess broke the silence with a question spoken in a low voice. "Why is it after her? Why her?"

Jonas answered reluctantly. "She died, but only for a few seconds before we got her heart started up again. This is a mistake. Gwen is on the mend and getting stronger day by day."

Was there no calling this beast off in circumstances like this? he had wondered a hundred times or more, sensing its presence in Miami, hovering like a dark cloud near their home as he and others from his pack took turns watching over his sister. A living, breathing being couldn't just end without cause. Gwen had survived her grievous wounds, so there had to be a system of checks and balances for instances like this.

At his left, Gwen issued another growl that alerted him to the Reaper's approach. Gwen's sharp teeth were bared. He feared what might happen next, and that with Tess and Gwen present, his plan to trade his life for Gwen's might go astray.

Tess called out to the darkness in front of them with a reasonable question. "If you goofed up where she is concerned, why not just admit that and call it a day?"

Jonas fisted his hands, inhaling the sour fragrance trailing this Reaper and loving Tess even more for standing beside him.

"What is the penalty for mix-ups?" Tess called out.

She was tense, brave, and could have been his life-long partner. He would have liked that.

Gwen growled again. His sister knew everything

now, including his feelings for Tess. If given the gift of hindsight, maybe he could have concluded that Gwen had helped by nudging him toward the hunter. The fact slapping him in the face now was that his sister must have known about Tess being a Were before he had.

Darkness coated the area beside them with a misty dampness that was incongruent with the weather. The swirling black fog began to gather, twisting itself into a manifestation straight out of nightmares.

The Reaper floated in a sea of fog—a creature so fluid that it probably took on the shape most likely to scare the pants off of everyone it faced.

Scare tactic, Jonas thought, with a fleeting bit of insight. In that respect, this sucker was a lot like a shape-shifter.

"You can't have her," Jonas said. "She lives. You've lost."

The insubstantial vision began to grow, stretching a few inches at a time until it had reached a height of nine feet, maybe more. Its face was a skinless skull with dark holes for eyes. A black cloak hid the rest. The thing hovered, never solid enough to be motionless. It didn't make an attempt to address Jonas's remarks. Jonas didn't see the scythe these creatures were famous for carrying, at least in mythology books.

Jonas had to wonder how Reapers actually absconded with the souls they sought. If those souls were still part of the living bodies that housed them, and weren't yet the misty essences that hung around for a few seconds after the body had shut down before heading off on their next adventure…then how did this Reaper extract them?

Reapers, by their very definition, were the purveyors of the souls they could snatch before those souls had gone heavenward. They took bad souls to a dark place. Tainted souls. Souls not destined to move on to something better or be rehoused in new bodies, as some people believed.

But Gwen was just a child. A good kid, an innocent soul not yet indoctrinated into the world of savages and killers until the senseless attack on her life.

Gwen didn't deserve a visit from this Reaper. Therefore, there had to have been a mistake. A grave error in perception.

As soon as that thought had arrived, Jonas's fear began to melt away. He took a step, leaving Tess and Gwen slightly behind. In a strong voice, he said, "You probably took the souls of the rogues that attacked my sister and her friends. You, or another creature like you. They all deserved to find you waiting for them. I'll be the first to agree with that. Maybe though, with my sister's body lying lifeless among those bastards, her name somehow got tangled up with that rest of the names on your list."

Jonas upped his volume. "I helped to kill those rogues and fought like a fiend. I have taken my share of lives on the job and on the sidelines, but always in the name of justice and to ensure the freedom of the many creatures on this earth. So if I offer myself up in my sister's place, would you even be able to accept my soul as an offering, especially when my sister could not have been slated for your hands in the first place?"

Tess was there with him now and tuning in. She had a hand on Gwen's ruffled fur and was giving off a chilling vibe of comprehension.

The Reaper faced them without responding, unless the blood beginning to seep from its empty eye sockets was meant to frighten everyone present into subservience.

From its back, two protrusions emerged and began to take the shape of wings. Black featherless wings, double the size of the Reaper. Those wings dripped the wetness of the mist that surrounded this dead, in-human, dark-hearted entity. The only sound now was that of droplets hitting the dirt.

Was this vision frightening? Yes. But again, Jonas told himself, these gyrations might be nothing more than a show. Had there been a full moon present, he would have offered his own show in return.

"Pretty damn impressive, I have to say."

Jonas started. He had not spoken those words. Tess had. And there was more.

"Still, arguments being arguments, yours pales in comparison to what's really the case," she continued. "So we're back to square one. You made a mistake that has to be rectified. Do that. Fix this and go after someone who needs your attention more than Jonas's sister does. You're wasting your time here."

Tess's latest challenge was so surprising that Jonas felt a grin tug at the corners of his lips in spite of the danger facing them. He also sensed Gwen's advance.

The Reaper's big black wings beat the air, causing dirt and leaves to fly in all directions. Jonas raised the claws that he had been hiding as if this were a show-and-tell game, rather than a thin line between keeping and losing something precious to him.

Claws were the best he could do without the moon, and a reflection of the anger that had been building in-side him for the past few weeks. However, the Reaper looked at them with its bloody sockets, and the big wings stopped flapping.

In a move Jonas had not been expecting, but should have, the sound of maneuvering muscles caught his attention suddenly, and his heart took a dive. ·

There was light in the darkness. The pale form of his sister, naked from head to toe and glowing with misplaced confidence, emerged from behind him... to face her tormenter.

Chapter 31

Tess stumbled back, struck cold by the evening's next surprise. One minute, she had hold of the white wolf's fur. The next minute, she was looking at the girl that had hidden inside that wolf's shape.

She had known that the two different shapes were aspects of the same being, yet seeing this for real in Gwen came as a shock.

Gwen moved forward, showing more courage than a frail teenaged girl had the right to possess. There was truly nothing typical about Jonas's little sister. And though the attack Jonas had mentioned in the girl's background remained a blank for Tess, she could not imagine what kind of courage it took for Gwen to confront her fears head-on here.

"I won't go with you," Gwen said.

Her voice was as light as the rest of her—an innocent young girl's voice, despite having been through hell in the past.

Hearing his sister speak had a strange effect on Jonas. Tess saw him blink. He renewed his position by rolling his broad shoulders. She was attuned to every nuance and change in his behavior and figured that Gwen must not have spoken to him for some time.

The Reaper's attention shifting to Gwen was like a tracking beam. Its black wings opened to span the length of the distance between two trees. Majestic things, those wings, if they had been on an angel instead of on the back of a representative of the Fallen One. That's what this guy was, after all…a lifeless member of the dark side. There was no other explanation for its appearance and failure to accept its mistakes.

Tess vowed to send this creature back to where it belonged if it so much as made one move in Gwen's direction.

"Go," Gwen said to the Reaper in a scene not unlike the old story of David versus Goliath. A small girl was challenging the Grim Reaper in a fight for her soul. No weapons. Nothing but the rightness of her stand.

"Go back and leave me alone," Gwen said.

The Reaper's wings retracted, folding over each other before being absorbed into the dark whole once more. The area became saturated with the odor of its anger. Hell, given where this thing probably came from and who it served, in its place, Tess wouldn't have wanted to come back empty-handed either.

Tess felt the creature reach out with its mind—not to her, but to Gwen. The fact that she understood this was a further surprise.

"Not going to happen," Jonas said. "She is not going to die, so get over it."

The figure it had presented to them began to collapse the way the wings had, pulling back, sinking into itself, until the skull was gone and only a patch of undulating fog remained.

But the Reaper didn't leave. Nothing so easy as that outcome occurred. Just when Tess had started to think it had heard them and was tucking its tail, another form reared up to threaten.

Jonas rushed forward to meet the dark warrior that presented itself to them in dark armor, wielding a flaming sword. Consumed by the heat of an angry passion, he threw himself at the latest incarnation of the Reaper, hitting the fog and passing right through it.

He stumbled, righted himself and spun around, focusing on the fact that this entity had no real physical form to fight and that weapons and claws were meaningless. So what would it take? That was the question plaguing him with an incessant chatter. How were the good guys going to win?

Tess had placed herself in front of Gwen with the kind of speed intrinsic to powerful she-wolves. She wore an expression of cunning, daring the Reaper to get past her. Her eyes flashed with anger. The hunter had merged with the wolf in her, and those two things coming together made for a strong, relentless team of fighters.

Her hands were raised. Her posture was set. She tilted her head to one side as Jonas had seen her do on another occasion, so that she could look at this problem from all angles.

God, how he wanted her.

"It's a trade I was going to offer you," Jonas said. "Then I discovered the secret."

He had the Reaper's attention. Feeling it turn his way was like being dunked into a vat of ice water. The thing had not reached Gwen. Even if it had, Jonas wanted to believe that it couldn't have done anything to her. It all circled back to reasoning versus action. The Reaper had not yet taken Gwen. All it had done so far was to appear at its most frightening and threaten with that.

The importance of that piece of the puzzle made Jonas shake.

"Secrets can be so annoying," he said loudly, garnering still more of the Reaper's chilling focus. "And I have just learned yours."

The flaming sword glowed red-orange. But it wasn't really a sword. And this entity had no real power here because it didn't belong here. The case for this had already been presented and had to be correct, because how long could it take a Reaper to do its nasty business? Minutes had passed since Gwen had shown herself, and nothing had happened.

The fact was that they didn't have to fight this Reaper and couldn't have if this visit was legitimate. What they had to do was convince the creature to give up and go away.

Jonas joined Tess and lowered his claws. Tess's thoughts rang loud and clear in his mind. *"What secret? What's going on?"*

Gwen came out from behind Tess. She slipped her hand into his, further strengthening his sense of the rightness of his theory.

"Your secret is that you can't solidify because you aren't supposed to be here," Jonas said. "I have to wonder, then, why you'd bother to come all this way, perhaps without the permission of the being you serve."

He heard Tess's muffled hiss and Gwen's soft sigh. Jonas spoke over those sounds.

"We have nothing to lose here, really. Do you?"

The fog seemed to lose ground. At the same time, the flaming sword disappeared, leaving Jonas with a shiver of satisfaction.

Maybe...but could this be right? The Reaper hadn't realized it was on the wrong path and was running on momentum? Were there mistakes like that, even for this creature? It had gotten this wrong and was just now beginning to see that?

Gwen moved. Still holding his hand, she walked right up to the entity they had been so afraid of and said, "We all make mistakes," as though this wasn't an entity that might have been forged in the fires of Hell.

A young girl's words caused the craziest result—a young girl that would one day become a revered queen of their species. Given all other outcomes and alternate scenarios of a night like this one, and given that Jonas's theory could just as easily have been wrong, the warrior looked Gwen right in the face. And though both Jonas and Tess had already moved toward Gwen, the warrior's semblance hovered briefly and then just melted away. One more whiff of its sour odor, and then all traces of the Reaper were gone.

Jonas and Tess stood there gaping, not quite sure how this result had been achieved. Tess spoke first.

"Too easy," she muttered, searching the area, expecting the Reaper's return.

"Yes," Jonas agreed.

Tess looked at him. "Is it over? Could it be over?"

He nodded. "I actually believe it is."

"You went head to head with a Grim Reaper and won?"

"I'm not sure anyone won," Jonas returned truthfully. Though his heart felt lighter than it had in weeks, he found it too damn dangerous to believe that thing had gone for good.

He turned to Gwen, who at that moment looked as regal and capable as her lineage suggested. "I'm sorry you had to learn all of this the hard way," he said.

Gwen smiled. Her gaze moved from him to Tess and back. "Maybe I'm not as mindless as you think, and never was."

Jonas was sure there was a story in what his sister had just said, one he'd have to explore. For now though, Gwen appeared to have put that Reaper in its place. It was unbelievable, and true.

He found smiling hard after everything. His eyes found Tess's. "You've earned hearing the truth about Gwen and about me. I owe you that. But now that the immediate danger is over and hopefully remains that way, you and I have some unfinished business to take care of."

Hell, yes, it was time to take a minute and shore these emotions up. He was still here. His soul had not been traded for Gwen's, and that meant he had time to look at the future. Plan a future. In fact, he had all the time in the world to cross the next hurdle...with Tess. He and Gwen could stay here for a while longer. He and Tess could get to know each other better.

Tess's sigh cut short the exotic leanings underscoring his immediate ideas about what kind of future with her that was. Tess was still wary and wore her anxiousness like a suit of armor. Without the danger of that Reaper looming over them, she would have to find out more about herself and her true nature. If she chose not to address those things, Tess would probably revert back to her old ways and shun all Weres.

However, the softness in Tess's eyes when she turned them on Gwen told him there was hope. And Gwen's returning smile confirmed it.

Possibly Gwen had been privy to all of those thoughts going through his mind. Facing Tess, his sister was the first to break a somewhat lengthy silence.

"You are, you know, even if you don't want to be," she said to Tess.

To Tess's credit, she didn't ask what Gwen meant. Instead, she said, "If it's true, my life has been a lie."

"Maybe just the part of it that occurred after you were injured by one of the werewolves you chased," Jonas suggested.

Tess let him take her hand, though she shuddered. Turning her wrist over, Jonas ran a finger across her scars. "And since you came into contact with whatever caused these."

She tried to draw her hand from his, and he held on. "In light of that, isn't it possible, understanding even, that your parents would help their daughter to survive such a change in plans?"

Her blue eyes were like fire when they again met his. Denial was there, and so was a flicker of curiosity. "Silver?" Tess whispered.

Jonas nodded. "The silver was to keep your wolf tethered. To make sure you didn't find out about the change and that no one else did either. It's the kind of protection a loving family would offer, Tess. Not a lie, but an act of love."

His explanation affected her greatly, and he still had more to say. "There's love in all kinds of strange places. There is fighting and enemies and friends among all species. There is justice to be sought and rogues to go after...all of the things you already do. You'll be welcome among us. You will never be alone again or have to live by yourself in the woods if that's the path you choose. I know you like my sister, and you know what she is. You like me."

He waited for her to argue with that. She didn't.

"We can help," he went on. "Gwen and I can stay for as long as you'll have us."

Tess's eyes were moist and glistening. "And then what? You go back to Miami and I carry on with my disguise?"

"You come with us for as long as it takes to get Gwen settled into a new life. Then we can..."

"We?" Tess asked.

His smile came naturally now. "You and I. Because that's how this works, as I've tried to explain. Only between Weres is it like this, Tess. I'm afraid you have me whether or not you want to. I'm just hoping you'll want to."

Jonas heard her heart beating. He fancied that he could hear the accepting growl of the wolf tucked inside her that would eventually show itself to Tess.

"Will you have me, Tess?" he was almost afraid to ask. He pointed to Gwen. "Will you have us, no matter what you choose to be in the future?"

He brought her close. They were tight together and Tess didn't squirm or pull away.

"Should I close my eyes?" Gwen asked.

But neither he nor Tess paid any attention to the teasing of a young she-wolf who was suddenly on the fast track to a full recovery and after regaining her voice, seemingly had not lost an ounce of her old wit. Tess had done this. Tess had somehow brought Gwen back to the land of the living.

"Yes. Close them," Jonas and Tess said together as their lips touched and their bodies caved to the urges now free to be taken seriously.

Because the future started here, now, right this minute, and he was going to prove that to the she-wolf in his arms if it took an all-nighter on the hood of her Jeep.

They were going to make love each chance they got. They were going to satisfy their cravings and create more of them. If Tess were to set her wolf free, they would howl at the moon and run naked in the fields…together.

He gestured for Gwen to return to the cabin, knowing it was safe now for her to be on her own for a while, and knowing his sister wasn't going to comply with that suggestion or any other. Gwen would run now, and be free. Chances were good that she'd return to Tess's cabin when fatigue set in, since she had always been drawn there. But it had been made abundantly clear to him that this young werewolf wasn't going to listen to anyone if she didn't want to.

He watched his sister go.

As for Tess…

His lover…

His future…

They would start by going back to where they had left off before being so rudely interrupted by the Grim Reaper, and then take it from there.

The heat and acceptance of Tess's mouth when he kissed her told him she was okay with this. She might have doubts, but she was going to overcome them, at least for tonight. After that, he'd have to convince her all over again…

And again…

Using the full extent of his powers of persuasion.

Even while kissing her, Jonas smiled.

"We're going to make one hell of a family."

It was a silent promise to Tess that everyone here would have heard, so he had waited until Gwen had taken off before saying it. Some things were best still kept from young she-wolves like his sister. Specifically, the things he and Tess were going to do.

He headed for the trees with Tess in tow to search for a perfect spot to get to work on those cravings and pave the way for the kind of happy-ever-after everyone on earth hoped to find.

Especially werewolves.

* * * * *

Get 2 Free Books,
Plus 2 Free Gifts—
just for trying the Reader Service!

 HARLEQUIN **INTRIGUE**

Get 2 Free Books,
Plus 2 Free Gifts—
just for trying the Reader Service!

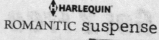

HARLEQUIN ROMANTIC suspense

YES! Please send me 2 FREE Harlequin® Romantic Suspense novels and my 2 FREE gifts (gifts are worth about $10 retail). After receiving them, if I don't wish to receive any more books, I can return the shipping statement marked "cancel." If I don't cancel, I will receive 4 brand-new novels every month and be billed just $4.99 per book in the U.S. or $5.74 per book in Canada. That's a savings of at least 12% off the cover price! It's quite a bargain! Shipping and handling is just 50¢ per book in the U.S. and 75¢ per book in Canada*. I understand that accepting the 2 free books and gifts places me under no obligation to buy anything. I can always return a shipment and cancel at any time. The free books and gifts are mine to keep no matter what I decide.

240/340 HDN GMWV

Name		
	(PLEASE PRINT)	

Address		
		Apt. #

City	State/Prov.	Zip/Postal Code

Signature (if under 18, a parent or guardian must sign)

Mail to the **Reader Service:**
IN U.S.A.: P.O. Box 1341, Buffalo, NY 14240-8531
IN CANADA: P.O. Box 603, Fort Erie, Ontario L2A 5X3

Want to try two free books from another line?
Call 1-800-873-8635 or visit www.ReaderService.com.

*Terms and prices subject to change without notice. Prices do not include applicable taxes. Sales tax applicable in N.Y. Canadian residents will be charged applicable taxes. Offer not valid in Quebec. This offer is limited to one order per household. Books received may not be as shown. Not valid for current subscribers to Harlequin® Romantic Suspense books. All orders subject to approval. Credit or debit balances in a customer's account(s) may be offset by any other outstanding balance owed by or to the customer. Please allow 4 to 6 weeks for delivery. Offer available while quantities last.

Your Privacy—The Reader Service is committed to protecting your privacy. Our Privacy Policy is available online at www.ReaderService.com or upon request from the Reader Service.

We make a portion of our mailing list available to reputable third parties that offer products we believe may interest you. If you prefer that we not exchange your name with third parties, or if you wish to clarify or modify your communication preferences, please visit us at www.ReaderService.com/consumerchoice or write to us at Reader Service Preference Service, P.O. Box 9062, Buffalo, NY 14240-9062. Include your complete name and address.

Get 2 Free Books,
Plus 2 Free Gifts –

just for
trying the
**Reader
Service!**

Get 2 Free Books,
Plus 2 Free Gifts—
just for trying the Reader Service!